My Heroes

To order additional copies, please contact us.
BookSurge, LLC
www.booksurge.com
1-866-308-6235
orders@booksurge.com

BARRY J. VEDEN

MY HEROES

The Men of Northern Indiana
Chapter XXX Veterans of the Battle
of the Bulge

BookSurge, LLC
2004

My Heroes

PREFACE

*M*y *Heroes* is not meant to be a historical depiction of World War II or of the Battle of the Bulge of which this book is primarily written. Memories recalled by some of the interviewees who are quoted herein may, in fact, be historically inaccurate. There has not been an attempt made on my part to verify each and every statement made by the men featured between the covers of *My Heroes*. Their memories are their memories — regardless whether they coincide with what history has written about the battle or not.

My father, whose story will be found in the pages that follow, remarked that the men in his outfit not only did not know that they were fighting in what would become the largest land battle ever engaged in by American forces, but that they seldom knew what country they were in. Belgium, France, Germany all blurred together during combat. It didn't matter to them where they were; they were being shot at and were only trying to survive. While some of the veterans who were interviewed could recount times, dates and places where events happened to them, others, like my father, merely followed orders to advance, dig in, or fall back. All they knew for sure was that it was cold, they were scared and war is hell.

There are volumes of information available on the battle, some of which I used for reference that will provide the hunter of facts with the information they are seeking. Where I did use other written material, the reference is noted, but this book is about the individual accounts of that famous battle. Few, if any, that have ever made it into the history books. As the veterans from the Battle of the Bulge join their fallen comrades left behind in Europe, their personal account of the battle and its impression on them are leaving with them. *My Heroes* is an attempt to capture as many of those stories as possible, as soon as possible. My only regret is that I waited so long to begin the task.

God Bless those members of the chapter who passed away before

I either knew them, or had an opportunity to interview them for this book. Chances are, if their accounts weren't captured in earlier issues of the *Bulge Battle News,* they have been lost forever.

INTRODUCTION
HOW WILL WE REMEMBER THEM?

They're old men now; even they will admit it. But they were young once, and they fought in a war and survived, when many others fought and did not. They returned home at the end of World War II to what they left behind—ordinary men leading ordinary lives interrupted by war, if you will, and worked hard to be part of the society they remembered.

Those veterans of World War II became doctors, steelworkers, meat cutters and owners of businesses. They married their high school sweethearts and had children and then grandchildren. Returning home at the end of the war, the veterans attended college on the GI Bill and became part of one of the largest expansions in personal wealth ever experienced in this country, while helping to create the middle class in America that we know today.

The years have passed by quickly, they will tell you, and other wars have interrupted the lives of other young men and women. And sometimes, society caught up in the now has a tendency to forget about the past. While time may have mellowed most of the boys-turned-old men, it hasn't erased the anguish of the years spent in Europe when they aged faster than boys should have to, nor has the passage of time deleted the memory of the battle that brought them together.

This is the story of northern Indiana soldiers who fought in the Battle of the Bulge—a last-gap push by the Germans that lasted from December 16, 1944 to January 25, 1945—as they remember it now, more than a half a century after the fact. The battle would become the largest land battle ever fought by the United States Army, and the memories of it some of the most enduring for the men who took part in the historic event.

I discovered that the lives of the men who fought in the Battle of the Bulge would all be changed by the events they encountered in a place so far away, yet upon arriving back home later they all seemed reluctant to talk about their ordeal. It took many years and the association of fellow veterans who fought in the same battle for their stories to be shared with others. What follows in these pages is a narrative not often found in history books, but merely in the occasional telling and retelling of their contributions to family and friends.

Long may their contributions remain alive.

I first became acquainted with the men of Chapter XXX Northern Indiana Veterans of the Battle of the Bulge on a snowy night in December 1997. That evening, my wife and I, along with my brother and his wife and my mother, accompanied my father to an annual dinner commemorating the beginning of the World War II battle that would become known as the Battle of the Bulge.

I was so impressed with what I witnessed that evening that I went home and wrote of what I saw and felt after attending the dinner. I would tell people later that I merely supplied the fingers on the computer keyboard – someone much higher than I actually supplied the words. I later showed my dad what I wrote about that evening and he, in turn, passed the writing on to the editor of the Chapter XXX news letter known as *The Bulge Battle News*. Bill Tuley, the editor, printed my letter in its entirety in the next issue and invited me to join my dad at the next quarterly meeting in Michigan City. The rest, as they say, is history.

This is what I wrote about that evening:

A TRIBUTE TO THE MEN OF CHAPTER XXX VETERANS OF THE BATTLE OF THE BULGE

Outside the snow was falling and a cold north wind gusting across the waters of Lake Michigan made its way south through town. Despite the Yuletide decorations and a hint of Christmas spirit in the air, it was an Indiana winter night to be spent indoors. Inside the Michigan City Holiday Inn, there were remembrances of another snowy, cold December, a half-century earlier and half a world away.

They gathered in the room amid family and friends and remembered a battle lasting forty-one days. A battle involving six hundred thousand allied troops, their program guide noted, of which 81,000 American soldiers were killed, wounded or captured – all in 41 days. Those forty-one days and the memories of them would shape the lives of the men gathered in the room forever. But you don't have to be told that. If you are reading this, chances are you are one of the many who already know about the Battle of the Bulge and the dates of December 16, 1944 to January 25, 1945. Those forty-one days probably mean more to you than to any other American. They now mean more to me as well.

Those of us who were attending as guests that evening sat spellbound as battle-scarred veterans interacted with one another and spoke of an occurrence in their lives as significant as any other. Humility, honesty, and friendship were the orders of the day as men who might not have known each other during the hard-fought battle, and have only recently bonded together as a group, displayed a camaraderie known only to those who have faced death and survived when others did not. Theirs are truly kindred spirits.

The men gathered on the evening of December 5, 1997, to enjoy the kinship of fellow veterans and to raise a glass in homage to life, freedom and democracy. But they also set an example that evening for all that have and those that will follow their footsteps in battle. There is a way to remember the horrors of war, they seemed to be saying, and still retain ones' dignity and humanity.

There were other, younger veterans in the room, myself included, and we watched with pride as our fathers or friends spoke of the roles they had in the 41-day battle. Fortunately, I never fired a shot, or slept in a foxhole wondering what the morning would bring, or lost a friend to an enemy's bullet, and I thank God often for that blessing.

Thank you, men of the Battle of the Bulge, for the freedom we all enjoy, for answering your country's plea for help, and for showing other generations the graciousness of your generation. I don't know the true definition of a hero, but somehow I have the feeling I was surrounded by a roomful of them one cold, snowy evening in December, that I, for one, will never forget.

Barry J. Veden
Proud son of Edward W. Veden
28th Infantry Division, 112th Inf. Reg. 3rd Bn I Co.

I'm still proud of my father, as he serves as an inspiration to me. I have witnessed him suffering through many medical problems, including heart by-pass surgery, cancer and diabetes, yet he never complains. To this day, he doesn't even protest the wounds and anguish he suffered during World War II.

As I write this, I am an Associate Member of the organization and I'm serving my third one-year term as Secretary/Editor of Chapter XXX, Northern Indiana Veterans of the Battle of the Bulge. In the years since I first began attending meetings in the organization, I have come to know members of Chapter XXX well. Some have become close friends. I cherish my relationship with the members of this organization—a true Band of Brothers—and took on the task of writing about their remarkable years of service to their country before their remembrances fade from memory or they join the fallen comrades they left behind in Europe.

I couldn't have told this story without the cooperation and help of many, many good people. I want to thank all those members of our chapter who took the time to relate their stories to me. For some, it was an emotional experience as I asked them to remember facts and situations that many have suppressed for years. To them I said that the rest of the world needed to know what they lived through and endured. Their stories should not be lost, but rather shared with loved ones and friends so that we never forget the sacrifices they made. We enjoy our freedom today because of their actions so long ago.

I especially want to thank Bill Tuley, whose story will be found in the pages that follow. Bill was the first editor of the Bulge Battle News and kept and passed on to me volumes of information that found its way between the covers of this book. In addition, Bill has become a very good friend of mine and has served as my mentor in the organization. Thanks to Bill Tuley, my dad, and all the men who took the time to share their stories with me, I have a much better appreciation of what those men endured during the years they spent fighting against a tyrant's wishes to dominate the world. I hope after reading this book, you will too.

I would also like to acknowledge two personal friends who helped tremendously with their expertise—John Hassell, a photographer who took the cover photo and many of the current photographs of the members of Chapter XXX, and Marcia Powrozek, whose editing talent saved this writer much work and possible embarrassment.

INFANTRYMEN OF:

The 28th Infantry Division

The 87th Infantry Division

The 75th Infantry Division

The 2nd Infantry Division

The 106th Infantry Division

The 1st Infantry Division

The 78th Infantry Division

The 90th Infantry Division

The 94th Infantry Division

The 99th Infantry Division

RICHARD BEES
28th Infantry Division, 112th Regiment, Co E
Hometown: Crown Point, Indiana

R ichard was born and raised in Youngstown, Ohio, and graduated from high school there in 1939.

"Before I graduated from high school, I saw an article in the *Youngstown Vindicator* about a test that would be held at Rayen High School," Richard said. "According to the article, those who took and passed the test, would be accepted into the Army Specialized Training Program (ASTP) and would be sent to college. I took the test and was informed that I had passed it. Later, I would learn that it took a higher score to pass the ASTP test than it did for OCS (Officer Candidate School)."

"I was called up on October 28, 1943, and rode a train to Fort Hayes in Columbus, Ohio, where I joined a company of ASTP. Since classes had already begun in September, it was decided that we would not be sent to college until January. In the meantime, we were told, we would attend infantry training at Fort Benning, Georgia."

"While at Fort Benning, Lt. Tuffy, a recent graduate of OCS, was my platoon leader. I've never met anyone who was as mean and nasty as he was. I finally came to the conclusion that he was so mean because when our training was completed, he would be shipped overseas while we would be going to college. It was little wonder that he hated us."

"I discovered that I would be going to Ohio State University in Columbus Ohio. One Saturday morning, Lt. Tuffy showed up with a big grin on his face. I knew that we were in deep trouble. He told us that Congress had cut the funding for ASTP, and that we were in the infantry. I wished then that I had taken an offer from a major and transferred to the Air Force."

Richard was eventually shipped to a camp in Louisiana for further training before heading overseas. When he shipped out across the Atlantic, he did so onboard the *Queen Elizabeth.*

"They assigned six men to a stateroom that was designed for two," Richard remembered. "We were told that we would be traveling across the ocean without any escort, because the *Queen Elizabeth* was so fast that it could outrun any enemy submarine. The overcrowding in the stateroom, and the thought of enemy subs possibly lying in wait for our ship to sail within torpedo range, caused me to spend all of my time on deck sleeping next to a lifeboat."

It took the QE five days to sail across the Atlantic, landing in Firth of Clyde, Scotland, where the men were billeted in barracks.

"The Scots had a reputation of being fierce fighters, in spite of, or maybe because of, the short skirts they wore. But they were not tall. I stood five feet, 10 inches tall, and my head and legs hung out over the mattress on my cot."

After a short stay in Scotland, the men were sent by truck to Crewe, located in England's Midlands.

"We enjoyed our stay in Crewe," Richard said. "We were free to go into town in the evenings, and we did. Food was scarce there though, so there weren't any places to eat. But there wasn't any shortage of beer, ale, or Scotch whiskey. Unfortunately, by the time we ate our evening meal in the Army mess hall and walked into town, we only had time for a couple of pints before the bars closed with the owners saying, 'Time, gentlemen.'"

Then it was time for combat, and the men traveled, first to Plymouth, and later across the English Channel to France. Once there, they traveled by the infamous 40x8 rail cars to their next destination.

"The trip onboard the 40x8's was miserable. We sat with our backs to the wall, stretched out our legs, and fell asleep. When I awoke, my legs were aching because they were on the bottom, and many more pairs of legs were on top of them. The railroad traveled at top speed for about 30 minutes and then sit at idle for several hours. Once, we stopped in a village, and I spotted a tavern. My friend and I decided to leave the train and visit the tavern. Inside was a non-English speaking bartender. Being well read, I ordered 'Dos Cognacs'. He replied, 'Nix cognac – calvados.' So, I ordered two drinks – they were so small – tossed them down and ordered two more. That stuff was like firewater! We were on fire by the time we left the bar and returned to the train."

"I regret that I don't have more information to relate about the Battle of the Bulge," Richard said sadly. "But we were constantly on the move, with little sleep and less food. During the battle, we were in a constant state of high anxiety."

"We eventually reached the front lines and I was assigned to Company E, 112th Regiment of the 28th Infantry Division. It was exactly one year from the time I entered the service. The division was at full strength, so we were what they called, supernumeries (extra men). The date was October 28, 1944. Our division was scheduled to attack the Germans in the Huertgen Forest on November 1. The attack was delayed twice, and an hour before the attack took place, all of the supernumeries were called back to be battalion guards. The Second Battalion was located, at the time, in the basement of a two-story schoolhouse."

"It appears that plans were made to attack German placements north and east of where the 28th Division was located, and we were ordered to make diversionary attacks to assist the main attack, which never happened. The plan was asinine!"

"Trees grew so close in the forest that men could not go through the forest very easily. There were a few ruts that Jeeps could use, but the use of tanks was out of the question. The enemy, however, had a good road network that allowed them to quickly deliver men and supplies to their soldiers. We learned later that the Germans had determined the arc of a fired bullet and contoured the ground in front of their machine gun emplacements so that when GIs hit the ground, bullets fired by the German guns would drop and hit the Americans in the upper part of their bodies. We attacked with M-1 and BAR rifles, and the Germans had excellent fortifications. It was easy to see why we were outclassed in the battle. The 28th Division was decimated during the fight for the Huertgen Forest, and eventually, the top brass, realizing the futility of the situation, ordered a withdrawal."

"We were then sent to Luxemburg to reform, re-man and rebuild. By then, there were so few of the original men left in the division."

During the reforming period, Richard was assigned to Company E Headquarters.

"In my new assignment, I carried the SCR radio, and stayed next to the captain all of the time. One of the officers, who was either killed in combat or transferred, was the battalion commander, and his replacement was a stickler for defense. I recall him visiting our positions two or three times each week to make certain we were digging in."

"When the Battle of the Bulge began, we were so well dug in that the enemy could not go through us, so they went around us to keep to their schedule. Captain Kauffmen knew that the Germans would return at their first opportunity and wipe us out. The order was given to move out and take only our ammo – no blankets or shelter halves, or anything else but weapons and ammunition."

"We wandered behind enemy lines for more than a week. We could hear the engines of the Panzer tanks from a long ways off, so we would detour around them. We would go up a ridge, hear the tanks, and go back down and try another way to get out of our situation. There was as many as five or six times that week that we actually engaged the enemy, and a fire fight would ensue. But both sides would break off the engagement because neither side knew the strength of the enemy they were fighting. I discovered that there are no more loyal friends than those fighting alongside of you in combat."

Like all of the Chapter XXX members have remarked, Richard agreed that it was the coldness that was as big an enemy as the Germans.

"We heard later that the winter that year was the coldest that they had experienced in many, many years. It was brutal! We stayed on the move constantly. I remember we didn't rest or sleep very much that week. When we took a break, we huddled together to stay warm. We roamed behind enemy lines from December 16 to late on the night of December 24. When we finally made it to friendly lines on Christmas Eve, I attended midnight mass at a monastery and gave thanks for our escape."

Richard was discharged from the United States Army at Camp Atterbury, Indiana, in January 1946. He would later take advantage of the G.I. Bill receiving a Bachelor's Degree in Business Administration.

When asked if he had any regrets about serving in the armed forces during WWII, Richard said, "I'm proud to have served, especially to have served in the Infantry and survived. We were fortunate! Captain Kauffmen's leadership got us out of a bad situation during the Battle of the Bulge. We did not lose one man during that week we were trying to get back to friendly lines."

BOB JACKSON
28th Infantry Division – Prisoner of War
Hometown: Buchanan, Michigan

L ife changing events happen to all of us. Typically, the significance of the life altering occurrence isn't recognized until some time later when there is more of an opportunity to reflect on our lives and the paths they have taken. Usually, we don't even realize that they happened.

A half century after Bob Jackson experienced his own life changing event, the story he hand wrote of his imprisonment in Germany as a POW was published. The title of the book is *KRIEGIE Prisoner of War.* (The word Kriegie is a shorten version of the German word Kriegsgefangene, and is the way German soldiers addressed the prisoners of war.) His account of those 101 days when he was held against his will by the Nazis is must reading for anyone interested in World War II, or for that matter, anyone needing to be reminded, as the author wrote, *that we live on the margins of an overly active and anxious world.* The book is now in its fifth printing and because of the success of his account of that life changing event, Bob Jackson has embarked on a career as a writer. He is currently working on a novel of the Pre-Civil War era.

Jackson was born in Crystal Falls, Michigan, in 1925. He graduated from High School in 1942 and volunteered for the service during the summer of 1943. He was put in a classification known as *Limited Service* because of poor eyesight. Very soon after that, the draft board ended Limited Service – draftees and enlistees were either 1A or 4F. Because Bob wanted to be in the military, he memorized the eye chart, passed the eye exam, and was reclassified 1A.

Nineteen is an awfully young age to fight in a war, but that is where the teenager from Crystal Falls was headed after completing training at Camp Blanding, Florida. While in Florida, he received training as a message center chief. Six months later, he was crossing the Atlantic on his way to Europe and the horror awaiting him.

"One day as we were out to sea during a time when the troop ship was on alert because of possible enemy submarine activity, I was standing on the deck looking out at the ocean," Bob remembered. "I saw a fin cutting through the water coming directly at the boat where I was standing. To me it looked like the fin of a torpedo. My first thought was 'My God we're about to take a direct hit.' As I watched in horror, waiting for that underwater blast to occur, a dolphin jumped out of the water near the boat and I realized it was just the fin of a fish I saw and not a torpedo. What a relief."

Landing in England, the boy from the Wolverine State discovered that he was one of thousands of soldiers shipped overseas as replacements for the men who were being wounded or killed on the Western Front. He was sent to the 109th Regiment of the 28th Infantry Division, a division which had already sustained heavy casualties.

Bob, along with 20 other replacements, was sent to fill in the gaps in the squads decimated by casualties and in need of replacements to continue the fight against the Nazis. He, like the other replacements around him, was scared and wondered what was in store for him in this place so far away from the Upper Peninsula of Michigan.

There was no waiting to acclimate himself to the sights and sounds of war. Bob's initiation into the arena of combat was immediate and deadly. The new replacement's first night on the front lines saw him take part in a night patrol where there was contact with the enemy and he had to silence a German soldier with a knife. Things would never be the same again for the young man from Michigan. He survived the patrol that evening, but knew then he was faced with a challenge in his life unlike any other. After the patrol, Jackson became the BAR (Browning automatic rifle) man in his platoon.

After a few days on the front lines rumors persisted that Jackson's outfit might be moving out. They heard that Aachen, the Ardennes and the Huertgen Forest were all possible destinations. Soon they were loaded into trucks and moved out for another location, another battle. They were transported to a thickly-wooded forest and dropped off in the mud. In the morning, while advancing toward a country village, they came under small arms fire.

I find myself squinting my eyes and tightening my jaw as I run across the open area, searching for meager cover; a plowed gully. Diving into it I can look from side to side, ascertaining my forward progress. I line up with the rest of the squad. Jumping up again, I zigzag toward the houses and finally reach the first squad's position. They, in turn, run forward, taking cover at the second row of houses, Jackson writes in his novel, *Kriegie.*

The battlefield was fluid, moving from house to house within the village to refuge behind a stone wall outside of the town. Casualties were heavy on both sides. The battlefield's importance was in the proximity of a road used to supply other units and the Germans were not going to relinquish it without a fight.

The battle raged on, punctuated by the sounds of artillery shells and bazooka fire, as German tanks fell victim to one or the other. Screams of men being wounded or killed were everywhere. Finally, the ranks of the enemy infantry were broken and they retreated from the battle.

Medics from both sides of the battlefield retrieved the wounded and the bodies of those who have died, and another day has passed for the young man mere months away from the world he knew in Michigan.

Rumors were again rampant, and the latest had the men of the 28th Division heading to Paris for some R&R (rest and recuperation). They were elated!

Moved out via troop-carrying trucks, the men reached their destination and were quartered in a village known as Diekirch, where they awaited rail transportation to the sights and sounds of "Gay Paree." They waited for three days for their R&R, during which time they bathed, shaved and mended their ragged uniforms. The train never came! They were finally told the train had been delayed and to pack up and be prepared to move out.

Two days later they were on the front lines again near the Our River, the border that separates Germany and Belgium.

Jackson's final battle was about to get underway. It is December 15, 1944.

"We only carried two days of rations and basic ammunition," Jackson recalled. "And there are only 45 of us, without any other company of soldiers on either side."

On a patrol that first night, they discovered German soldiers building a bridge that is strong enough to support men and tanks. It was being built inches under the top of the river water. The water hid the progress of the work from Allied planes and foot patrols. The bridge meant one thing – the Germans were about to come across in force to the side the Americans were holding.

The patrol returned to their posts, reported the discovery to their commanding officer and returned to their foxholes. They were awakened the morning of December 16 by sounds of artillery shells falling all around them. Hours later, when the incessant shelling stopped, the men of Jackson's outfit peeked out from their foxholes to see a line of German tanks interspersed with German infantrymen, poised to attack. Jackson was about to fight in the last battle prior to his capture.

The battle raged for three days and the men of Jackson's outfit endured heavy enemy artillery fire, withering small arms fire from German infantry, and finally the deadly roar of tanks firing into their positions. After three days, they lost their 30 cal. and 50 cal. weapons and crews, and all of their officers. Their ammunition was all but gone.

"On the third day, with us out of ammunition, the Germans just came at us, foxhole by foxhole, taking prisoners," Jackson recalled. "That was about noon. There were only 18 of us left. They searched each of us and took away anything and everything they found. Before they got to me, I slipped a ring off my finger that belonged to Jean, a girl back home, and hid it in my shoe. I rubbed dirt on my finger so they wouldn't notice the white mark where the ring had been. They didn't find it. The Germans did let me keep a rosary I had in my pocket."

The ring would be used later to barter for much needed food.

The POWs didn't know what would happen to them next as they watched the enemy set up a machine gun in front of them. They stood with their hands above their heads as the guards moved away.

"I thought they were going to kill us all," Jackson said.

There was no sound as the men stood silently awaiting their fate. Then the machine gun fired – inches over their heads and the men dropped to their knees believing they were being shot. The German soldiers just laughed at their predicament.

"That was the first of many tortures we endured as POWs," Jackson recalled.

The prisoners were marched away from the battlefield, not knowing their destination.

"We were harassed and beaten with clubs the entire time we were marched – some 24 hours of non-stop walking. We finally ended up in a cold barn. We had not eaten since we were taken prisoner and are only offered a cold cup of water in the barn."

In the morning they heard voices – English-speaking voices – and they were joined by more American prisoners. There were now more than 50 of them. There was no food available. They drank a ladle full of water dipped out of a freezing bucket.

Again the men set out on foot, and as they progressed, they were joined by still more prisoners. By the time they stopped that night, they numbered more than 200. The men were given a cup of water, a slice of hard bread and a used blanket. It was their first food in two days. They slept outside in the cold and snow, blankets wrapped around them providing the only protection from the nighttime weather.

The next day, the day before Christmas, they were herded down a road and again marched all day. On the way, they passed a sign indicating they are in a town called Gerolstein. On the outskirts of town, they are stopped, searched again for weapons and put inside a large warehouse-type building. Outside the building there are towering huge cliffs. Inside there are more prisoners.

"There were more than 600 of us in that building," Jackson remembered. "There wasn't even enough room for us to lie down. We were there for a few days when American planes flew overhead and dropped their bombs, hitting the cliffs outside our building. They didn't know there were POWs inside. Huge pieces of rock came crashing down on us, killing and maiming many of the men inside."

Broken legs protrude from the debris. Pools of blood are everywhere and screams for help cannot be answered fast enough. We work as a team, helping

as many as we can. Three prisoners are pounding on the door shouting, Medic!
Medic! Doctor! Doctor! Send us a Doctor! Let us out of here!

Their cries go unanswered. The door remains locked, Jackson writes.

Later, when the guards opened the doors, the wounded are carried out and put on trucks, never to be seen again. The Americans are forced to go back inside the building and carry out their dead comrades.

At the end of a week in the bombed out warehouse, during which time more American planes dropped bombs on the area, 40 men were chosen to leave and participate in a work detail. They were told they will march 10 miles, be housed in a barracks, given three meals a day and be able to write and receive mail from home. Jackson was one of those chosen.

"We marched for more than 30 miles with nothing to eat or drink," Jackson said. "When we did stop, it was to work at repairing areas that have been bombed by our planes."

The men were given worn-out shovels and had to fill in craters created by falling bombs. They worked tirelessly for more than six hours moving twisted rails and broken concrete before being given a break. Then they were given a tin can of soup and a slice of bread. It was almost daybreak.

The prisoners again marched all day and ended up in the village of Heidweiler.

"The building that we stopped in front of in the village was made of red brick and looked like a school house."

It was. And that building was what the 40 men called home. The room they had to sleep in was a mere 18 by 24 feet – big enough for a classroom of school age children – but not sufficient in size to sleep 40 grown men.

The men discovered they were going to be a work gang for the Nazis, half going into a forest each day to load fallen timbers on to an ox-drawn sled, the other half into a courtyard to unload and work on the logs. The frozen hardwood logs they had to load onto the sleds were approximately eight feet long and 12 inches in diameter. The other prisoners cut the logs into small blocks with nothing but handsaws, keyhole saws and one old crosscut saw missing a handle. The pride of the operation was a saw-like machine which ran on a low-grade kerosene. The POWs made wood chips that would be used as fuel in wood-burning trucks. The trucks, having a large tank on the side, were loaded with this fuel and it was burnt to provide steam power.

About three in the afternoon, one cold day, with approximately two feet of snow on the ground, the men were still in the woods carrying logs to the sleds when they heard a roar overhead. They looked skyward to see four American planes, their machine guns blazing as they attacked the ox-drawn sleds. The pilots must have believed they were part of a supply line for front line troops. On a second pass, the planes dropped bombs on nearby barns and as the bombs met their target, collapsing roofs disclosed trucks full of supplies inside of them. That convoy didn't make it to the front lines.

The next morning, the prisoners were punished for the attack by the airplanes the day before. They were denied their meager allotment of bread, and as they were marched outside, they saw a pile of shovels awaiting them.

A moment of fright holds the group motionless at the foot of the stairs. The gloating eyes of the silent guards survey the mass of disheveled men. Stacked neatly in the middle of the yard is a supply of shovels and picks. We have heard of men having to dig their own graves and that thought crosses our minds. The guards may have been tormented past the point of reason by yesterday's bombings and now they want to be rid of us.

We are marched over to the tools and are told to pick them up. Men's arms reach for the handles that we do not want to grasp. They lay heavy and cumbersome on our shoulders as we march down the road. The left rank is not detoured into the barnyard and at the next intersection we turn right, down a narrow side street. Suddenly my despair turns to delight as I realize we are marching in the direction of the bombed supply trucks.

The men were assigned to clear out the rubble of the attack and fill in bomb craters—a task much more desirable than digging one's own grave.

Then one day, the prisoners discovered that there are Red Cross packages in the recently bombed trucks nearby and they devised a plan to steal food from the parcels – food that was meant for them in the first place but kept by their German captors. It would be a scene that would make James Bond proud, as the GIs stuffed food cans into their clothing and hid them in a wooden trunk that sat in the middle of the area where the men were working. When they completed their subversive activities, there were approximately 150 – 160 cans of foodstuff hidden for their consumption later. After being without food for so long, it must have been terribly tempting to eat it right away, but the hungry men didn't. The food stayed in the trunk until there was a better opportunity to take it without being caught. They had already been warned by the guards that anyone caught stealing food off of the trucks would be shot. They stole it anyway – that's what starving people do.

The men were beginning to hear the sounds of artillery fire and they knew the Allies were moving closer to where they were being held. That presented a good news/bad news situation; good that the war is being pushed further into Germany and hopefully closer to ending, bad that the prisoners might be transported elsewhere for the safety of the guards, as well as to keep the prisoners from being liberated by their own forces.

When the day arrived to steal the food out of the wooden trunk,

Jackson discovered a harmonica along with the cans of food. It was rusty and he has not played a tune for years, but he took it anyway. That evening, after the guards passed out the daily ration of bread and the men have settled in for the night, he began to play a song, *Home, Sweet Home*.

There was silence in the room for a moment as if the men weren't sure what was making the music, but when Jackson played an old Polka song, the room filled with laughter and the sounds of stomping feet. Men who could barely walk were dancing, and for a moment, civilization returned to the prisoners. The men were thankful, and with tears in their eyes, they hummed along as Jackson played, *How Great Thou Art*.

The guards, hearing the noise and believing a riot was starting, broke into the room, their rifles at the ready. When they discovered the men dancing to the sounds of a harmonica, they left them to their moment of frivolity. Then the feast began and the much needed food the POWs recovered from the wooden trunk was eaten. Afterwards, the cans were stomped on and hidden between the walls.

A few days later, after an aborted escape attempt, Jackson and the rest of the men were told they were being relocated to new quarters. They had been at their location for more than two months and it almost seemed like home to them. The men were marched continuously for four days with no food or water. They ate freshly fallen snow for moisture.

Their feet were wet, some nearly frozen, some frozen. When they stopped in a small village similar to the one they left five days earlier, the men discovered a barn with cows inside and snuck in to the stalls and milked the cows for the nourishment it would provide. They milked the cows dry and stole the animals' fodder – old potatoes.

More prisoners were brought in from other small villages where they too provided slave labor and soon there were more than 200 – all in the same weak physical condition. They were all forced into a continuation of their march. Some of them were so weak they couldn't continue and fell along the wayside. When a guard ordered them to get up and they couldn't – they were shot and killed. As other prisoners saw the brutal murder of some of their fellow GIs, they began moving towards the guards and the Germans fired into the group killing 20 more starving, dying prisoners. The men stopped then and were told through an interpreter that the same fate awaited anyone who dropped out as there weren't enough guards to stay with those who couldn't make the march.

As if dying by the hands of the enemy wasn't bad enough – the march took a turn for the worse when an American fighter plane, seeing the mass of men below and probably thinking they were all German soldiers, fired on the marchers, killing and wounding many.

The pilot must think we are German infantry and will not be discouraged from his mission of death. Two more passes completely unnerve us as we scramble farther into the open fields to escape.

I bury my face in the snow and pray as reverently as I ever have. When I finish praying, I raise my head to find the plane has left. Death is everywhere.

The prisoners were gathered back on the road and the march continued. While there were only 140 left out of the original 200, they were soon joined by other marching prisoners and the numbers swelled to more than 500. They walked for seven more days and shots rang out every day as men who couldn't continue were killed.

After another three days, during which time they endured additional strafing from American planes, the weary men reached their destination – Stalag XII near a town called Limburg.

Inside the barbed wire fences were buildings housing different nationalities of prisoners – English, French, Canadian, Polish, Russian, Turkish, Indian, and American. The men believed the compound would be their home for the rest of the war – some three hundred miles from where they began their journey.

Each day saw more prisoners arriving and dying. The camp became overfull and men were forced to sleep and die outside of the barracks. Those who didn't make it were buried in mass graves outside of the camp. Eventually, the German guards begin taking 100 prisoners a day out of the compound, uniting them with thousands of others, and then they were marched away, presumably to another camp somewhere.

On March 17th, the compound was emptied and the men were marched to a railroad yard and loaded into boxcars called 40 x 8 (Designed to hold 40 men or eight animals). Seventy men were packed into each car. The men sat in the cars for hours before an engine coupled onto them and they departed for an unknown destination. Less than a half hour later, the engine uncoupled and the cars were left unattended on a railroad siding. They were sitting ducks for any American fighter plane flying missions nearby, and it wasn't long before the men in the boxcars heard the roar of planes overhead.

Our fighters come over. Their attack is deafening. Lead rips up and down the boxcars, killing, tearing and punching death into men like rain.

Screams of agony and fright fill the boxcar accompanied by the well-known whistling of rushing air that is followed by earth shaking explosions of bombs. Men stampede where there is no room to move.

It wasn't over. The planes came again and again for seven days. The men who were still alive were trapped inside the locked boxcars. Death was all around them.

When the German soldiers return on the evening of the seventh day and opened the boxcar Jackson was in, only five men out of the 70 were left alive. Looking around, the men saw that hundreds of boxcars had been destroyed by the airplanes; bodies were sticking out of some, strewn on the ground around others. It was March 24th, three days before Jackson's twentieth birthday.

On March 29, 1945, 101 days since being taken prisoner of war, Jackson and 500 other POWs were still being forced to march down a never ending path to nowhere. The previous day, an American spotter plane flew overhead and that simple activity gave the men hope that the Allies were near.

Around noon, the 500 bone weary, starving GIs had enough and as if on cue, they all sat down in the middle of the road. The guards lashed out at them cracking skulls and breaking ribs with the butts of their rifles – Jackson was hit twice, knocking him almost senseless. The men didn't move from their sitting positions. Amidst the chaos, there was the sound of an airplane and the American spotter was back circling the mass of men sitting on the ground. Then the roar of tanks was heard and then the tanks were seen fast approaching the men.

Spreading out over the fields, the tanks maneuver a flanking position. We run to them, tumbling and falling at every step. A discord of voices holler and sing, tears pouring from our sunken eyes. The tears dam up in our matted beards which refuse to part and let them fall. We hug each other and dance together as the tanks come abreast of us. Hundreds of us kneel. Bare headed, we bow. I have my rosary in my hands as I give thanks to the Lord for our liberation.

Jackson was hospitalized in Europe and the U.S for seven months after his liberation. He was awarded the European-African-Middle Eastern Theatre Ribbons, two Bronze Campaign Stars for the Ardennes and Rhineland campaigns, Good Conduct Ribbon, the coveted Combat Infantry Badge, the Prisoner of War Medal, and the Bronze Star.

STEW MCDONNELL
28th Infantry Division
Past President and Founder of Chapter XXX
Hometown: Michigan City, Indiana

There is one thing that is becoming increasingly clear as I interview the various members of Chapter XXX. They have far more in common than having fought in the Battle of the Bulge. They are easily the most patriotic group of Americans anyone could have chosen to write a book about.

Stew McDonnell is no exception.

There is an American flag flying from the second story porch of the condo that Stew lives in and a World War II vintage O.D. Green Jeep parked in the garage as I arrive for a scheduled meeting with the founder of Chapter XXX Veterans of the Battle of the Bulge. Inside the home near the Lake Michigan shoreline books and photographs of WWII fill shelves, while medals, awards and other photos hang on walls. An array of *Army Times* newsletters sit atop a small table by the entranceway and two neatly pressed and decorated Army uniforms hang in view in the bedroom – one of a Pfc who served in the 28th Infantry Division during WWII, the other of a Captain in the 3rd Army Reserves. Stew is wearing a sweatshirt this day that says, simply, *Army*.

A brief tour of his memorabilia sets the stage for reminiscing and once the interview begins, it is non-stop 1940s for several hours. I am reminded once again as to how the war years imprinted data so deeply in these aged veterans that they speak of occurrences of fifty years past as if they just happened.

Stew remembers the events from those days with a fondness associated with good times. It is always the good times that stay close to the surface for those who take a walk down memory lane. The hard times are there in the memory bank, but don't come to the forefront as easily.

We begin with pre-war information about his early life in Chicago and build quickly into the time spent fighting Nazis in Europe.

Born on the South Side of Chicago, in a working class, blue collar neighborhood, Stew lived across the street from Hirsch High School where he graduated from in 1942. While in high school, he was a member of the Junior ROTC, attaining the rank of Captain. His dad was working for the Illinois Central Railroad at the time, but when he died at age 44, Stew was left to help his mother and younger brother, while a war was being waged an ocean away.

When the draft board discovered that his mom was working and helping to support the family, a deferment that Stew hoped would keep him from combat didn't materialize. Instead, a draft notice arrived in June of 1944. At the time, after attending the Illinois Technical Institute for a year on a scholarship and deciding he didn't want to be a fire prevention engineer, Stew was working at Carnegie Steel in the Metallurgical Lab making $150 a week — very good money in those days. Uncle Sam's wages weren't nearly as appealing, but the draft notice he received didn't exactly include options.

Stew was inducted into the service in downtown Chicago and would be sent to Ft. Sheridan, Illinois, for indoctrination. Before he left Chicago, however, he received a visit from his best friend who was a year and a half older. His friend was already in the service and proudly wore his uniform when he arrived to see Stew off.

"I remember thinking at the time that before I finished my training, the war will probably be over." Nice thought — didn't happen.

Because of his background in the Junior ROTC, Stew was given command of the recruits heading from Ft. Sheridan to Camp McClellan, Alabama. When they arrived at the Infantry Replacement Training

Center (IRTC), they discovered that they would be living in tar paper shacks with wood burning heaters – housing that only a GI could appreciate.

After 16 weeks of Basic Training during which time Stew learned the workings of every weapon an Infantryman would use in combat, he was approached by two officers. They wanted to know if he might be interested in attending Officers Training at Fort Benning, Georgia.

"I heard that officers were being shot at pretty regularly in combat, so I thought if they had openings in Ordnance and not Infantry I might be interested in attending Officers Candidate School (OCS). They didn't. That helped make my decision easier for me." Stew would not be joining the ranks of the 90-day wonders being sent into combat and being shot at merely because they were of rank.

After completing Basic Training, Stew received a week's furlough. On a train en route to Chicago, a trip that included a stop over in St. Louis, he met his first WAC (Women's Army Corps). The remainder of the trip home was much more enjoyable.

The week at home ended much too quickly and soon it was back to the real world of Uncle Sam's Army. A train ride again took him from home, only this time its destination was Fort Meade, Maryland, where, according to Stew, "All we did there was busy work." He did have opportunities to visit nearby locations and saw the Baltimore area as well as Washington D.C. While in the nation's capitol, he met a girl from Wisconsin at a USO dance. The good times wouldn't last long, however, and soon he was being shipped overseas.

"Crossing the North Atlantic in the winter on board a troop ship is not exactly something I would want to do again," he said. It took them two weeks to make the crossing – two weeks of being seasick and watching others who were sick. What a way to prepare men for war.

Disembarking the troop ship in European waters was a lot harder than boarding at an American port. Rope ladders were thrown over the side of the ship when they anchored outside of Le Havre, France, and the men, loaded down with their bags and carrying rifles, climbed over the sides and into LCIs – a landing craft that took them to shore. Once ashore, they were loaded into a train car referred to as a 40 x 8. The term meant that the car was designed to hold 40 men or eight horses.

"It was so cold inside those wooden cars," Stew remembered. "Here they're having the coldest winter in 40 years in Europe, and we're riding inside of rail cars fit for animals."

The cold train ride ended at a "Repple Depot" in Givet, France where new replacements were assigned to the units that needed men. The Battle of the Bulge had already begun.

"I was sent to G Company, 112th Regiment, 28th Infantry Division, a company that had sustained heavy casualties. We heard there were only 20 men left out of the original 180 that were there when the battle began," Stew said. By the end of the war, the 28th ranked 17th out of 68 units with a total of 12,292 casualties. Having the 17th most casualties out of all the units in a war meant that the men who served in that division were truly in harms way.

"I was told by one of the veterans, 'If you want to stay away from night patrols on the front lines, join a machine gun unit.'" He did. "As a result, I never went out on a night patrol – something most men did not cherish doing. And neither did I."

The sights and sounds of combat are something all of the veterans will tell you that they will never forget.

"I really didn't think I was going to make it through the first night. I lost a good friend the very first night." Nothing would ever be the same again for Stew. How do you ever tell people who have never been in combat what the horror of war is like? Even if they tried, no one would really understand, so for the most part, the veterans didn't talk very much about what they saw during combat when they arrived back home.

"We moved out from Givet the next morning – it was so cold! We were trying to retake ground that had been lost to the Germans during the initial push. At the time I was an ammo carrier for a light machine gun squad." An ammo carrier did just what the name implies – he carried boxes of ammunition for the machine gun. By the time the war was over for Stew, he had made it to the position of gunner – that meant he only had to carry the tripod the machine gun rested on.

"It began to snow. No one even knew where we were at. All we knew was that we were pushing the Germans back to the Rhine River. We just followed the sergeants who were getting their instructions from the officers."

"After two weeks of fighting in the Bulge – sometime in January – the 28th Infantry Division was pulled off the line. The Germans were falling back quickly. They loaded us into 6x6 trucks and we took off for an area known as the Colmar Pocket. It was a trip of about 100-150 miles – in the back of trucks. The Germans were trying to push through in that area so we were rushed there to help stop them. I think it was even colder when we got there. The area was probably a great place to visit in peace time, as the Alps were in the background and they looked beautiful, but we didn't have much time to enjoy the scenery."

"We were stationed right next to an outfit of French Moroccans. Those guys were like wild men. We stayed out of their way. They used to cook their dinners in huge pots. I never ate anything that they were cooking because I'm not certain what was in those pots."

It was about that time when there was a rumor going around that the military pay truck had been stolen – a truck that had the paychecks for the entire division.

"At the time, I think I was only making $60 a month, and fifty of that was going home, so I didn't exactly break the bank with my paycheck." They would discover later from General Cota, the Division Commander, that the truck really wasn't stolen. It had secret information on board the vehicle and they wanted people to think that it was missing.

After the Colmar battle, it was off to the Alsace-Lorraine area where Stew's outfit spent two weeks. They passed through Nancy and Verdun France on their way to Aachen, which was the first big town the Germans gave up. The fighting was continuous. It was in this area that Stew would hear the sounds of small arms fire more than anyplace else. There were lots of German snipers shooting at any target in their sights. Stew's machine gun squad put down a field of fire for the infantrymen firing M-1s.

The Rhine River, where they were now fighting, was wide and each side of the river had high embankments. Most of the gunfire they were taking was coming from across the river. There were lots of houses by the water's edge and that's where the German snipers were firing from.

"Suddenly, we heard what we thought was some kind of boat coming down the river. We heard it long before we saw it. After awhile, here comes this United States Navy vessel steaming down the river. They recognized the American troops on our side of the river and pulled over. They told us they were heading for a town called Koblenz to look for some Cognac. Imagine that! Here we are in the middle of a war and these sailors are on a mission to find booze. They came back later with cases of Cognac. We had shot some rabbits for dinner so we ate and drank Cognac with them that evening."

In March 1945, Stew's unit crossed the Rhine River on small portable bridges. He was an assistant gunner at the time.

"When we got into Germany, we saw lots of German prisoners and they were either kids or old men. We knew the end of the war couldn't be far off." While guarding some prisoners, a mortar shell landed nearby and fragments from it wounded Stew in the hand. Some of the prisoners tried escaping, but Stew was well enough to keep that from happening.

"I pointed my gun at them and told them to 'Sit.' I don't know if they understood the word I spoke, but they knew my intent and they sat."

Returning from having his wounds treated, Stew rejoined his old outfit. By this time, they were traveling on the Autobahn, the German highway system that Hitler had built, moving quickly across the country.

"Our Armored Divisions were advancing so quickly that we couldn't keep up with them. We found ourselves basically cleaning out pockets of resistance. There were lots of Nazi soldiers surrendering." They made it as far as Geissen, and around May, the 28th Division was taken off line. "We crossed the river into Hessen and all of the companies in the 28th were split up and sent into towns to man checkpoints."

Stew was sent into a town called Neiderholm, about ten miles from the Rhine River.

"Our job was to check everyone for papers. If they didn't have the proper credentials, we called the MPs. There was a distillery in town that made Cognac. We were able to build up our cash reserves by selling the Cognac to other units."

On May 7, the Germans surrendered, and sometime in May or June of that year the French took over the duties that Stew's unit was responsible for, sending his outfit to France to prepare for deployment back to the States. When they arrived home, they were given a 30-day furlough after which they were to begin training for an amphibious assault on Japan. They would be in the third wave going into the mainland of Japan – not exactly good news for men who had already seen their share of combat.

On August 15, 1945, while at home on leave, Stew was having

breakfast at a restaurant on the corner of South 79th and Cottage Grove in Chicago when he heard the news that the Japanese had surrendered. He went next door to a tavern for what turned out to be a three-day drink. Later, when he made it to the Loop in downtown Chicago, he recalled, "Everyone wanted to buy a man in uniform a drink."

At the end of his furlough, Stew had to report to Camp Shelby, Mississippi. He had only accrued 30 points, not enough to be discharged. The 28th Division, which was a National Guard unit prior to the war, was broken up and the men sent to other Regular Army divisions. Stew was sent to the 2nd Infantry Division at Camp Swift in Texas.

"It was a God-awful place in the middle of nowhere," Stew remembers. He was assigned to Company "M" of the 23rd Infantry Regiment of the 2nd Division.

Sometime in September, the 2nd Division was sent to Ft. Lewis, Washington, the division's home. On the way there, they stopped in San Francisco, California to participate in an Armed Forces Day parade. They ended up spending three weeks in San Francisco before boarding trains for Washington. "Marching in the parade was special because so many people turned out for it and they were very appreciative of our efforts," Stew said.

Ft. Lewis is located just outside of Tacoma, Washington, and Stew stayed there for two months. While there, he was given an opportunity to re-enlist. If he accepted, he would be given the rank of Sgt., but he said, "No thanks!"

A train ride which was much better than the 40 x 8 cars he rode while in Europe, would bring Stew to Ft. Sheridan, Illinois, for his discharge. The war was finally over for him, and he was back to the world he knew before he was drafted.

Using the G.I. Bill of Rights, Stew went back to school, but while there, he heard about the Columbia College of Radio Broadcast in downtown Chicago. He enrolled there and attended classes for three hours every Monday through Friday in the morning. In the evening, he was a guide at NBC, then located in the Merchandise Mart. It took him a year to complete his education at Columbia and in November, 1947, he saw an ad for a new radio station that was opening in Michigan City, Indiana. He auditioned for the position of radio broadcaster at WIMS and got it.

Stew met Marge, his wife-to-be at a soda fountain in Chicago. They married on September 10, 1949, and would eventually have ten children, seven boys and three girls.

In 1950, Stew joined the Army Reserves as a Corporal. After completing a series of tests in 1951, he was commissioned a Second Lieutenant. He would stay in the Army Reserves until 1961, during which time he was promoted to Captain. He resigned his commission because of the time he was putting in with his radio assignments.

In August 1993, Stew saw a story in a VFW magazine about the Veterans of the Battle of the Bulge Association (VBOB). He called the national office and asked if there were any chapters in Northern Indiana. He was told there weren't any chapters in the entire state of Indiana. They asked Stew if he would be interested in starting a chapter.

"I told them that I would look into starting a chapter for northern Indiana veterans, but not for the whole state," Stew said.

With the help of the National Headquarters, letters and news releases were sent to the news media in November 1993.

"I had a list of all those veterans who belonged to the national, and I was hoping we could get a good turnout for a local chapter."

An organizational meeting was held at the VFW in Michigan City in December. Twenty-three local veterans of the Battle of the Bulge showed up.

"They came from all over northwest Indiana," Stew said. "Everyone there was interested in starting a local chapter, so we formed a committee and agreed to have a second meeting for the purpose of selecting officers. One of the men, Paul Graham, said, 'Why do you want to form this organization now?' "I said if not now, when?""

In January 1994, Grover Twiner, Chapter Coordinator for the National VBOB, presented the chapter with its charter and flag. Stew was elected president and served in that capacity for four years.

Since the inception of Chapter XXX in 1994, veterans from that organization have participated in parades and set up displays to help educate students as well as adults about the Battle of the Bulge. Stew's World War II vintage jeep is used to participate in parades in the Michigan City area. The membership of Chapter XXX has swelled to more than 100. Other presidents of the chapter continue to seek the advice and counsel of Stew McDonnell, a man who in 1993 wondered if there would be any interest in forming the organization.

In 1994, Stew traveled back to Belgium, Luxembourg and Germany on a division tour commemorating the 50th anniversary of the Battle of the Bulge. The trip really brought back the memories of his time spent fighting for the freedom we all now enjoy.

"The 50th Anniversary in St. Louis was the best meeting I've ever attended," Stew said. "There were more than 2,500 veterans from the Battle of the Bulge in attendance, and I think they would all tell you that they are proud to have served."

Asked what his best times were while in the service, Stew deferred instead to saying that he will certainly remember the things that happened to him and others while they were in combat, and that he was proud to be in the service of his country.

"I'd do it again!" he remarked.

When asked about how he feels about the chapter that he helped start, Stew's comments were, "The baby has grown up."

EDWARD VEDEN
28th Infantry Division, 112th Regiment
Hometown: Michigan City, Indiana

E d marched off to the dark cloud of war in Europe as a 22 year-old draftee in March 1942. He was married and worked as an apprentice meat cutter with the Atlantic & Pacific Food Store (A&P). Like most of the young men and boys reporting to service at the time, Ed had little idea of what war was like. He knew, however, it was his patriotic duty to serve his country in its time of need, and so he reported to the U.S. Army and began a four-year odyssey that took him to hell and back.

Reporting first to Fort Benjamin Harrison in Indianapolis, Indiana, Ed was eventually sent to Camp Livingston in the Bayou State of Louisiana where he underwent Basic Training. While there, he attained the rank of Corporal and was trained in, and received a Certificate of Proficiency for completing instruction in, Defense Against Chemical Attack. He was named the Gas Non-Commissioned Officer of his unit. He was later sent to Camp Gordon Johnson in Florida for advanced infantry training.

While at Camp Jordan in Florida, part of the training the men received was in preparation for an invasion. They practiced landing on beachheads, using LSTs (landing ship – tank, nicknamed "large, slow targets" by sailors because they had a top speed of only 11 knots) to bring the fully equipped soldiers to shore. One of the practice sessions was scheduled at night, a night when weather made an amphibious landing fraught with danger. The commander decided to go ahead with the mock landing despite the weather conditions.

As the landing craft headed towards shore, one of the boats became disoriented in the foul weather and struck a sandbar. The coxswain, unable to see clearly and believing they were on shore, dropped open the front of the craft and 28 men marched off the boat and drowned in water that was over their heads. It was a sobering experience for the remainder of the men in the outfit and made them realize that there were more dangers in war then just an enemy opening fire on them.

In October of 1943, Ed, who was now part of the 28th Infantry Division, sailed out of New York harbor on board a liberty ship. His recollection of the 11-day crossing of the Atlantic Ocean includes sleeping in double shifts (each man had rights to a bunk for 12 hours, then spent the next 12 hours on deck so someone else could sleep in their bunk), as well as eating in double shifts. He remembers meals in the mess hall and trying to prevent the food trays from sliding off the tables during turbulent seas. On board the liberty ships, the food supply was used as ballast, so as the food was eaten and the ship became lighter, it became more susceptible to high seas.

During the crossing of the Atlantic Ocean, there were two separate incidents when the ship went on high alert because of the possible presence of enemy submarines, but they never saw any enemy subs and were never fired on. Out of their convoy though, two ships went dead in the water for reasons unknown and were left behind as the convoy continued its voyage to Europe.

"I felt sorry for those men on board the ships that were left behind, as they were sitting ducks for enemy submarines," Ed said. "We never did hear what happened to either of those two troop carriers that were left behind."

The convoy landed in Cardiff, Wales, 11 days after departing New York and began preparation for action. At that time, despite knowing they were heading for battle, there wasn't a great deal of concern for their own safety. As of that time, no one was shooting at them.

As they crossed the English Channel at night on D-Day plus ten (ten days after the initial D-Day invasion on June 6, 1944), they watched the lights of tracer shells being fired at the enemy and heard the rumble of distant bombing. They knew that very soon, the 112th Infantry Regiment was going to part of a very large invasion force and that they would be in harm's way.

"You know it's the real thing and not a training exercise anymore when the bombs start falling around you," Ed remembered.

Landing in Normandy, the men of the 112th moved off the beach inland. Their first combat encounter took place at St. Lo. There, they relieved elements of the 29th Division, which had taken a lot of casualties. It was in this area where Ed would be wounded for the first time.

As his platoon was advancing toward an enemy position among the infamous hedgerows that populate the area, German troops opened up with mortar fire – one shell landing close enough to the platoon that Ed suffered shrapnel wounds to his right leg.

Evacuated to a hospital in England, the metal shards were removed from his leg and Ed spent the next two weeks recuperating from his injuries. He then spent the following three weeks in the hospital as CQ (Charge of Quarters) while his wounds healed completely. After five weeks recuperating from his combat injuries, he was shipped back to his outfit.

After returning to his combat unit, where he discovered only two men were left of the 42 that were there when he was injured, the next major battle that Ed was involved in took place in the Huertgen Forest. In the forest, the men of the 112th took a beating from tree burst bombing and learned a new phrase – "Screaming Meemies." The forest was made up of close-ranked fir trees, some towering as much as 75-100 feet. The height and thickness of the trees made the forest a gloomy, forbidding place to fight a battle. The shells fired by the Germans burst in the treetops sending hot steel downward on the soldiers.

"All you could do was dig in," Ed recalled about the tree bursts. "The sights and sounds of those explosions are something you never forget. You couldn't do anything but try to survive. You couldn't shoot back – there wasn't anyone to shoot at."

Stretching northeast from the Belgian-German border, the Huertgen Forest covers an area of about fifty square miles within the triangle formed by the towns of Aachen, Duren and Monschau. From September to December 1944, 120,000

American soldiers advanced upon the Germans through this forest. Other battles in World War II have been more dramatically decisive, but none was tougher or bloodier.[1]

More than 24,000 Americans were killed, missing, captured and wounded. Another 9,000 succumbed to the misery of trench foot, respiratory diseases and combat fatigue. In addition, some 80,000 Germans fought in this battle and an estimated 28,000 of them became casualties. [2]

After surviving the Huertgen Forest, Ed and the rest of his Company were sent to the Siegfried Line (along the border between Germany and France) to await replacements. His company alone covered approximately a 28-mile front. Everything was quiet.

"We could see the Germans over the hill," Ed remembers. "And they could see us." But one day, a member of Ed's platoon watched as a group of German soldiers came over the ridge and began setting up a mortar emplacement.

"We went after them and ended up killing two of them. The third was captured and he turned out be a Major in the Wehrmacht."

"Believe it or not, that major told us exactly when and where the final push was coming from," Ed recalled. "He said the battle would begin the next day at 5:30 a.m. and that we would know it because first there would be bright lights, then "Screaming Meemies" would be fired at us. Boy! Was he ever right!"

The next day, the final push of the war by the German forces began. It would become known as the Battle of the Bulge. Twenty-nine divisions of German soldiers, approximately 600,000 men, took part in this last gap attack against the Allied forces.

"We got knocked off the line and started evacuating the area," Ed said. "We didn't know where we were or where our lines were. Thank God we had some officers who really used good judgment and they led us back to the rear where we regrouped with the rest of our Regiment.

Once they regrouped, Ed's platoon was sent back to the front lines to bolster another platoon, which had lost a lot of its men.

"We were walking down this road when we came to an intersection. We didn't know it at the time, but the Germans had the road crossing zeroed in with mortars. Just as the main part of our platoon arrived at the intersection, they let loose with a mortar round. It hit our platoon dead center, killing eight men and wounding twelve." Ed was one of the 12 that were wounded.

"That shell blew me completely off the road, shattering my rifle. I lie in the ditch unable to hear anything or see anything for awhile. The Medics picked me up. They saw the severity of my wounds and once again, I was sent back to the rear where they removed some of the shrapnel, and then was sent to a hospital in England."

After having his wounds treated, the Processing Officer at the hospital told Ed that he would not have to go back into combat after being wounded twice.

Ed refused to stay in the rear, opting to go back to combat once again, but he had a seven-day delay en route to the front lines, and on the fourth day of that delay, while in London, the war ended.

"That day was unbelievable," Ed recalled. "The British people are tough and they endured so much during the war, but on the day the war ended, they were jubilant – ecstatic. I have no complaints about the English – they treated us great."

Eventually, Ed was processed to go home – four long years after leaving Indiana. "I was sick of war and combat by then. I was ready to get out."

When asked about his best memories of the four years he spent in the war, Ed said it was the camaraderie he experienced. "Meeting so many men from so many different walks of life. Despite our differences, we all got along. We stuck up for one another. And we had good times too. There were times when we played tricks on one another, and who could ever forget the wine cellars we found in the French homes? Those Frenchmen liked their wine – and so did we."

The worst times? "The bombings," he answered without hesitation. "There wasn't anything you could do but dig a little deeper and pray a shell didn't have your name on it."

"I never engaged in any hand-to-hand combat, but one time, as we were advancing toward an enemy position, we were ordered to fix bayonets. That was an eerie feeling. Fortunately, when we arrived where the Germans had been, they had already left. We were all relieved."

There are other memories, some good, some not so good.

On December 17, 1944, the American 7th Armored Division engaged the Sixth Panzer Army at Saint Vith. Saint Vith was a major road that led to the Meuse River and to Antwerp. The Army division was successful in halting the German advance and this caused the Germans to take a path that was out of the way. On this day, American soldiers were taken prisoner at Baugnez and then shot while on a road to Malmedy. Of the 140 men taken prisoner, 86 were shot and killed while 43 managed to survive and escape. Rumors of this event spread quickly through the American divisions causing the Americans to fight much harder and with more resolve.[3]

"After we heard about what happened at Malmedy, we didn't take any prisoners," Ed recalled. "That one event made us fight much harder and with a different attitude about the Germans we were fighting."

Another incident Ed recalled had to do with a GI in his platoon who took a direct hit to the helmet he was wearing. "The bullet entered his helmet, tearing a big hole in it. The soldier never got a scratch. But, he was in such disbelief that he hadn't been killed that he lost his mind. The medics took him away screaming. We never saw him again."

Staff Sgt. Ed Veden was discharged from the U.S. Army on the 31st of Aug. 1945. He was awarded the Combat Infantrymen's Badge, the EAME Theater Ribbon with 2 Bronze Stars, the Purple Heart with one Oak Leaf Cluster and the Good Conduct Ribbon.

Included in his mementos is a "Candidates Pass" dated 5 Aug. 1945. It reads: "Veden, Edward S/Sgt. 35111543, 194 (Reinf Co) is authorized to be absent from his organization between the hours of 1800 to 2400 hours daily except Sunday. He is authorized to be absent on Sunday from 0600 to 2400 hours. This pass is good within a radius of ten (10) miles of Compiegne ONLY. This pass is good for ten (10) days from date of issue. Signed by Capt. Donald L. McFarland, Captain Infantry Adjutant."

Also included in his keepsakes is an AWARD OF DISABILITY COMPENSATION OR PENSION, dated Sept. 29, 1945. It states: "In accordance with the provisions of Pub.2-73rd Cong. Pub. 144& Pub.312-78 Cong. You are hereby notified that as a Sgt. Co. I., 112th Infantry who was discharged from the Military service of the United States on the 31st day of August 1945, you are awarded Pension in the amount of $46 monthly from September 1, 1945 on account of your disability resulting from the following conditions held to have been incurred or aggravated during your War Service WWII. Wounds in right leg – 30%, wounds in left leg – 10%. In order that your consideration may be given any necessary adjustment in your award of monthly pension, a physical examination of you will be scheduled at a later date of which you will be subsequently informed. The monthly payments pursuant to this award will continue during the period in which you are 40% disabled subject to the general conditions mentioned on the reverse side of this communication to which your attention is directed." It is signed by A.B. Chadwick, Adjudication Officer, Hines, Ill.

Ed returned to his wife and the child that was born while he was in combat and had never seen, and resumed his career as a meat cutter for the A&P Food Store in Michigan City. He would eventually have two sons, Barry J. born during the war, and Walter E. Veden, born ten years later. They would each marry and have one child. Barry, the oldest, has a daughter named Laura. Walter has a son named Chris. Ed and two sons continue living in Michigan City. His wife, Rilla, passed away in 2003.

WILLIAM J. WILKIN
28th Infantry Division, 229th Field Artillery Battalion
Hometown: Long Beach, Indiana

Along with information sent from Bill is a copy of a photograph from *Time* magazine, dated April 1944. It is a photo of hundreds of young men in uniform standing on a dock. None of the men are carrying rifles. The hull of a transport ship with a multitude of thick ropes lashed from ship to dock sits in the background. The men in the picture are looking up at the photographer, and one of those men looking towards the camera is Bill Wilkin, identified by an attached note.

All of the men look apprehensive. They have just landed in Southampton, England, after being part of one of the largest convoys of ships crossing the Atlantic Ocean, and are much closer to the war than when the ship left Boston on October 8, 1943.

Bill, along with the other men in the picture, was about to enter a world much different than the one he left behind in Rochester, New York.

Bill was born on July 14, 1924, to a family of four brothers and five sisters. His dad had served in the United States Marine Corps in World War I, the "war to end all wars," and had been wounded during action in Belleau Wood. The U.S. Fourth Marine Brigade lost nearly 7,800 men in the fight for Belleau Wood, and later, the French renamed the spot, *The Wood of the Brigade of the Marines* to honor their heroic stand.

At a very early age, Bill became involved in American Legion athletic programs, but he knew when he graduated from high school in 1942 there was a war in progress, and that he would be drafted when he turned 18.

"I was inducted into the U.S. Army on March 23, 1943," Bill remembered fondly. "I was sent to Fort Niagara for processing, and a few days later, was sent to the Field Artillery Replacement Center at Fort Bragg, North Carolina."

In addition to being trained as a cannoner, Bill also received training as a battery clerk because of his typing ability.

"After completing 13 weeks of Basic Training, I was assigned to Battery B, 229th Field Artillery Battalion, 28th Infantry Division at Camp Pickett, Virginia. I was immediately assigned to the machine gun section."

For the next few weeks, the men of the 229th took part in mountain training in West Virginia, and practiced amphibious training in the Chesapeake Bay region.

"I was given my first three-day pass before we were slated to leave the states onboard a liberty ship, and was able to go home," Bill related.

After ten days at sea, the ship carrying its human cargo landed at Southampton, England, and the men were sent to a camp in Wales.

"The camp we were sent to was an old flour mill that had barracks for the men to sleep in, but little else. We had very few food rations except hard biscuits and stew. There weren't any guns, trucks or any kind of vehicles there for quite a few months after we arrived.

"Our activity, when we first arrived, consisted of a 10-15 mile hike everyday over the Welch countryside. Of course, every evening there was also a hike of about six miles to the nearest pub. But that meant we had to walk the six miles back to the camp afterwards."

"Our battery also took part in some water training programs, and became acquainted with landing craft during some awful weather."

"In May 1944, we were shipped to an embarkation point near Salisbury, England. We had every expectation that we would be part of the coming invasion of France. We didn't know it at the time, but the 28th Division was to be the spearhead invasion at Omaha Beach up until about six weeks before the invasion on June 6, 1944. Instead of the 28th, the 29th Division took the role on D-Day, and that probably saved my life, as I would have been with an Artillery forward observation party in the second wave going ashore."

"We watched the news of the invasion that we missed on D-Day, and learned later that the 28th was to be held in reserve until July 1944, when our division was attached to Patton's Third Army. On July 20, we left England on LSTs (landing craft) for France, were assigned to the First Army, and immediately were sent to relieve the 29th Division which had been in combat since June 6. They had taken numerous casualties."

According to a document entitled, *Outline of History of 229th F.A. BN,* the battalion was committed to the line in the vicinity of Villebaudon, France, in support of the 28th's 112th Infantry Regiment. During the months of August, September and October, the artillery battalion continued their support of the 112th in Compiegne, France, and Berg Reuland, Belgium. In November, the battalion was in support of the 112th Infantry Regiment at the Huertgen Forest.

During the 24-hour period of 050600 to 060600 November 1944, the Battalion fired 3,949 rounds, believed to be a record for a light Field Artillery Battalion. Battalion continued heavy fire in support of the 112th Infantry in its attack on Schmidt, Germany. There were heavy losses during this period of the fighting in the Huertgen Forest. During this period, the Battalion expended 16,892 rounds, believed to be a record. After Huertgen, the Battalion moved to Oberhausen, Belgium. The end of November found the Battalion still at Oberhausen, Belgium.[4]

"This period of time is when I was first exposed to enemy fire," Bill remembered. "We were taking small arms fire as well as enemy mortar fire and artillery shelling. A covered trench was an absolute necessity due to the continuing incoming artillery fire. I received a laceration to my left thigh, from enemy mortar fire, but the wound didn't require that I be sent back to the rear for medical attention."

"During the breakout at St. Lo, and our push across France, we had to slug it out at every crossroads where the Krauts left roadblocks. The hedgerows were a disaster, but our infantry boys did their jobs well. I continued in my job as a radio operator in a forward observation party, and I was promoted to corporal about this time."

"On August 28, 1944, we entered Paris and camped in a local park until the following day when the 28th Division paraded through Paris in combat formation. That night, we continued our pursuit of the retreating German army."

"Although we continued to expend artillery shells in support of the 112th Infantry Regiment as they neared the Siegfried Line, and were assigned to protect Luxembourg, our next big assignment was the battle of the Huertgen Forest."

The 28th smashed into the Huertgen Forest, 2 November1944, and in the savage seesaw battle which followed, Vossenack and Schmidt changed hands several times. On 19 November, the Division moved south to hold a 25-mile sector along the Our River in Luxembourg.[5]

"The 28th Division was finally relieved in the battle of the Huertgen Forest after taking 2,000 casualties," Bill remembered. "Several other divisions met the same fate in that unfortunate campaign. I made the rank of sergeant about the time we were moved to a quiet sector of the Ardennes, a move designed to give the division time to replenish the troops that had been lost."

On December 16, 1944, the Battle of the Bulge began. The 28th Division was thinly spread across the area that the Von Rundstedt offensive targeted.

"The 28th Division served gloriously in this battle," Bill said. "By fighting a delaying battle, our actions caused the German timetable to be delayed. The 112th Infantry Regiment became separated from the remainder of the division, and operated independently for several days in fighting and delaying the enemy."

"When our forces arrived near St. Vith, the remaining infantry regiment of the 106th Infantry Division joined with our combat team and together, we fought a delaying battle, which gave the 101st Airborne Division time to take up positions at Bastogne. Our success during this battle was a testament to the leadership abilities of Col. Nelson of the 112th Infantry, and of Lt. Col. Fairchild of the 229th Field Artillery Battalion. Not one piece of equipment was lost during the withdrawal phase of the battle."

The 112th continued its artillery support for the 3rd Army forces going to the relief of the beleaguered city of Bastogne, and after the city was relieved, the division was sent to Colmar, France where it supported the II French Corps.

The 229th continued to support the 112th Infantry as it crossed Germany on its way to the Rhine River before being assigned to occupation duties at Oberzeuzheim, Germany.

"When the war ended in May 1945, a point system was developed, and if a soldier had accumulated 85 points, he could be discharged and not sent to the Pacific Theater to fight against the Japanese. I only had 76 points, so I was sent to a camp in France where I was issued a 30-day leave before being re-assigned to the Pacific. While I was home on leave, the war in the Pacific ended when the atomic bomb was dropped on Japan."

After his leave ended, Bill reported to Camp Kilmer, New Jersey, and from there was sent to Camp Shelby, Mississippi, to help prepare the battery for transfer to the 2nd Division. When that assignment was completed, Bill was sent to Camp Rucker, Alabama, for discharge, and was one of the earliest discharged veterans on October 26, 1945.

"After my discharge, I spent a few months acclimating myself back to civilian life before returning to my previous position as a payroll clerk at General Motors. I later took a position as a claims adjuster for an insurance company. It was about this time I met a beautiful woman and we were married on September 3, 1949. She encouraged me to take advantage of the G.I. Bill and I enrolled at the University of Rochester. After four years of night school and summer school, I finally achieved enough credits to apply for law school. My application was accepted, and I began my legal training at Albany Law School. My graduation day was in May 1959, as I lost a year in school due to a service-related pulmonary problem."

"I was admitted to practice in New York State on March 17, 1960. During my legal career, I have been involved in many jury trials, and have handled many industrial problems. On November 9, 1981, I was appointed a U.S. Judge, and have served in that capacity since."

"I am proud of my service in the 28th Infantry Division and the five battle stars that I have on my European Service Ribbon."

ROGER HOLLOWAY
87ᵗʰ Infantry Division, 345ᵗʰ Reg. Co L
Hometown: Michigan City, Indiana

Each veteran of the Battle of the Bulge has his own memories of, not only the battle that has brought them together as members of a fraternal organization many years later, but also of the years since those cold days in the 1940s when, on a daily basis, they stared death in the face. They simply did not fight in a war, survive, and retreat into a cocoon when they came back home. They have lived full, rich, meaningful lives since arriving back on American soil. But the time they spent fighting Nazis in Europe when they were young lads, helped shape them into the men they became later. It also gave each of them remembrances that are still in the forefront of their minds as they reach their eighth decade and beyond.

Roger Holloway is no exception.

Roger will gladly share information about the battle with a visitor, and he will proudly point to accomplishments attained in the years since then. He has accomplished much in his lifetime, completing a career at a local utility company that saw him promoted a number of times to positions of authority, marrying the love of his life and raising three sons, and playing the tuba in a band for years. But there are still vivid recollections of the time fighting the war that cause him to shudder at the thought.

"I have memories that haunt me to this day," he will tell a visitor. And then he relates one such incident.

"It was toward the end of the war – things were moving fast. We were in a firefight with the Germans, and we were trying to get them to surrender."

Sometime before this engagement began, Roger's outfit had liberated prisoners of the Nazis – one of them a young Italian man. The Italian civilian began hanging around with the American forces after he was freed, even picking up a rifle somewhere along the way. He followed them for a few days before the following incident took place.

"During the firefight, we saw three people coming out of the woods with their hands up," Roger said. "I don't think they were soldiers because they weren't wearing uniforms. One of them appeared to be an older man. The other two were much younger. The Italian civilian charged at them, wildly firing his weapon. The older man coming out of the woods shouted, 'Mein kinder!' (My children in German.) One of the younger men was hit by a bullet and fell to the ground. The older man was then shot and also fell to the ground. Then the third man was shot. The last man shot attempted to get up. The Italian finished him off by hitting him with the butt of his rifle. I was approximately 30 to 40 feet away when this incident occurred. The Italian disappeared that day, and we never saw him again."

The situation continued.

"On the road, leading the American forces that day, was an American Sherman tank. A German officer had been captured along with a woman wearing a Red Cross arm band. The German officer was ordered to stand on the front of the tank – the intention was for him to call out to the German soldiers in the woods and have them surrender to the GIs. The officer shouted at the men in German, ordering them to surrender. They continued to fire their weapons. The officer was hit, either by his own men, or by one of ours, and he fell off the tank. About that time, the tank began moving and ran over one of the German officer's legs. One of our men ran forward and shot the German officer in the head, killing him while the woman stood by screaming. About the same time, 10 to 12 German soldiers came out of the woods with their hands on their heads, a gesture that signified they were surrendering. One of our squad leaders, a buck sergeant, shot all of the soldiers who were attempting to surrender."

"Sometime before these barbaric acts took place, our Company Commander, Capt. Wahl, had been killed in action. I don't know if his death had any influence on the men involved or not."

Sometime later, after the war ended, Roger was ordered to report to Command Headquarters. An officer from another company had witnessed the shootings and had reported it to headquarters. When Roger arrived and was told why he was there, it was said to him, "You didn't see anything, did you?"

"I knew then not to say anything, so I didn't."

The incident that Roger witnessed in the woods that day became a nightmare that he has carried with him for more than 50 years.

His time in the service of his country began for Roger on October 18, 1942, at Fort Benjamin Harrison, Indiana. He was 18 years old at the time, and couldn't have imagined what was awaiting him in combat.

On November 15 of that year, Roger was assigned to the 241st Coast Artillery at Fort Dawes in Boston Harbor. While there, he took and passed the Aviation Cadet Exam and was assigned to Wofford College at Spartanburg, South Carolina, where he was enrolled in the 40th College Training Detachment for Air Crew. Later, he was assigned to Pre-flight Training at Maxwell Field, Alabama, and then Primary Flight Training at Palmer Field in Bennettsville, South Carolina. While there, he flew solo in a PT-17 Stearman, but that would be the end of Roger's flight training. A short time after D-Day, he was transferred to the 87th Infantry Division, 345th Regiment, L Company after washing out of flight training.

"Because of the need for infantrymen after the invasion forces landed in Europe on June 6, 1944, we heard that more than 15,000 men had been washed out of flight training," Roger said.

The 87th Inf. Div., the Golden Acorn, was organized as part of the National Army at Camp Pike, Little Rock, Arkansas, on August 5, 1917. The division served in World War I, scattered throughout Western France, and after the war ended in 1918, was reconstituted a few years later in the Organized Reserves. The division was re-activated on December 15, 1943, at Camp McCain, Mississippi, in preparation for their mission in Europe. On October 17, 1944, less than a year later, the division was transported to Grenock, Scotland, on board, first the Queen Elizabeth, and later, the remainder of the men of the division sailed on the H.H.T. Pasteur.

"The first day at sea on the Queen Elizabeth, there were dirigibles flying above the ship watching for enemy submarines," Roger remembered. "I had mixed emotions about what I was about to get into. I couldn't even comprehend what fighting in a war was going to be like."

After arriving in Scotland, Roger's outfit was transported to Leek, England, where they were stationed in an old silk factory. From there, they crossed the English Channel with the 87th Div. on their way to Le Havre, France. Roger remembers the channel was rough that day, making the crossing difficult.

On 5 December the Division began its movement to the combat area in the vicinity of Metz where the 345th Regimental Combat Team was committed to preliminary action by temporary attachment to the Fifth Infantry Division to assist in the reduction of the remaining fortresses surrounding that city.
The 345th Regimental Combat Team remained in he lines at Metz until December 13 when it was relieved by elements of the 26th Division.

After the 345th left Metz, they moved into the SAAR region, near a town called Medelsheim.

"We really took a beating at Medelsheim," Roger remembered.

According to James R. McGhee's book, *Golden Acorn Memories,* in reference to the shelling of "L" Company at Medelsheim, Germany, 16 Dec. 1944…*"The Captain then asked me to try and break up the tank activity to our front across the valley while he returned to his troops who were still being "plastered" by the German artillery in front of the Seventh Army. One of our other observers, Lt. Guy Allee, "A" Battery Reconnaissance Officer, could actually see the muzzle flashes of the enemy guns —but—it took him almost four hours to get clearance to fire into Seventh Army's zone and silence the enemy guns! That incredible blunder resulted in "L" Company being reduced from that fresh, full-strength Infantry Company all the way down to some 30 effectives!"*

Roger Holloway was one of the 30 men remaining in "L" Company after the enemy shelling stopped.

"I'll never forget that day. It was terrible," Roger said, remembering the battle at Medelsheim. "It was December 16, 1944, the date that the Battle of the Bulge officially began. We were annihilated. The enemy artillery shells kept falling on us, and there wasn't any place to hide. It's a saying that has been used before, but it's true – there weren't any atheists in those foxholes. I saw grown men cry and pray for their lives – we were all scared."

The artillery shells kept raining down on the GIs, sending a constant shower of hot shrapnel on the men.

"The Germans waited until we were in the open before they started firing at us. The ground was frozen so hard that you could barely dig a hole deep enough to protect your backside."

"I was fortunate that I was never wounded," Roger remarked. "The closest I came to being hurt was a time that we were under attack and shrapnel tore through the sleeping bag I carried on my back."

One of Roger's fellow GIs wasn't as fortunate, being severely wounded during the battle for Medelsheim.

"It was a terrible battle, with death and destruction all around us, and this kid, a private by the name of Dombroski, who was from Forest City, Pennsylvania, got hit. I went to him – he was still alive at the time. I held him in my arms – I knew he was seriously wounded – and he died while I was holding him. The last thing he said was, 'I have to take a s____t.'"

The battle seemed to rage forever, but when our own 155mm howitzers zeroed in on the enemy, four hours of heavy shelling by American guns reduced the town of Medelsheim into a dense cloud of black smoke and silenced the enemy guns. Roger had survived his first major combat battle.

On December 23, orders were issued for the 87th Division to break contact with the enemy in the Saar region, turn its sector over to another division and get going to Belgium in a hurry.[8]

On Christmas night, 1944, Roger's division took a 200-mile ride in the back of trucks. Their destination was unknown.

"The temperature was around 15 degrees that night and we were huddled in the back of trucks all night long. The convoy wound its way through France, avoiding the large towns and most of the main roads," Roger remembered.

At 3 p.m. the next day, the 345th set up a bivouac area 15 kilometers from the Cathedral City of Rheims. They were there to provide protection in the event of a German breakthrough. There they waited and rested.

Two days later, they were on the road again.

"Our outfit was reassigned to General George Patton's Third Army and we were heading for an assembly area in the Luchie Woods, close to Belgium. As our convoy traveled the roads, we came across the remnants of the 106th Infantry Division. They had taken the brunt of the German attack as the Battle of the Bulge began, and shot-up and burnt vehicles littered the roads. We didn't find one GI who was alive in that convoy. When we neared the town of Moircy, dead German soldiers, their bodies frozen, lay in piles like firewood. There were also many bodies of GIs."

The battle was joined at Moircy about 1000 hours (10 a.m.) the next morning. By evening, the three companies had won Moircy, destroying a number of enemy tanks in the process.

The enemy counterattacked and the Battalion Division Artillery zeroed in on Moircy. "We certainly did a job on that town," was the consensus of the gun crew. The next morning the First battalion, 345th Infantry, attacked again. This time the Nazis had enough of Moircy and the "Golden Acorn" chalked up another town on its captured list.[9]

"One time we were in the basement of a building and had a telephone line running to a machine gun outpost about a ¼ mile away. The line broke and we weren't able to communicate with the outpost. So me and another GI went out to find the break in the line. As we were making our way in the woods towards our outpost, we heard the sounds of men talking. We lay perfectly still and waited. Pretty soon, two German soldiers walked by. We didn't make a sound, and they never saw us."

Roger repaired telephone communication lines despite the fact that his MOS (Military Occupational Status) was 745, a rifleman.

"We didn't use walkie-talkies very often, because the enemy could get a fix on your position as soon as you got on the air, and pretty soon artillery shells would be falling all around you."

"Another fellow from Michigan City by the name of Ralph Jahnz was a member of "M" Company in the 345th Regiment. Our moms back home became friends, and they would exchange letters that Ralph and I had written to each of them. Ralph eventually received a battlefield commission. We both made it home after the war."

On December 8, 1945, Roger was discharged at Indiantown, Pennsylvania. In January 1947, he enlisted in the Navy Reserve and stayed in the Reserves until January 1955.

On June 1, 1952, Roger and Annette Emmons were married and they had three sons – Steven, Paul and Mark, and three grandchildren. Annette died in 2003.

After Roger's discharge from the U.S. Army in 1945, he worked at Bodine Printing Company in Michigan City, and attended Valparaiso Technical Institute, where he graduated in 1950. He was hired by Northern Indiana Public Service Company where he worked his way to Superintendent of Substations before retiring in 1983 after completing a 33-year career.

Roger continues living in Michigan City, and with the recent passing of his wife, has taken up interest in the tuba again.

BILL TULEY
87th Infantry Division
Past President Chapter XXX
Hometown: Merrillville, Indiana

There is a presence about Bill Tuley. Even though he is 86 years of age and no longer in the military, he makes a visitor feel as if he should be saluted. He commands respect, and gets it.

"I always wanted to be a soldier," he will tell you, and a soldier he became. It didn't happen easily.

Bill's military career could actually be documented as beginning with a summer spent in the Civilian Military Training Corps (CMTC) at Fort Benjamin Harrison in Indianapolis, Indiana, during the summer of 1935. While there, he underwent basic military instruction and discovered that he loved playing soldier.

The next year, even though he passed on the opportunity to attend the CMTC again so that he could study Journalism at the University of Denver, Bill joined the United States Marine Corps Reserve unit in Hammond, Indiana. All hopes of being a Marine faded, however, when he flunked the eye exam during a physical examination prior to summer camp. There would be no Semper Fi for Bill.

With the bombing of Pearl Harbor, Bill was certain he would be called up. Instead, he kept getting deferments because he was the sole support of his widowed mother after his father had passed away.

Bill knew that it would break his mother's heart if he enlisted, but he wanted to go into the service. He also knew that if he were drafted, his mother would accept that because "his country had called him."

In June 1942, he paid a visit to the Draft Board in Hammond and explained his situation to them. On June 17, 1942, he was ordered to report to active duty. Bill Tuley was in the Army.

A train would take the new enlistee to Fort Benjamin Harrison in Indianapolis to begin his life in Uncle Sam's Army, a train that left Hammond from the station one block south of the Post Office at the corner of State and Sohl Streets. Bill's mother wanted to go along but he wouldn't let her. She found a way to go there anyway when she asked a person who was renting a room from her to take her to the station. Bill wouldn't find out until years later that his mother hid behind a building and watched her son leave for war on board that train. He cried when he discovered what she had done.

Being in the military is what Private Tuley "always wanted to do," so when he arrived at his first assignment at Camp Campbell, Kentucky, he thought he finally had "made it." What he made was a clerk's job. He didn't even have to carry a rifle or participate in drills. He merely performed a civilian desk job while wearing a uniform. Before being drafted, Bill owned and managed a semi-professional baseball team in Hammond. At Campbell, he coached the 5th Corps Quartermaster basketball team. He was still a long way away from where he wanted to be in the Army.

A promotion followed in three weeks and Private Tuley became a T-5 grade clerk.

In January 1943, T-5 Tuley heard that the 87th Division was being reactivated at Camp McCain, Mississippi. He asked for a transfer to that division and got it. He was assigned to "E" Co, 345th Inf. Reg. 2nd Battalion. He was made Company Clerk – "I didn't want it. It looked like I would never be a soldier."

A Colonel by the name of Warren pulled a surprise inspection while Bill was in the office one day. He talked to Bill and asked him where he was from and what he did in civilian life. "Why are you here?" he asked. "Because I want to be a soldier," was the response. "I'll see to that tomorrow," the Colonel said, and the next day the Company Clerk who was itching to be more involved in being a soldier was transferred to a rifle platoon, promoted to sergeant and given his own squad. "Finally, I'm a soldier," Bill thought.

Sgt. Tuley stayed at Camp McCain until June 1943. While training, he fell in a ditch and broke his ankle in two places. The next eight months were spent in a hospital with an ankle injury that wouldn't heal. The Army considered releasing him with a medical discharge because of his condition.

The division, meanwhile, left for maneuvers in Tennessee and never came back. Bill was left in the hospital to recover from his injuries. The division then went to Fort Jackson, South Carolina. After eight months in the hospital, Bill was released and rejoined his old squad in "E" Company, 345th Infantry. He was immediately promoted to Staff Sergeant and in early summer was named manager of the Regimental baseball team.

It was at that time that "we prepared for war." In late September or early October, the division was restricted to their barracks. They weren't even allowed to write letters or make phone calls. Eventually, the whole division rode a train for New York City, and with the exception of the advanced party, boarded the cruise ship *Queen Elizabeth* for transportation to the European campaign. There was no convoy and no escort as they crossed the Atlantic Ocean – they were assured the QE could outrun or outmaneuver any enemy submarine in the water. After six days, during which time Bill joined other landlubbers in being seasick, the entire division landed in Scotland.

They departed the ocean liner in South Hampton and boarded a train for Stone, England. They crossed the English Channel in late October during the night, so Bill wasn't sure if the Channel was rough or not, but he didn't get seasick. Landing in Le Havre, France, in a downpour, the men marched to the area where they would bivouac for the night. Once there, the drenched soldiers tried to pitch their tents but the field was so muddy that the tent stakes wouldn't hold. So the men rolled up inside their tent halves and tried to get some sleep. "I was already mad at the Germans for causing me that discomfort," Bill remembered.

The next day, the men boarded a train to Metz, a city surrounded by four medieval forts. The Allies had already captured the city but the

Germans still occupied the forts. The Army's plan was to isolate the Germans in the forts from their supplies of food and water, and play a waiting game. Hopefully, they thought, the Germans would eventually run out of supplies and have to give up. The Army posted patrols between the forts and waited. The Germans would come out at night foraging for food, and eventually, the enemy soldiers in two of the forts surrendered. They were loaded in trucks and sent to the Saar Valley where there were other American forces. After Bill's outfit pulled out of the area, the German soldiers in the other two forts surrendered to other GIs.

Staff Sergeant Tuley's first combat assignment took place in Medelsheim, Germany, on December 16, 1944. It would be the day after the Battle of the Bulge began, but of course, they didn't know that at the time. Officers and Non-Commissioned Officers were briefed at 6 p.m. on December 16 and were given their assignments for the following day. One Company of men was to clear the woods west of Medelsheim. The following morning the men reached the assigned area where they would leave for their mission. They only carried with them what would fit in their backpacks – they didn't even take blankets along. The rest of their gear was left behind to be picked up and held for their return.

Bill's squad led the platoon into the woods. They had to cross a wide-open area, and though there were concerns that it could be a place where the Germans would open fire on them, nothing happened. The squad of GIs then entered a densely wooded area and was ordered to advance while firing their weapons. No one shot back. About half way through the woods, the Germans opened up with artillery and mortar fire. Tree bursts rained shell fragments down on the men below. Instead of digging in though, the men kept advancing. The enemy fire followed them into the woods.

"We didn't realize what the tree bursts were, at first," Bill remembered. "We kept looking in the trees for the Germans."

A soldier by the name of Roger Issacs, who would someday become a fellow member of Chapter XXX, and a good friend of Bill's, was the first one in the platoon to be wounded. The GIs finally withdrew after realizing the Germans weren't in the woods. Their mission was declared a success. The Battalion Commander sent a message to the Regimental Commander saying that "E" Company had suffered 49 percent casualties, but had stopped a German counter-attack.

Checking on his men after they withdrew from the woods, Bill realized he was missing one of his men. Charlie Titone, a close friend of Roger Isaacs, was not in the platoon when they took a head count after they withdrew.

"I'm going back into the woods to look for him," the Staff Sergeant told his men. "If you're fool enough to go back into the God-damn woods to look for Charlie, I'm fool enough to go with you," Max Wirick, a shorter but bigger soldier from Hudson, Michigan, told him.

The two GIs left then and went into the woods looking for Charlie. Everything was quiet. They searched the area but didn't find anyone alive. They saw a lot of dead bodies, but they didn't find the man they were looking for. They started back to their own lines and the Germans must have seen them. They opened up fire again and Max was wounded. He cried out, "I'm hit!" Bill turned and looked at Max. He was already turning ashen gray. He asked for a drink of water but Bill didn't give him any. He had been wounded in the stomach and lower abdomen and Bill knew you weren't supposed to give water to anyone with those types of wounds. The Germans continued firing shells at them as Bill picked up Max and began dragging him to safety. As the shells came in close to them, Bill would lay Max down and lay beside him. He kept that up for about a half mile until they finally reached safety. Sgt. Tuley would later be awarded the Bronze Star for that deed. Max survived, although he spent seven months in a hospital recovering from his wounds.

Bill visited him years later and Max said that he never felt better in his life. Bill and his wife Helen would visit Max and his wife in Michigan a number of times after the war. Years later, after Max had died, his house was broken into and all of his medals were stolen. Bill arranged for the government to re-issue the medals to Max's wife and Bill presented them to her. "You can't imagine how appreciative she was of that," he said.

The Battle of the Bulge had started, and once it was determined that it was a serious offensive by the Germans, the 87th Division was one of two sent into Belgium. Before it was over, 31 divisions would take part in the battle. His division traveled 200 miles overnight in the back of trucks to get to the battle. It was bitter cold and Belgium had more snow on the ground than they had in the past 20-30 years. The men were re-issued gas masks because of the rumor that the Germans were going to use poisonous gas. Two weeks later though, the gas masks were picked up again from them as the rumors turned out to be false.

The 87th Division entered the battle south of Bastogne. The Germans had been stopped, but the task confronting them now was to push the German assault back. There were lots of night attacks by the Germans.

Using spotter planes that the GIs called "Bed Check Charlie," the Germans tried to spot American troops below so they could call in artillery or tell the infantry where the GIs were. It became a game, albeit a serious one, where the Americans knew the planes would fly overhead each night, and they tried to hide from them.

One time during the battle, Bill's company was in a wooded area. There was a peaceful little village nearby, nothing more than a half dozen or so houses, with maybe a church or two, which the Germans occupied outside of the woods. There was only one road in and out of that small village. "C" Company was to enter the village and weed out any Germans that might be there. Bill's outfit lie in wait for the enemy in case they tried leaving the village. It was frigid cold and snowy. One of the men in his outfit, Joe Brizonis, complained constantly about the conditions. His comments were starting to wear thin on everyone, especially Bill, because he knew it was demoralizing the men. He finally had enough of Joe's complaining and placed his rifle to his neck telling him if he didn't shut up he would shoot him. The Germans never did come out of the village while Bill's squad was there, and Bill didn't have to shoot Joe.

There was a building in the middle of the battle that was occupied by doctors from both sides. The Germans occupied it first and used it as a field hospital. When the Americans drove the enemy out and took control of the building, they also used it also as a field hospital. The German doctors were allowed to continue to treat their wounded soldiers. Each side respected what the other was trying to do and no one ever did interfere with the doctors' work. Bill didn't recall what the end result of that was but felt like the wounded German soldiers probably were taken prisoner and the doctors were released.

In another battle, Bill's company had to cross an open, snow-covered field with 200 men. He said there was no way they would be able to do that without suffering heavy casualties. Taking a patrol of four men, they started across the field. A German artillery spotter saw them and called in artillery fire. The patrol went east out of the clearing to confuse the Germans and avoid the shells landing around them, and they were able to make it safely across the clearing. Once into the wooded area, they found a three-man enemy outpost that was well concealed. The Germans had a radio and plenty of provisions inside. The Americans surprised the Germans and killed two of the three soldiers inside. The third was wounded and tried to run away, but Bill shot and killed him. After they checked out the outpost to make sure the area was secure, they sent one man back to signal that it was okay to cross the clearing. For years after that incident, Bill wondered if he shouldn't have taken the German prisoner rather than shoot him. "I've replayed that incident over in my mind many times."

Bill ended his career in the military government after the war. His first assignment was in East Germany and he had quite an experience with Russian soldiers.

Immediately after the war ended, or a few days before it officially ended, Bill was named Chief Clerk for the Military Government Detachment #77. There were 15 enlisted men and 7 officers assigned to this detachment. There were hundreds of GIs available for this duty, but each detachment tried to take the men they needed (clerks, cooks, etc.). Bill was sent to Darmstadt where they were forming units to take control of the government. Their job also was to weed-out wanted Nazis and get the civilian population back to living normal lives again.

Bill was sent to Zwickau, East Germany, a city of 80,000 people that were basically untouched by the war. The men were told that they were in Russian territory and that eventually the Russians would come and take control of the city. At the outskirts of town was a Displaced Persons camp that had civilians from Poland, Belgium, Lithuania, Latvia, and other areas of Europe living in it. They had been a forced labor workforce for the Germans. They lived together in one camp, but were separated by their nationalities. Bill's unit was to keep them in the camp until they could be processed and sent home.

The American forces took over the City Hall building called the "Rathaus," and were housed there once the Germans evacuated the building. There were no stores open in town at the time, and one day some of those from the DP camp walked into town and broke into a store. They began stealing bottles of wine. Someone came into the Rathaus building and told them that DPs had broken into a wine store in town. Bill went to talk to the people but they didn't understand English and he didn't understand the language they spoke. To get their attention, he fired shots from his P-38 into the ceiling. That got their attention, and they eventually put everything back onto the shelves, left the store and went back to the camp. The people invited Bill to the camp before they left. He went there that evening and enjoyed live music and lots of drinking and dancing. The women were dancing with everyone. Bill stayed until late at night before going back to his quarters.

The sleeping and dining quarters in the building where the Americans were housed was on the second floor of an apartment building. The enlisted men stayed on one floor, the officers on another. They had clean, white sheets on their beds, china, silverware and tablecloths on the tables, as well as servants. Bill said they thought they were "in heaven."

There were three civilians assigned to their unit, including a father and daughter. The daughter was 18 years old and a high school graduate. The father was a professional translator. They spoke and wrote several languages. The daughter worked as a clerk and translated German into English. She had a girlfriend who was also 18, and who also spoke several languages. She worked in the office with them. Bill didn't' know how much, if anything, any of them were paid because that was all handled by the officers.

One time, a call came in the office from one of the banks in town that a former Nazi was in the bank trying to withdraw funds from an account so that he could make a run for it. The bank guard called Bill and told him what was going on – Bill drove a Jeep to the bank and went inside. The guard told Bill that the man was on the second floor of the bank. Bill walked into the office and saw two men – one sitting behind a desk and one in front of the desk. Bill pulled his pistol, put it to the head of the man in front of the desk and told him he was under arrest by the U.S. Government. He put the man in the Jeep and took him to the Army's office. The man was obviously scared and probably would have tried to escape if he thought it was possible. The security forces were called and they came and took him away.

"I have no idea what ever happened to him," Bill said.

After four or five weeks there, the unit was notified to pack up and be prepared to leave. The Russians were ready to take over the town. They told all of the civilians that they would be leaving and that the Russians were coming. The translator talked to Bill and asked him to take his daughter and her friend to West Germany.

"We had to say no, despite the fact that the Russians had a horrible reputation for raping and pillaging towns that they took over. They went back to being barbarians. We heard stories about all the raping that occurred in Berlin when the Russians took that city."

Everyone in this city was aware of the Russian's reputation.

"From what I've read," said Bill, "there were two types of Russian soldiers – the professionals and the men who were conscripted into the Russian military. The conscripts were probably the ones causing most of the problems, because they were from the Hinterlands. They had nothing to go back to. They never saw running water, indoor plumbing or electrical lights. They were ruthless, barbarians. The professional officers didn't condone these men's actions, but they didn't try to stop it either." All of the Germans were aware of their reputation and the translator wanted his daughter out of harms way.

When the Russians arrived, all of the Americans were in the office. Soviet troops pulled up and the officers, speaking in English, presented themselves. After the formalities, the Americans withdrew and pulled out. There were two strange-looking GIs with them in the back of the truck. The two sat in the back, next to the cab, dressed in American soldiers clothing, but they were the translator's daughter and her girlfriend. Successfully smuggled into West Germany, the girls stayed with Bill until he went back to the states.

When they arrived in West Germany, Bill was assigned to I-85 and sent to Obernzell, a town on the Danube River across from Passau, Germany. The men lived in tents in a small village next to the Czech border because the village was so small there wasn't any place for them to stay. The Inspector General visited the area and talked to Bill. Bill told him it was a disgrace for the men to be staying in tents and the next day they were sent to Obernzell where they had good quarters. The two girls were still translating for them.

The unit took over two buildings in town. One was the past Nazi official's residence and was a two-story house. All the officers stayed on the ground floor. Everyone ate all of their meals there. They had civilian cooks and mechanics. The enlisted men now totaled seven and the officers were reduced from seven to five, for a total of 12 in their detachment. The enlisted men stayed at another house on a hill. They had indoor plumbing and a hired maid to clean for them.

Life began to be grand again. Bill's office was in the building with the officers. The commanding officer of the new detachment was a captain from Austria. The job was the same as before – get things going in the country, maintain law and order, and keep plundering from happening. There was no show of force. They could get help in minutes if need be. The Captain commandeered a Mercedes-Benz for his own personal use and Bill became his chauffeur. Bill had an Opal for his use if he wanted it. The Russians stole food and occasionally raped some of the local women. The Russian officers said it would stop, but it didn't. Sometimes Bill would have another soldier drive him to the Russians to complain about their soldiers' behavior. The Russians admired and respected people in authority, so by having someone else drive Bill to register complaints, it appeared as if he were a person of stature.

"Life was good there. We didn't even have to make our own beds."

There were saddle horses left behind by the previous owner, and the Americans could ride them if they wanted. Also, in town there was a barbershop where Bill went every morning for a shave. If there were other customers in the chair, the barber would make them get out until Bill was shaved. Bill paid the man for his morning shave. "We didn't take anything for free."

Military Government was something fairly new. Sgt. Tuley was asked to devise a weekly report that would be sent to the district HQ. He devised the form and sent it to Regensburg. Bill and the captain from Austria had to attend a meeting in that city. When they arrived, the form that Bill had devised was held up as an example for everyone to see, and they were told to use that form for their weekly reports.

Working in another military detachment was an American legal officer by the name of Lt. Dalton. He was transferred to Bill's outfit. He brought his German secretary, Ursula, with him. She became the third civilian working for them. The lieutenant was eventually sent back to the states and discharged, but he came back to Germany as a lawyer and married Ursula. Ursula had lived in Koneigsburg, where her father worked in a bank. He transferred to a small bank in the city and hid from the Nazis until they found out about him. One day a big black car deliberately ran him down, killing him. It was said that it was an accident.

At the time, civilians were fleeing from the Russians. Railroad tracks were being blown up and civilians had to walk into towns in order to get onto trains. French officials advised people to get out of Berlin because there might not be anymore trains allowed to leave. Ursula and her mother arrived at the train station and a friend literally pushed them into a window to get them aboard the last train leaving Berlin. Ursula now lives in Burlington, North Carolina. Bill and his wife have visited Ursula several times on their way back from Myrtle Beach.

Bill had arrived at the new assignment at the end of June. Sometime in early December he was notified that he would be going home. The captain had put Bill in for a promotion – to Tech Sergeant, and asked him to stay. Bill thought, "Maybe I better go home."

Returning to the United States, Bill landed in Boston on Christmas Day. He would stay there for three days. After spending years in combat in Europe, he was finally back in the states. He left Boston on a train for Camp Atterbury in Indiana, and was discharged from there on December 31 – now that's a New Year worth celebrating!

"I saluted and cried at my discharge," Bill said. "I was going home to be a civilian and didn't know how to be one." He actually arrived back in Hammond, his hometown, on New Year's Eve – too late to get a date for the night.

"I had worked at W.B. Conkey as an apprentice printer before leaving for the service," Bill said. "But I wasn't in a big hurry to go back to work after arriving home." It took five weeks, some of the time spent reminiscing over a drink or two, to decide it was time to return to the workforce. "I just got tired of drinking every night, so I went back to work in the printing business. I stayed at Conkey's for twenty years."

The printing company in Hammond was the biggest binary in the country, and printed everything from The World Book and Encyclopedia Britannica to catalogues for hardware companies.

In 1947, Bill married Helen who he had met at a wedding. Bill was an usher at the wedding that saw his best friend's sister get married, and Helen was the maid of honor. They lived in an apartment in Hammond after they wed.

W.B. Conkey was eventually sold to Rand McNally and the company moved the typesetting operations to Kentucky where wages were lower. After spending 20 years working in a printing room, Bill went to work for the Hammond Times newspaper in the same capacity. Twenty years later, management at the Times informed the union workers that due to an impasse with their union in negotiations for a new contract, they were letting 105 union printers go. The company wanted to downsize the workforce through attrition and the union said no, so the Times took the position of firing the union printers. Bill was one of the 105.

It was on to the Hoosier State Bank. Bill would replace a man who was retiring and who had run the in-house print shop there. Bill would work in that print shop for another ten years.

"That was the best job I ever had," Bill said. "Those were some of the nicest people I've ever met." He had a key to the bank door and often worked in the shop on Saturdays when the bank was closed.

"They trusted me and I even carried money for them to other branch banks. I carried the money in a brown paper bag."

Bill would eventually buy the print shop business from the bank and move it, first to Dyer, then to Schererville, before selling the business to another company. That wasn't the end of his printing career, however, as he remained in partnership with the company that bought his business for another 10-12 years. He finally retired at age 81.

It has been said that once printers' ink is in the blood of a person, it became hard for that person to be anything else but a printer. Bill is testament to that adage, and even after final retirement at age 81, found a way to stay active in the business by becoming the first editor/publisher of the *Bulge Battle News*, a publication for the Veterans of the Battle of the Bulge, Chapter XXX.

The years spent in Europe helped shape Bill Tuley, as well as the rest of the men who served during World War II, into the generation that Tom Brokaw, a renowned journalist and author, has called "The Greatest Generation." Their generation saw so much horror and endured so much suffering it was as if each veteran of World War II set out on a mission to help make the world a better place to live again. It could be said that they helped rebuild America, struggling to climb out of the depths of the Depression in the 1930s, into one of the most successful economies the world has ever seen. Bill Tuley, like the other brave men of Chapter XXX Veterans of the Battle of the Bulge, did his part, first in the military, and later as a civilian.

A Catholic priest by the name of Father Doody was in Bill's regiment during the Battle of the Bulge. Father Doody is now a member of Chapter XXX and a friend of Bill Tuley's. One afternoon a phone call came in from Father Doody after the priest saw an article in a magazine about Bill. They arranged a meeting and have been friends since. (Bill remarked that in battle it didn't matter what faith or denomination a soldier was, if there was a service and prayers, they tried to attend. Also, there are no atheists in a foxhole during an artillery attack.)

RICHARD W. SCHNICK
75th Infantry Division, 275th Eng. BN. Co C
Hometown: Michigan City, Indiana

Richard Schnick is tall and is an imposing figure as he walks into the McDonald's Restaurant in Michigan City to discuss his years of service during World War II. His white hair and glasses give a hint to his stage in life, but he still looks like he could beat a man half his age in a one-on-one basketball game. Like several of his fellow chapter members, Dick has recently lost his wife and now lives alone. If he is lonely, it doesn't show. He is always cheerful when I've been around him, and this day was no different.

He came to the meeting prepared with memories and mementos. I once wrote to a friend of mine who was moving to Tucson, Arizona, that there are two things that can't be taken from you – dreams and memories. I don't know how many dreams Dick Schnick still has, but he carries with him a lifetime of memories. On this particular day, he was willing to share a small bit of those remembrances from his war years.

Dick has with him this day one book entitled: *PHOTOGRAPHIC Cavalcade, a Pictorial History of the 75th INFANTRY DIVISION 1944 - 1945,* and another, *THE 75TH INFANTRY DIVISION IN COMBAT.*

There are hundreds of black and white photos of soldiers and the aftermath of destructive battles, as well as blow-by-blow descriptions of the action the 75th Division was involved in during the years 1944-1945 amid the pages of these two aging books. There are two photographs of Dick that he proudly points to. They are photographs taken a very long time ago of a young man in fatigues in the middle of a war.

In one photo he is helping to carry a wounded soldier on a ladder made into a stretcher. He has a story about the photograph.

It was around February 5, 1945. Dick's unit was fighting in an area that would be called The Colmar Pocket Battle.

WOLFGANTZEN AND APPENWIHR FALL – 5 FEBRUARY

During 5 February, the division succeeded in securing APPENWIHR, WOLFGANTZEN, and HETTENSCHLAG. In the APPENWIHR-HETTENSCHLAG area, which was defended by elements of the 305th Volks Grenadier Regiment and the 198th Division, patrols observed enemy activity early that morning. At 0645 attacking elements of the 289th Infantry moved south. Leading elements were permitted to reach the outskirts of the village of APPENWIHR before the enemy commenced firing with small arms and mortar. In the attack the 1st and 2nd Battalions encountered anti-tank and anti-personnel mines and booby traps on all approaches to the town, delaying the advance considerably. The 1st Battalion, supported by Companies B and D of the 709th Tank Battalion, and Company A of the 772nd Tank Destroyer Battalion, secured the town at 0950. On being rejected from APPENWIHR, the enemy retired to his delaying position in HETTENSCHLAG, which was taken by the 2nd Battalion at 2000. The 289th Infantry's speed and firepower had thus severed all important roads south and southeast of Colmar.

In capturing WOLFGANTZEN from the north, the 291st Infantry took the enemy completely by surprise. All enemy defensive positions were prepared in the south and western edge of the town, where the enemy expected the attack. At 1500 Company C moved rapidly down the canal on the left, hitting the town from the north, while Company A, accompanied by tanks, came in from the west. All resistance ceased by 1730.[10]

It was during this battle that a GI next to Dick was seriously wounded.

"While we were fighting in Wolfgantzen, my outfit got caught at an intersection by Germans lobbing mortar shells at us," Dick remembered. "One shell landed within three feet of where I was at. I saw the shell hit—it didn't go off immediately, but rolled down a hill where it exploded. If it had exploded where it originally landed, it would have surely killed me. Why wasn't I killed when others were? How you can explain things like that?"

There isn't any explanation except that it wasn't Dick's time to die.

While still behind cover from the shells landing around them, a GI close to him was shot in the helmet, the bullet ricocheting around the man's head until it finally hit him.

"He wasn't dead, but he was wounded pretty severely, so a couple of us looked for a way to carry him to a medic and saw a ladder lying nearby. We put him on the ladder and carried him to safety. That man lived, maybe because of the actions we took that day, but he told me years later at a reunion, 'I know you saved my life, but I still don't like you.'"

The caption under the photograph in the book reads: *As in everything else, the sight of men in pain falls into the same dull pattern of war which makes youngsters hard, old men. Scenes of dead and injured being removed from the fighting areas was commonplace. The treatment given the wounded was the finest and most sympathetic that could be gotten anywhere under the circumstances.*[11] Another photo in the book shows Dick with a mine detector, clearing an area of buried land mines.

"There were mines everywhere,' Dick commented. "The Germans laid mines made out of all kinds of material such as glass and wood. We had the standard type of metal detectors to detect mines with, so when they were made out of other types of material, it made it difficult for us to find them." One day as he and other men assigned to clear an area of hidden land mines were leaving for the day, a German machine gunner opened fire on them.

"What was strange about that," Dick said, "was that they had seen us out there before, and we saw them. But they had never shot at us. Then on this day they opened fire and we ran like hell. The bullets were hitting the ground all around us as we dove off the road and hid under some cover. I never did get a scratch out of that either."

The caption under the photo depicting Dick with a land mine detecting device says: *Although Tellermines and S-mines still predominated in German land-mine warfare, the trend later was toward weapons which were cheaper to make and more difficult to detect. Glass, wood, plastic and clay were replacing metal wherever it was possible. It was with the standard electronic type of mine detector, however, that most of the work of mine removal was done. Upon the efficiency of the equipment, and accuracy with which adjustments were made, depended the safety of our men. The heavy snow hampered the work and increased the danger factor, but the difficulties were dealt with and the job well done. Dry, white snow crunched under foot as men slowly and cautiously labored to gain ground.*[12]

Nineteen is an awfully young age to be heading to war, but that's how old Dick was when he left Michigan City, Indiana, on March 18, 1943. At the time, he was single and working at Clark Equipment in Buchanan, Michigan. The war in Europe seemed a long way away.

After completing basic training at Fort Leonard Wood, Missouri, Dick spent time in both Louisiana and Texas before being sent to Camp Breckingridge, Kentucky. He shipped out to Europe from Camp Shanks, New Jersey, crossing the Atlantic Ocean in five days on board a cruise ship-turned-troop carrier. They made the crossing without an escort.

The 75th Division landed in Wales then took a train to Scotland.

"There wasn't any place for us to train in England, so they had these make-shift camps set up in Scotland," he remembers. "Actually, the buildings we stayed in were nothing more than chicken coops. There were two small stoves in each building."

They stayed in Scotland only long enough for their equipment to arrive, then boarded buses to Plymouth where they crossed the English Channel on LSTs. "Our outfit was headed for the Ninth Army sector in Holland when the breakthrough occurred at the Battle of the Bulge," he said.

Ideally, a new division's introduction to combat should be a relatively easy one, but Field Marshal Gerd von Rundstedt's December offensive in the Ardennes presented such a threat to the Allied cause that the 75th Infantry Division was obliged to start combat with the toughest fight encountered in the whole war in the west. During its month in The Bulge – the first half on the defensive, the second half on the offensive – the 75th Infantry Division won its spurs by helping to smash the German advance and by retaking the ground that had been lost. The rookie division had become seasoned in a battle described by Prime Minister Churchill on 19 January 1945 as one that would live forever as a famous American victory.[13]

"On Christmas Eve, we were taking enemy fire and things were looking pretty bad," Dick said. "The situation deteriorated so badly that we were given orders to blow up our own trucks and equipment so the Germans couldn't use them if they did over run us. Fortunately, we didn't have to do that."

During the period 24 December-24 January, the Division suffered 407 killed, 1707 wounded, and 334 missing. The intense cold proved as serious an antagonist as the enemy. Non-battle casualties, largely trench foot, frostbite and cold injury, accounted for 2623 casualties.[14]

"It was so cold," Dick remembered. "We were all miserable. All we had to eat was frozen C-rations." It was during this period when tank and infantry attacks were being made by the 166th Panzer Division in the vicinity of Hotton and Soy.

"One night while I was on guard duty, I watched as these two German paratroopers dropped into the town we were at. I'm not certain what their intentions were, but we were able to capture them before they made contact with whoever they were trying to meet. That was such a strange sight watching those two parachutes coming down toward where I stood. I thought I was seeing things at first."

After the Battle of the Bulge, Dick's unit fought at the Colmar Pocket Battle then on to Holland and the Ruhr Valley. On the 29th of March, 1945, Dick, along with six other Infantrymen and three engineers, crossed the Rhine River in small salt boats pinned together. They used old mattresses on the floor of the boats to deaden any noise that might be made while they were on the water. Their mission was to capture German soldiers from three houses the Germans occupied on their side of the river and bring them back. When they made it to the other side of the Rhine, the Germans fired flares and began shooting at them with machine gun fire, so they left the area and headed back to their lines. As they were crossing back to their side of the river, they almost rammed a rubber raft with German soldiers in it.

"I don't know if they had been on our side of the river trying to capture prisoners, or what they were doing," he said. "But they didn't see us and we made it across to our own lines."

Dick Schnick was discharged from the United States Army on March 6, 1946, at the Separation Center in Camp Atterbury, Indiana. He returned home without suffering a scratch during combat. He would be married in September of that year. He and his wife, Marian, would have one son, Marshall. Dick worked as a tool and die maker from 1946 until 1985. Twenty-eight of those years were spent at Waterford Tool & Die. Dick and his son Marshall continue to live in LaPorte County, Indiana.

MY MEMORIES OF THE BATTLE OF THE BULGE
By John E. Stanley
75th Infantry Division, 291st Reg.
Hometown: Hobart, Indiana

I was 16 years old when I came to Indiana, straight from a farm in Tennessee. At 18, I was inducted into the U.S. Army at Fort Benjamin Harrison, Indiana. It was Nov. 4, 1943.

From the base in Indiana, I was sent to Camp Walters, Texas and assigned to the 75th Infantry Division. That's where I received Basic Training. The second time we came in from a march, the Sergeant asked me if I would accept the position of Temporary Corporal. He offered me that position because I was good at marching and good with directions. I accepted and wore the band of Corporal around my arm until I was discharged. The troops always recognized me as a Corporal.

We departed for the war in Europe from New York City. We were heading to Le Havre, France. I was told that the ship I was on sank three German submarines as we crossed the Atlantic Ocean, but I cannot substantiate that. I do know that one night we were ordered to wear our life jackets and we stood all night while the ship fired depth charges into the water. There wasn't any other artillery or weapons to defend the ship with, only depth charges.

Active duty in Europe for me began on Nov. 26, 1943. Our division went out on patrols, missions and fought in many battles. I fought in three major battles in Europe. They were the Ardennes, Rhineland and Central Europe. There were other battles that I fought in as well, and they were all major battles to me because my life was on the line each time.

I received the Purple Heart, three Bronze Service Stars, Arms of the City of Colmar, Combat Infantryman Badge, Rifle Sharpshooter, the Good Conduct Medal, European African Middle Eastern Campaign Medal, and the Bronze Star for bravery and the World War II Victory Medal. I am especially proud of the Sharp Shooter Medal.

I only had two or three days of training when I was put in charge of training other boys how to shoot. I didn't have any problem hitting a bull's eye target with an M-1 rifle, and I'm certain my childhood training while I lived on a farm, and the hunting I did while there, attributed to my shooting ability.

I have a distinct remembrance of one battle that I took part in. We were ordered to take the town of Wolfkansin, France from the Germans. The enemy had us pinned down with machine gun fire. Our outfit would advance out of the woods, machine gun fire would begin blasting and we would flatten out on the ground. When the Germans stopped firing their guns, we would crawl on our bellies to advance toward the German position. I saw a cornfield in a valley and crawled to it. At the time I was a First Scout. I remembered the direction the machine gun fire had come from, so when I arrived in the cornfield I worked my way to the edge and watched for the point of origin of the gunfire. When the German soldier fired again, I saw his exact position. The next time he fired, I zeroed in on him and when he rose to fire again, I shot him. The machine gun fire stopped and our troops began to move up. When the other German soldiers realized what had happened, they started coming out of a pillbox. I shot the first German who came out, he fell to the ground and I emptied my whole clip on him. I repeated that on every German who came out of the pillbox.

I don't know how many men I shot. Each clip held eight rounds and I'm not certain how many clips were in a bandoleer, but I would guess about twenty-five. I used my entire supply of ammunition. Thinking about it now, I realize it wasn't necessary to empty my clip on each one I shot, but at the time, in the middle of a war, it seemed like the appropriate thing to do.

When the other troops arrived at my position, I borrowed ammunition from a buddy. I went to check out the German who had been firing the machine gun. He was dead; my bullet hitting him between the eyes. I took his P-38 pistol and bayonet and carried them with me the rest of the war. I still have the pistol. We eventually secured the town of Wolfkansin. As I recall, we went from there to Holland.

As I mentioned earlier, I was raised on a farm and was hunting rabbits at the age of 10. Therefore, my natural instincts and training became a real plus for me in combat. I had no problem while on patrol to take the patrol out on rounds and return them back to the point where we were dug in at. I did this at nighttime and part of the secret for me was watching the sky. I suppose that would be no minor accomplishment for someone with no such background, but I guess that is why I led so many patrols. My natural instincts for that kind of duty helped keep me and others safe.

One night we had just returned from a patrol when the Sergeant yelled for me. A Lieutenant Colonel had arrived at our location and he wanted to see the area. I was told to take him around. There was a German dugout in the patrol area, and because it hadn't been checked out yet for booby traps, we were told not to enter the area. During the patrol with the Lieutenant Colonel, he saw the hole and asked what was in it. I told him what our orders were and why, but he said he wanted to see what was in the hole. I told him I couldn't stop him from going in but my orders were not to enter and I wasn't going to. He took a flashlight, entered the hole and there was an explosion. I took the rest of the patrol back to where we were dug in at and reported the incident. The Sergeant went out to check on the Colonel while we waited in our secured area. I never heard anymore about it, but I knew he was dead.

My memory of the Ardennes Battle (the Battle of the Bulge) is that the Germans had made a full attack against our American troops near Bastogne, Belgium. Our troops were trying to hold ground and secure Bastogne. The Germans had managed to penetrate the American lines and had practically wiped out the 28th and the 106th Infantry Divisions. Our division, the 75th, went in to relieve them.

As we marched into battle, we saw bodies of American soldiers stacked upon each other on both sides of the road. The sight reminded me of how we used to stack firewood on the farm. It was an unforgettable, horrible sight that still lives in my memory.

When we reached the area where we were going to relieve the other GIs, we dug in. My buddy and I dug our foxhole and I suggested that we use a railroad iron that I found to place across the top of our foxhole. We put boards on top of that and then put dirt on the boards. We could see the German soldiers walking back and forth in the woods ahead of us, but we couldn't fire because we knew some of our soldiers were somewhere behind the Germans and we were afraid our bullets might hit them. After several days of being confined to that foxhole, it was my buddy's turn to go for rations.

I was sitting in our foxhole watching the Germans. The sun was setting, just topping the trees in the woods. I heard a mortar shell coming and I knew it was going to hit the foxhole. After you've heard shells long enough, you can tell by the sound they are making when the shell is going to hit you. I crawled back farther into the hole as the shell hit. I was told later that my buddy returned the next day and found me unconscious. He went for a medic, and when they returned they pulled me out of the foxhole and took me to the medic's station. I regained consciousness sometime later that day, and found that I was blind. The medic treated my eyes, the blindness was temporary, and I stayed with him until Patton's army arrived with tanks.

I was told that the first shell hit the back of the foxhole I was in, a second shell hit the foxhole in the middle, and a third shell hit the front of it. I believe if we wouldn't have used the railroad iron, there is no way I would have survived that attack. I had to be reissued a rifle and a full pack because mine had been destroyed. It seemed like an eternity before General Patton arrived with his tanks.

The 75th Division fought in the Battle of the Bulge for 26 days. I was told later that our division alone lost 1,409 soldiers. That's an average of 54.2 men a day. Every time I get really cold now, I can't help but remember the extremely cold weather we endured during this time. We were in snow that was knee-deep or higher all through the battle. I remember times when the snow was up to my hips. I found out later that it was the coldest winter in the history of Belgium.

When I was suffering through blindness, I was told to stay put and that someone would pick me up. However, I wanted to stay with my group. My buddy, Raymond Foxworth, tied a rope to his pack. I held onto the other end until we reached the next place that we were to dig in at. About this time, about 12 days after the shells hit my foxhole, I was beginning to see some light, and I eventually regained my sight. The medic brought me my Purple Heart.

In some of the battles, I remember incidents, but don't remember whether they were in France, Belgium or Holland. I remember the time we were pinned down on the edge of a town. It could have been when we were in the Colmar Pocket. There was a German machine gun in a house in an upstairs window. The Sergeant and other men in the outfit had been shooting anti-tank grenades from their M-1 rifles, evidently from their shoulders, but the grenades were falling short of the target. The Sergeant sent for me to come up from the back. Once I got there, he explained the problem and asked me if I could put a grenade into the window. I told him that I would give it my best shot. I put the butt of my rifle on the ground, installed the grenade on the end of the rifle and elevated the barrel toward the sky. I knelt behind the rifle and kept elevating it until I could see the top of the grenade and the window. When I had the window in my sight, I fired my rifle. The grenade went up toward the sky and then came down and dropped directly into the window. That ended the machine gun fire that had been coming from that window. We moved into the town and liberated it from the Germans.

During another battle that we were in, one of our soldiers was shot and was lying in the line of fire. I crawled out to him, grabbed him by his feet, and dragged him back out of the line of fire. I was later awarded a medal for bravery for saving the life of that soldier.

While fighting in Belgium, I was still an acting Corporal. The officer in charge assigned squads from the company into different areas to be lookouts. We had just taken a town and the Germans had retreated. There were 12 soldiers in a squad. I was sent with the rest of my squad to a hilltop where there was a small house and a barn. Three of the men in the squad had only been with us a few days. I told all of the men to keep an eye in the direction that the Germans had retreated. I was going into the barn to do my personal business. I went into the barn and had just started dropping my pants when I heard a voice in my head tell me to "scatter out." I ran outside, still holding my pants, yelling for the men to scatter and take cover.

Everyone did just that except for the three new men. They were still sitting at the corner of the house when a mortar shell hit them. I yelled for a medic and they came running to where the shell had hit. I believe if those boys had been in combat longer, they probably would have taken my advice and scattered. During combat, anytime someone was wounded and not killed instantly, we never heard the end of the story about their condition, and we never heard any more news about those three men.

Later, when we were all getting ready to move out again, two Army officials interrogated me for several hours. They wanted to know how I knew our squad was in danger. How did I know beforehand that the men should scatter and take cover? I explained to them over and over again that I heard a voice inside of my head telling me to take cover. That was the way it had been all through the war. When I heard the voice, I didn't question it. I just obeyed it. I know it was hard for them to believe me, and I doubt if they ever did, but it was the truth. I believed then, and I still believe today, that it was God speaking to me. My mother was dead, but I knew there were other people praying for me, and I prayed and asked God for direction and protection.

Once, after a battle, I reached for my canteen and realized it had been shot off my belt. Upon further inspection, I found that I had three bullet holes in my overcoat between my legs. The company commander issued me a new canteen and overcoat.

In one battle, the Germans had us pinned down in some tall grass. I was lying flat on my stomach. The only protection I could find was a rut – like a car rut. Machine gun fire cut the weeds and tall grass over my head. I remember laughing and telling a buddy next to me that if they ever lowered their aim, we were dead men. They didn't and we didn't die.

One time, we had captured some German prisoners. Two of us were assigned the task of taking them back to our rear lines. We had to walk through about a half mile of woods to get back to where our troops were. One of the German prisoners could speak English. When we started into the woods, I counted the prisoners. I told the prisoner who could speak English to tell the others that I had counted 24 prisoners. I said that if when we got through the woods there weren't still 24, I would shot the rest of them. They were all still there when we came out of the woods.

Another time there were three of us from the 75th Division on boat patrol. We were on the Rhine River trying to determine where the Germans were and what type of equipment they had. We weren't paddling the boat we were on, instead, just letting it drift across the river. We saw two German soldiers with a machine gun. We knew if they saw us that it would be the end of us. We were delighted to find that they were both asleep. We drifted right on by, quieter than mice.

There were so many battles and I was such a young man at the time. Now, 56 years later, I can't recall each battle, but there are some memories that are still very vivid.

I make no apologies for the actions I took during the war. I've never been sorry that I served my country. Actually, I've always been proud of my service record. It has been said that our past influences our present. Therefore, I have zero tolerance for people who take this great country and our freedom for granted. We have paid the price for freedom. All I have to do is remind myself of the scene of dead soldiers stacked like wood and I know we deserve the freedom we all enjoy.

I was discharged from Camp Atterbury, Indiana, on March 26, 1946. My serial number was 35 898 226. I was in Company "C", 291st Infantry Regiment, 75th Division. I was a Private First Class.

GEORGE STRICKLAND
2nd Infantry Division, 23rd Inf. Reg.
Past Director Chapter XXX
Hometown: Munster, Indiana

George Strickland is a quiet man. Like many of his WWII friends, he is not in the best of health, but, despite his physical limitations, he has always taken an active role in the Northern Indiana chapter of the Veterans of the Battle of the Bulge, serving as one of the first directors in the organization. He continues to attend quarterly meetings in Michigan City, Indiana, and on one of those Saturday mornings, he spoke about his time in the service of his country.

George was inducted into the United States Army on the 27th of July 1944. He was 19 years old.

A resident of Munster, Indiana, George was sent, first to Camp Atterbury, in the Hoosier State, then on to Camp Walters, Texas. He received 17 weeks of Basic Training before being shipped overseas as a replacement. He traveled across the Atlantic Ocean with other replacement soldiers on the troopship *William H. Berry*. After two weeks at sea, during which time the ship was on alert a number of times because of the possible threat of German U-boats, they landed at Le Havre, France.

"I remember there was a terrific storm while we were crossing the Atlantic. That, plus the possibility of being targeted by a submarine, made for a very stressful crossing of the ocean," George said.

After landing in France, the men were loaded on train cars called 40x8 and transported to the end of the rail line. The railroad cars were designed to hold either eight animals or 40 men. George was a private at the time.

"It was so cold inside those cars," George remembered. "We were in those boxcars for two days – it was terrible. We knew we were on our way into combat, and spending two days riding in a rail car gave us lots of time to think about the consequences of that."

"We finally got off the rail cars and found ourselves close to Omaha Beach in Normandy where our division landed on D-Day plus one. The harbor was in terrible shape. There were boats half sunk with big holes in their sides. Smaller ships called Ducks were unloading the supplies. There was a lot of activity in the harbor."

"We were taken to two or three different Repple Depots where the men were dropped off and assigned into divisions that were in need of replacements. I was taken in a small truck to the 2nd Division at the Elsenborn Ridge."

While at the Elsenborn Ridge, a Chaplain asked if any of the men would like to attend service one Sunday. George and two of his friends attended. George would be the only one of the three to make it home when the war ended.

According to an article from the U.S. 2nd Infantry Division, *On June 7, 1944, D Day+1, the division stormed ashore at bloody Omaha Beach. While other units were stalled by the determined German resistance, the Indianheads blasted through the hedgerows of Normandy. After a fierce 39-day battle, the 2nd Inf. Div. took the vital port of Brest, which was liberated on Sept. 18, 1944. From positions around St. Vith, Belgium, and throughout the Battle of the Bulge, the 2nd. Inf. Div. held fast, preventing the enemy from seizing key roads leading to the cities of Liege and Antwerp.*

Even a key German General praised the efforts of the 2nd Div.

"We failed because our right flank near Monschau ran its head against a wall," said General Von Manteuffel, Commander of German Fifth Panzer Army after the Battle of the Bulge. That wall was the men of the 2nd Inf. Div.

George remembers the V2 rockets the Germans were using at the time. "They sounded like Model A Fords as they passed overhead."

"We were walking down a road one time when a shell came overhead and landed 20 feet away from us. Shrapnel from the shell wounded one of the men in our outfit. The Captain looked at us and said, 'You're veterans now.'"

"As we progressed across Europe, we were in the Black Forest when we came under intense machine gun fire. We all hit the ground, hugging anything that might afford us some protection. The bullets were so close, not only could you hear then whizzing by, you could see pine tree needles hit by the passing shells falling right over our heads."

"During my four and a half months of combat, it seemed like my outfit always spearheaded advances against the enemy. We were always the first to go into a situation. I carried my bible with me all the time I was overseas," George said. "The only time I thought about dying was the time when our outfit was pinned down by mortar and machine gun fire. I really didn't know if I was going to make it out of that battle. All the time you are in combat, you have to constantly be on your guard. I spent a lot of time looking around to see who might be taking a potshot at us. I also did a lot of praying."

Another tense situation George remembered concerned enemy planes.

"I was in a truck convoy and we were driving down this road on our way to another battle site when enemy planes attacked the convoy. The trucks pulled off the road into a field. Twelve German planes came over and we all ran for cover. I was scared to death."

Toward the end of the war, George's outfit liberated Czechoslovakia.

"We were scheduled to go to Berlin but ended up in Czechoslovakia instead. We spent six months there where we took part in the liberation of many towns and where we lost more than a few men. During this time, I crossed the Elbe River in a rowboat."

George shared with the author an account of a battle that he took part in. It is called *Explosion in the Quiet Zone* and is written by Charles B. MacDonald, one of the country's foremost military historians before his passing in 1990, and a company commander during the Battle of the Bulge. It reads:

Captain Charles MacDonald shivered from the cold. A company commander in the 23rd Infantry Regiment, 2nd Division, MacDonald had spent the night listening to German Nebelwerfer rockets shriek overhead. The Ardennes front was supposed to be quiet. But in the early hours of 17 December 1944, the forests around Elsenborn Ridge shook with the sound of battle.

Deployed outside the twin villages of Krinkelt and Rocherath, MacDonald's company was blocking a road that led to Elsenborn Ridge. His riflemen stood right in the path of the first SS Panzer Corps; spearhead of the Sixth Panzer Army.

German infantry attacked the company line seven times, screaming and waving their rifles. Seven times the GIs stopped them dead. Then came the tanks. Five heavy Tigers, with their 88mm. guns, came thundering down MacDonald's exposed left flank. There was only one bazooka in the entire company, and its tube had been dented by a German bullet. It would not fire.

The big Tigers opened up from 75 yards away. Their shells snapped tree trunks in half, throwing deadly burst of wood fragments in all directions. The company's first platoon, blasted away from their positions, fell back in a daze.

At a nearby firebreak, MacDonald tried to rally his men, but a flanking force of Germans hit them before they could form a line. When he looked up from his radio, only three of his soldiers were still there. It was time, as MacDonald said, to "run like hell."[45]

At the end of the war in Europe, the men who hadn't accumulated enough points were retained in the service for a possible invasion of Japan.

"I was shipped out to a fort in the state of Washington to prepare for the invasion," George remembered. "I met Stew McDonnell while in Washington. We were both obviously relieved that the bomb was dropped on Japan and we didn't have to take part in another battle."

"When it was all over, I can honestly say I was with a good bunch of guys and I'm glad I was able to serve my country in its time of need," George said. "But being in combat and being under enemy fire is something that I'll never forget. The sights and sounds of combat stick with you for a lifetime."

George Strickland was discharged from the Army on July 2, 1946. He was a Pfc at the time and had earned three Bronze Stars for combat in the Ardennes, Rhineland, and Central Europe campaigns. He also earned the prized Combat Infantryman's Badge and an additional Bronze Star for Meritorious Achievement in Ground Combat Operations Against the Enemy.

Returning to civilian life, George was employed by Union Carbide and Amoco Oil Company.

TEO ESPOSITO
106th Infantry Division
Hometown: Portage, Indiana

Teo Esposito is not a big man. But what he lacks in size, he more than makes up for in heart and courage.

Teo fought in WWII with the 106th Infantry Division, 422nd Infantry Regiment. Like many other GIs who fought the war in Europe against the Nazis, he was taken prisoner by the Germans. American POWs weren't afforded the same treatment as their German counterparts while in captivity, and many died as a result of being captured.

For some of those who survived, anguish and dark memories from that time in their lives have been a constant reminder of when they served in the military defending freedom. Emotions from the time spent as a POW are never far below the surface for Teo – even more than 50 years after he was liberated from a Prisoner of War camp, but he was kind enough to share his story with the *Bulge Battle News*.

A graduate of Emerson High School in Gary, Indiana, Teo joined the Army in October 1941. He graduated from Basic Training about the time Pearl Harbor was attacked.

Teo's initial assignment was as a Basic Training instructor teaching new recruits every facet of the training manual. It wouldn't be until September 1944 that he would see Europe, arriving in Belgium via Scotland and England.

Serving as an Infantryman with the 106th, Teo manned forward outposts and sent patrols into enemy territory.

"As one of those in a forward position, I could see German soldiers' everyday, not far from where we were at," Teo remembered. "I was concerned that because we were so close to the enemy lines, we would be some of the first to be shot or captured."

His worst fears were about to come true.

On Oct. 19, 1944, while guarding a group of 15 German soldiers that Americans had captured, Teo and six other GIs were themselves captured by German soldiers.

Six months of hell lay ahead of him.

"There was never a time while I was a prisoner that I wasn't scared," Teo said. "If we didn't do exactly what the Germans told us to do, they shot us."

One of the more tragic events happened as he was being shipped via rail car to another POW camp in Germany. Allied planes bombed the trainload of American prisoners without realizing the cargo the trains carried. Many men perished.

"Someone opened a hatch on the car we were in and we all began running when the bombs began to fall," Teo said. "I was knocked unconscious, and when I came to, I was half covered in rubble and was bleeding from cuts that I sustained. What I saw then was something that looked like it was from a prehistoric time. It was cold, around 18 below zero, and everything around us was white. I thought I was dreaming at first. The German soldiers had found ox-drawn wooden carts, and they were throwing the bodies of dead GIs into the carts. That's a scene I'll never forget."

Teo would be in four different camps while a prisoner; Stalag 12A, 3B, 4B and 3A.

"The conditions were horrible. We had little to eat, and what we did was rotten enough that it made us sick."

One such delicacy was called soldier's bread, a soggy, poor excuse for bread. On one march to another camp, Teo and a few other prisoners saw frozen rutabagas lying in a field and ran over to pick them. The frozen rutabagas were some of the better food they ate as prisoners.

On April 22, 1945, Russian soldiers broke through the German lines and liberated the imprisoned Americans.

"We walked for five or six days after being liberated, trying to find the American lines."

They eventually found the American 30th Division emplacement, and were taken to safety.

"I remember thinking at the time, 'Thank God we made it.'"

While recovering from their wounds and imprisonment, the recently-liberated GIs were visited by General Eisenhower.

"Ike told us that he would make sure that we all made it home safely."

The men did arrive home safely, and while at home recovering from his months as a POW, the Japanese surrendered and the war was over.

"I'm no hero," Teo will tell you. "The heroes are the ones we left behind on foreign soil. But, I'd do it all over again. I love my country and I'm glad I had a chance to serve."

(Note: Teo died not long after this interview was completed in March 2001.)

PHIL HUFFINE
106ᵗʰ Infantry Division, 422ⁿᵈ Inf. Reg.
Prisoner of War
Hometown: Crown Point, Indiana

There is no pain on his face as he relates the story, and one wonders how that can be. Phil suffered so much as a soldier fighting for his country during World War II, and could have justifiably carried a chip on his shoulder for the remainder of his life. But he hasn't.

The onetime prisoner of war tells a visitor of the horrors he experienced during his imprisonment by the Nazis and how close he came to death. He shares the story while wearing a smile that could melt an icicle on the coldest day in Iceland.

Maybe because of his ordeal as a POW, Phil now embraces life with an outlook that many people half his age wish they possessed. Perhaps the pain he endured in Europe, during the time when he wondered if he would ever see home again, or the light of the next day, for that matter, helped shape the future of Phil's life into what it has become. He has not forgotten the dark period – the cold, the hunger, the near-death struggle to survive—but the days when he was held against his will by the Nazis did not keep him from being successful later. And it is obvious that he has accomplished much by keeping a positive attitude about life.

Like other Battle of the Bulge veterans, Phil was a young man when he enlisted in the 1940s – a student at Indiana University in Bloomington, Indiana.

"As a young man, I wanted to work in the world of finance, perhaps be a banker someday," Phil related with an ever-present smile. "I was a student at IU, studying in the field of finance when Pearl Harbor was bombed. The next day, December 8, 1941, 10 fraternity friends and I decided that we wanted to fight for our country."

Getting to the fight became a lot harder than what the young man from Tipton, Indiana, thought it might be.

The Sigma Nu fraternity brothers from IU who were intent on enlisting, traveled to Indianapolis to sign up for the Air Corps, but once there, Phil failed the eye exam. There would be no flying in a war for Phil in 1941 – he would have to enlist first in the Army Reserves and wait for a call to active duty. The call came in May 1943, and Phil reported for service at Fort Benjamin Harrison, Indiana.

Because of his college background, Phil was sent to Fort Benning, Georgia, under the Army's ASTP program – a program designed to keep educated men in college until they graduated. The universities were all full, however, so after Basic Training, Phil was assigned to the 98th Infantry Division in Tennessee.

"My first assignment was at the Division Finance office in the Enlisted Man's Payroll Section where we determined the monthly pay for enlisted men. It was like a civilian job," Phil remembered. "We didn't have to stand any military formations, and our hours of work were from eight to five. It was a nice job, but I still had a burning desire to contribute in other ways."

The 98th Division was eventually transferred to Camp Rucker, Alabama. Once he arrived there, Phil applied for a transfer to the Army Air Corps, hoping to be able to fly an airplane someday. The permission to transfer was awarded and Phil was soon sent to Miami Beach, Florida. While in Florida, he was tested and qualified for flight training. All of the schools were full, however, and the young man from Indiana who wanted to fly, along with others, would have to wait for vacancies in the program before they could begin their training. It didn't look like he was ever going to be in the war.

After leaving Miami, Phil was sent to Lockborne Air Field in

Columbus, Ohio, where, he said, "We didn't do anything there but wait for a call for pre-flight training." The call never came.

The war in Europe was claiming the lives of many young Allied soldiers, and by the spring of 1944, the Army was in need of more ground forces for the invasion that would take place in June, and to replace those men who had already been wounded or killed in combat. Men in the States who had transferred during the previous six months were reassigned to ground force units – Phil included.

It was back to Indiana and the awaiting 106th Infantry Division at Camp Atterbury.

The 106th Division was activated at Fort Jackson, South Carolina, on March 15, 1943. After completing maneuvers in Tennessee in late March 1944, the entire Division was transferred to Camp Atterbury. IN. While there, the Division lost more than 7,000 enlisted men and 600 officers who were sent to replacement depots. Many of the men from the 106th were sent to the replacement depot at Fort Meade, Maryland, and ended up in divisions that became part of the invasion force on D-Day, 1944.

During the summer in 1944, the 106th was filled with replacements from other training units, such as the Army Air Corps, the Army Specialized Training Program (ASTP), the Coast Artillery, AAA Artillery units and others. In October, 1944, the Division shipped overseas to England for a brief period of training before shipping across the channel to Le Havre, France.[16]

"We shipped out for Europe out of New York harbor," Phil remembered. "I was on the *Aquitania*. As we were leaving the harbor, we ran to the decks to see the statue of liberty, and after looking at the moving water passing under the ship, I became sick. I was seasick for four days." Not a good way to start a journey to a place where he would be called on to fight for his life. As if being seasick wasn't bad enough, the food being served onboard the ship was lamb. "My God, that stuff smelled terrible – you could smell that food all over the ship," Phil recalled. "And that only made me sicker than I already was."

The cruise across the ocean would take approximately six days and when the troop carrier landed, it did so in Grenoch, Scotland. From there, a train would take Phil and the rest of the division to a small town outside of Oxford, England. While there, Phil would learn a new trade for the military – truck driver.

"I was awakened one morning about 4 o'clock by my first sergeant.

He told me I had two hours to be at the train station. When I asked why I was being sent there, he said, 'You're our Jeep driver and the division needs drivers for a special assignment.' So, I reported to the station and discovered I was being sent to Glasgow, Scotland, where vehicles were being unloaded and reassembled after transportation from the States. After assembly, the vehicles were then driven to Liverpool, England. The Army needed men to make the round trip which took about 22 hours. I wound up driving everything from a Jeep to an 18-wheeler. I even drove some Ducks, which are amphibious vehicles used for beach landings. When I complained that I didn't know how to drive some of the vehicles, I was told that manuals were in the glove boxes and I should read them. There were hundreds of drivers making that round trip everyday. We would drive the vehicles to England, spend the night there, and then take a train back to Scotland the next day. " The vehicles being delivered were replacements for those that had been destroyed in combat.

After about six weeks of the special assignment, Phil was called back to Oxford where the Division prepared for its first combat assignment.

"We loaded all of our vehicles on LSTs, ships designed to carry men and equipment and capable of disembarking the cargo on a beach by lowering the front door. I had a friend by the name of Danny Mattingly from my hometown of Tipton who was in the Navy onboard a LST, so I began looking for him. There had to be 100 or more LSTs there waiting to be loaded, but, believe it or not, I ended up on his ship. I looked him up once we got onboard and found him. It was so nice seeing a friendly face from home."

After being loaded with cargo and men, the LSTs lie at anchor in the English Channel for three days waiting for a pilot to take them up the Seine River. Eventually, they would land at Le Havre, France, and on December 11th, replace the U.S. 2nd Division on line, which was in the Schnee Eifel area of the German/Belgium border east of St. Vith, Belgium.

The 106th Division had just arrived from the United States and was new to action. The General, Alan Jones, a quiet, methodical and conscientious commander, was unhappy about the fact that two of his regiments, the 422nd, and the 423rd Infantry, had taken over positions well forward on the crests of the mountainous feature, the Schneee Eifel. His third regiment, the 424th, held positions somewhat to the south and west of the Schnee Eifel with a gap between them and the 423ʳᵈ, covered by a reconnaissance troop. The whole division was responsible for more than 21 miles of front, including the Losheim gap in the north watched by the 14ᵗʰ Cavalry.[17]

"We were on the front lines only a few days before the battle that would become known as the Battle of the Bulge began," Phil said. "At first, there wasn't anything going on – no contact with the enemy. We were sleeping in two-man dugouts with log roofs. Despite the fact that it was bitterly cold, staying in the dugouts and sleeping in sleeping bags enabled us to stay somewhat warm."

On the night of December 15, things took a turn for the worse for the 106ᵗʰ and the rest of the men in the Ardennes Forest.

"We could hear tanks moving around that night, and we knew they weren't ours. The next morning at 4 o'clock, I was sent to Regimental HQ to tell them what we were hearing, but by then, the battle had already begun."

On 16 December, 1944, the Germans launched their ARDENNES OFFENSIVE. The 106ᵗʰ, positioned in the Schnee Eifel salient, was hit with their full force. After three days, the 422ⁿᵈ and 423ʳᵈ Regiments were surrounded and completely cut off from the rest of the U.S. Army.[18]

"While at Regimental HQ, I became separated from my company," Phil remembered. "Twice we saw tanks and thought they were ours. They weren't. They fired at us, but we were able to get away."

Getting away from the tanks, the men joined up with other men from the 106ᵗʰ on a hilltop near the town of Schonfeld. There were approximately 100 GIs gathered together there.

"The Germans attacked us there and we were able to repel them the first time," Phil said. "But after two days, we ran out of ammunition. On the morning of the third day, we saw a German vehicle approaching waving a white flag. A German officer told us that we were surrounded and that if we didn't surrender, they would wipe us out. They also said that our resistance was keeping the Germans from getting to some wounded American soldiers on the other side of the hill. We didn't believe that the enemy was concerned about helping wounded GIs, but one of our officers went with the Germans and saw for himself the condition of the GIs on the other side of the area that we were defending. He came back to our lines and told us what he saw."

After discussing the situation among themselves the men decided to surrender to the Germans, and around 12:00 noon, the Germans came and took them prisoner.

"They stripped us of heavy coats, gloves, and overshoes, leaving us wearing only field jackets over our fatigues. It was bitterly cold and they took away any clothing that might keep us warm."

The men were then marched toward the town of Flammerschein.

"During the entire time we were being forced marched, if any one of our guys fell out because of injury, sickness or just being tired, the Germans shot them," Phil said. "We lost about a fourth of our guys during the march because they were shot by German soldiers who were guarding us. It was so cold, and we were so scared. When we stopped at night, we had to sleep on the ground outside in the weather."

"The first day we were captured, we were coming into a small German town when American B-25 bombers flew overhead at tree-top level and dropped bombs on a hospital clearly-marked with a red cross. The hospital was destroyed. As we were being led into town, the civilians recognized us as Americans and they went crazy. They began throwing rocks and anything else they could find at us. Our captors didn't try to stop them. I really felt like we were all going to die right there. The guards put us in a barn that night, and we all felt that the soldiers would probably either kill us or let the civilians do it for them. We stood all night in that barn, afraid to lie down – scared to go to sleep. Men were on their knees praying. We just knew we were all going to die."

Later, after being loaded in boxcars, the men faced death at the hands of Allied airplanes.

"While en route to the camp that was to be our final destination, American fighter planes flew overhead and the German soldiers onboard stopped the train and ran into the woods. The planes strafed the boxcars, probably thinking they contained materials for the German war effort."

Talk about fate – all of the men sitting across from where Phil sat in the boxcar were wounded or killed by the bullets, while the guys who were on Phil's side of the cars were not. After the strafing, the train continued on to the Prisoner of War camp. The men onboard were discovering that death lurked around every corner.

"We arrived at a prisoner-of-war camp known as Stalag 4B. There were around 200 of us by then, as more captured American soldiers were added to the group as we moved deeper and deeper into Germany. Along the way, we saw lots of German artillery pieces being pulled by horses – even trucks pulled by horses, and we knew the German Army was out of fuel, and not in good shape. We kept hoping that meant the war would end soon."

At Stalag 4B, there were somewhere between 18,000 and 20,000 captured soldiers already there – mostly Russian prisoners who were treated more harshly by the German guards than what the American or British prisoners were treated.

"We were placed in the area that contained mostly American and British captives. There were about 1,000 of us," Phil said. "Most of the prisoners in that section had been captured during the North Africa campaign in 1942, so they had been there awhile. There was an English sergeant major who was the ranking non-commissioned officer in the area, and he ran that POW camp like an Army unit. We had bunk inspections and we did calisthenics each day. He would not let us feel sorry for ourselves."

Some of the older veterans, who had been held prisoner for awhile, received Red Cross packages while at Stalag 4B that contained everything from musical instruments to clothing.

"The American/British compound had a band that put on a concert every Friday night – something quite unexpected for POWs in their captors' hands. But it was enjoyable, and we looked forward to the entertainment."

Food was running out for the German Army and the POWs suffered as a result of those shortages, receiving only a cup of coffee and slice of bread for breakfast, while the evening meal consisted of two boiled potatoes and a slice of bread. The meager rations were only enough to sustain the men, and as a result, all of the captives suffered considerable weight loss, Phil included.

"There was a radio hidden in one of the barracks, and every night at 7 p.m. BBC Radio in London would report the news of the war. We would all gather around to hear how the war effort was going. The German guards tried on numerous occasions to find that radio—they heard that we had one someplace—but they never did. I don't honestly know where it was hidden. Those radio broadcasts helped us immensely. I never gave up hope of being rescued because of the news we heard on the radio. We knew what was going on in the war, and how close the Germans were to losing it."

"When I first arrived at the camp, I was interviewed by English noncoms who told me if I wanted to try and escape, they would help me, but their advice was to sit it out. So I did."

While Phil never saw anyone tortured while he was a POW, he did witness the Nazis shoot fellow prisoners.

"One time English planes bombed a railroad yards nearby and we were taken there afterwards to fill in the bomb craters. When we arrived at the worksite, an American sergeant told one of the German guards that according to the Geneva Convention, prisoners didn't have to engage in that type of work. A German guard pulled out a pistol and shot him between the eyes. The rest of us began filling in the bomb craters."

"I was only in the camp for a short while when I contacted pneumonia. I became really sick with it," Phil remembered.

"As the illness worsened, the Sergeant Major in our section of Stalag 4B was able to have me transferred to a French hospital, one of two hospitals that were located right outside of the camp. That was in late February or early March 1945."

It was around that time that the Russians began closing in on the area where the Prisoner of War camp was located, and the hospital was evacuated.

"They loaded all of the patients in boxcars and sent us to an old beer hall that had been converted to a hospital and staffed by English doctors. My pneumonia was really bad by then and my lung had collapsed," Phil said. "The doctors drew fluid out with a long needle, and my lung eventually became infected. I was in pretty bad shape, drifting in and out of consciousness."

Prior to the 4th Armored Division liberating the area where Phil was being held, he was to be repatriated through the Swiss Red Cross. By then, his conditioned had worsened to the point where he couldn't even move.

"I was flown first to a hospital in France, then to the 155th General Hospital in England. My weight had dropped, from the 150 pounds I weighed when I was captured, to 95 pounds."

After arriving at the hospital in England, Phil was operated on to remove the infection that had invaded his body, and after a short stay there, was flown back to the States.

"I was sent to Kennedy General Hospital in Memphis, Tennessee, where I began the slow recovery to good health."

Phil recovered enough so that he was able to leave the hospitals and military life behind and enroll at IU for the Fall Semester.

"I was anxious to return to school," he said.

While at school, Phil met Joanne Mott, who was a student in the School of Music, and asked her to marry him. Her parents were against the marriage unless she finished school first. She stayed in school to get her degree, and Phil continued his education, receiving a Masters Degree in Finance while awaiting Joanne's graduation. They were married in 1947.

The world of finance was moving at a fast pace at the conclusion of WWII, and Phil and his wife moved to the Lake County area in Indiana where he went to work for Calumet Title Company. The company eventually changed its name to TICOR, and Phil stayed with them until 1953, when he bought into a company known as Calumet Securities Corporation. He was the third owner of the business. The company moved from its original location in Gary to Schererville, Indiana, in 1974. Phil would continue in the business until he retired in 1994. Phil's wife, Joanne, passed away in 2001.

"You know, I'm torn between two beliefs about what happened at the Bulge," Phil said. "How could the Germans amass a half a million men waiting to attack us without our intelligence knowing about it? If they didn't know that there were troops readying to attack our guys, why not? If they knew that an attack was imminent, why did it take them so long to react and get reinforcements up to the front lines?"

"While I was being held prisoner, every time I had a chance, especially at night, I couldn't help but think that by being taken a prisoner, I had let everyone down – my country, my family, everyone. It was really a period of shame, and I think a lot of the men felt that way. Our division had been in combat such a short period of time when the Battle of the Bulge began, and we lost so many men. Later, the history books would show that we slowed the German army advance long enough to throw off their timetable, and that allowed American reinforcements time to get to the front lines, stop the offensive, and eventually push the Nazis back into Germany."

"I understand that Stalag 4B is still standing, but I have no desire to go back and see it. I wouldn't take a million dollars for the experiences I lived through, but I wouldn't do it again for a million dollars either."

"When the movie, *Saving Private Ryan* was playing in theaters, my son took my granddaughter to see it. She didn't know that America was ever at war with Germany. I don't know what they teach in History classes in our schools today, but obviously, they don't teach the students very much about WWII," Phil lamented.

"I have a daughter-in-law who is from Germany. Her mother was part of the Hitler Youth Movement. And my daughter-in-law's grandfather fought on the Russian front for the German Army receiving the Iron Cross decoration for valor."

Phil continues to live in the comfortable home in Crown Point, Indiana, where he and his wife resided for 7 years. He is kept company by his faithful canine companion, Katie. As this story is written, Phil is serving as Vice President of Chapter XXX, Veterans of the Battle of the Bulge. In 2005, he will become president of the organization. He will serve the members of the chapter well while wearing his ever-present smile.

WILLIAM TOMASZEWSKI
1st Infantry Division
Director, Chapter XXX
Hometown: Portage, Indiana

Bill is one of the many Chapter XXX veterans who accomplished extraordinary deeds during the Battle of the Bulge. Modest and humble, he does not look like a hero, but when the situation called for action, Bill knew what he had to do. Besides, who knows what a hero looks like?

As a result of action he took in battle near the town of Ruthen, Germany, Bill was awarded the Bronze Star. His citation reads:

William Tomaszewski, 35895407 Company M 26th Infantry
For heroic achievement in connection with military operations against the enemy
in the vicinity of Ruthen, Germany, 1 April 1945.
When a unit encountered a roadblock consisting of logs and a vehicle, Private
Tomaszewski, despite intense hostile automatic and small-arms fire,
Fearlessly maneuvered the vehicle off the road and enabled tanks to destroy the
obstacle.
Private Tomaszewski's heroic actions exemplify the dauntless initiative of the
American soldier.

The presentation was made to Bill, along with a Purple Heart award by a Colonel Corley. By the time the war had ended, Bill was the recipient of the European-African-Middle Eastern Theater Ribbon with five Bronze Stars, the Good Conduct Medal, the Purple Heart, Bronze Star, also the Bronze Star with Oak Leaf Cluster, the Sharpshooters Badge and the cherished Combat Infantryman's Badge.

A chest full of medals that Bill proudly displays even in 2003 is what a hero looks like to me.

Born on June 18, 1925, in Gary, Indiana, Bill was inducted into the Army on September of 1943 – barely 18 years old. He was sent to Camp Wheeler in the state of Georgia for Basic Training.

In March 1944, Bill landed in Belfast, Ireland, for training for the invasion of Europe. Later, he was one of the many to come ashore at Omaha Beach during the D-Day invasion where he, and others in his outfit, walked until dark. The next day, they continued their trek to a town called Caumont, which was 22 miles inland, the furthest penetration by the Allies at the time. The enemy was on three sides of the men. In Caumont, Bill joined forces with the First Division, "M" Company 3rd Battalion, 26th Regiment of the 1st Army.

Joining a machine gun squad, he became a machine gunner on a .30 caliber water-cooled weapon. He also drove a jeep during combat and was in battle until the war ended without ever being wounded. When the war ended, Bill was in Czechoslovakia.

Bill's unit was involved in the battle for Aachen, the first German town the Nazis lost to the American forces. He remembers fighting for 30 days cellar-to-cellar to root out all of the Nazi soldiers. His battalion commander, Col. Corley, received the surrender papers from the German general in charge of the town of Aachen.

After returning to the States, Bill went to work for Linde Company-Union Carbide where he would retire from in 1981 after 30 years of service. A widower for a number of years, Bill has one daughter, five grandchildren and five great-grandchildren. His hobby is making stained glass projects such as Tiffany lamps and picture windows.

HENRY C. "HANK" VORWALD
1st Infantry Division, 16th Inf. Reg., HQ and C Companies, 1st & 2nd BNs
Hometown: Demotte, Indiana

Hank registered for the draft on October 16, 1940.

"After registering, I decided not to wait for my draft notice and tried to enlist in the Air Force instead," Hank remembered fondly.

He was put on temporary hold.

"In April 1941, my father became ill and was unable to work. I had been told to report any changes in my enlisted status to the Draft Board, so I did. They in turn informed me that because of my dad's poor health, the fact that my brother James was already in the Air Corps, and that I was now the sole support of my mother and two small siblings, I would be put on a temporary release from the service."

On December 7, 1941, Pearl Harbor was attacked, but Hank's father was still very ill. Hank's father remained very ill through 1941 and 1942.

Hank was married in 1942, and in February 1943, his wife gave birth to a son.

"In May of 1943, my father recovered from his illness, and I reported to the draft board. I was inducted into the service in September of that year. I was still supposed to be sent to the Air Force," Hank remembered, "and at the induction center five of us were told to report to Camp Wheeler to help fill the quota for the ground forces."

Hank was assigned to the 1st Infantry Division, the "Big Red One" while at Camp Wheeler, Georgia, where he underwent Basic Training.

"We fired all types of weapons in Basic Training, and underwent many hours of tough PE (Physical Education). We went through an infiltration course and practiced hill attacks while taking live shelling," Hank remembered. "We also set through many hours of classes and lectures, especially classes in radio communications and cryptography. We had a total of two one-day passes in 17 weeks."

Hank remained at this station from November 1943 until March 1944. Leaving Georgia, he traveled, first to Fort Meade, then to Camp Shanks, New York.

"We knew we would be going to the war in Europe once we arrived at Camp Shanks, and shortly after we arrived, our battalion of men shipped out on a small liberty ship that crossed the Atlantic Ocean on its way to Ireland. The trip took 12 very long days, during which time both the weather and the food was bad. We arrived in northern Ireland the last week of March 1944."

Hank was sent to England late in April 1944 and assigned to 16th Regiment, HQ Company, 1st Division. There, the men trained for the D-Day Invasion.

"From June 1944 to May 1945, we not only fought the Germans, we had to endure heat, rain, mud, cold, sleet, snow, ice, and freezing temperatures. As far as our food was concerned, it was as good as could be expected, considering the conditions. Our cooks were okay, and our Colonel insisted that we received hot food as often as possible. But, we still ate our share of C rations, and by the time the rear echelon troops picked them over before sending the rest to us, about all that was left was hash."

"We were transported occasionally by trucks to our destinations, and every once in awhile we got to ride on tanks, but mostly we covered a lot of ground on foot."

On November 28, 1944, Hank was wounded outside of the town of Eschweiler, Germany, during the Battle of the Huertgen Forest.

"I believe the three worst operations the 1ˢᵗ Division took part in were D-Day and the battle for Normandy, the Huertgen Forest, and the Battle of the Bulge," Hank remembered.

"Prior to the invasion in June 1944, we had excellent West Point graduate officers, but the war took its toll on officers, and we ended up with some officers and non-coms who were not good leaders. Thank heaven we kept our Major and Colonel to the end."

As the war was winding down in 1945, Hank had occasion to see German prisoners.

"We were rounding up Germans and taking them prisoner. We especially looked for the SS troopers. Some of the prisoners we captured looked beaten down and tired. Others were arrogant and tough. We didn't trust any of them."

Describing his experience taking part in WWII, Hank said that, "It was a real experience. I wouldn't have missed it for anything, but I wouldn't want to do it again. I spent 300 plus days in combat – it was all blood, sweat and tears."

Hank was discharged at Camp Atterbury, Indiana, on October 19, 1945. He was awarded the Marksman Badge, the Combat Infantrymen's Badge, the Good Conduct Medal, the ETO with five Bronze Stars, the Purple Heart, Bronze Star, three Presidential Unit Citations, the French and Belgium Forrageire, the Victory Medal and the Jubilee of Liberty.

Asked about the difficulty in adjusting to civilian life following his discharge from the military, Hank remarked, "After 300 plus days of combat, during which time we were shot at, strafed by planes, shelled at by artillery and tank shells, there seemed to be too much of a rush to discharge us. I believe combat troops should have a little more time and consideration given to them to make the adjustment back to civilian life easier."

In conclusion, Hank said that combat forms a great brotherhood, and even though their ranks are thinning, he still corresponds with some of his buddies from the 1ˢᵗ Division, and has attended 1ˢᵗ Division reunions.

WILLARD CLARK
78th Infantry Division
Hometown: Rochester, Indiana

Willard Clark entered the service of his country on March 3, 1943. He was 18 years old at the time and part of the first 18 year-old draft held in this country. The war was a long way off, but Willard knew that he would end up in battle – he just didn't know where. Like almost everyone else entering the service in the 1940s, Willard was anxious to serve his country, but like most other recruits marching off to war, he had no idea what was awaiting him when he arrived.

Beginning his 13-week Infantry training at Camp Butner, North Carolina, Willard was destined to remain in North Carolina after his training and assist in the training of other recruits entering the U.S. Army.

Receiving his first stripe, the young Pfc spent the next 26 weeks helping to train recruits who eventually wound up in Cassino and Anzio, Italy.

By the time recruits were being trained for the invasion of Normandy, Willard was a three-stripe sergeant and assistant squad leader. He took part in that 13-week cycle of training and then spent the next three months in the hills of Tennessee on maneuvers. A stop at Camp Pickett, Virginia, provided Willard with orientation classes before he finally arrived at Camp Kilmer, New Jersey. The next stop would be overseas.

Willard shipped out in August 1944, on the troop ship *John Erickson*. None of the GIs knew where the ship was heading, but after one and a half weeks at sea, the ship docked at South Hampton, England.

The English Channel was too rough to cross when they arrived in England, and it wouldn't be until a week and a half later that they were transported across the channel on board a LCF to Le Havre, France. From there the men were transported to somewhere in Belgium, although Willard will tell you that they walked as much as they rode in trucks, bypassing the fighting in France.

As a member of the 78th Infantry Division's 309th Infantry Regiment, F Company, Willard saw his first action on December 13, 1944. He would never forget it.

"Combat action is something that you never forget," Willard said. "The sights and sounds of death are all around you, all the time."

Willard was on the front lines from December 13, 1944, until February 24, 1945, a lot of that time spent in the Huertgen Forest.

Of the 200 men in F Company, 74 were killed and one proclaimed missing in the Battle of the Bulge. During the battle, 593 men went through Company F due to the high casualties the Company sustained.

"The Germans would shoot artillery tree burst over us and we tried to dig in, but it's hard digging through tree roots. We suffered heavy casualties. There was lots of confusion on our part, and panic too. We couldn't sleep at night because we never knew if the enemy might be advancing under the cover of darkness. So we catnapped whenever we could. Flares also lit up the sky like daylight, making it hard to sleep."

"God, it was so cold! The water in our canteens was frozen most of the time. We would get water from the new recruits who were replacing those who had been killed or wounded – ammo too. The Army couldn't get food to us, and when they did, it was too cold to eat."

On two different nights, German paratroopers dropped into the American lines dressed as GIs.

"We could tell by the sounds the planes made that they were German and not ours because they had a different sound to them, so when we heard German planes overhead, we knew we were in for trouble."

Willard arrived on the front lines in combat as an assistant squad leader. By the time he was evacuated from combat because of frozen feet, he was a squad leader. He would spend nine months in a hospital recovering from his injuries.

"The fist six months I couldn't even walk," Willard remembered. "But the main reason I survived combat was because of the good training we received. That's the reason I'm here today."

Willard received the Combat Infantryman's Badge, the Bronze Star and two campaign stars for the Ardennes and Rhineland Campaigns.

The WWII survivors of the 78th Division, now numbering about 700 men, meet once a year throughout the country for an annual reunion. The men of Company F hold their own get together at those reunions, and on alternate years, they meet on their own.

"There's never been a day that goes by that I don't have some thought or remembrance about the war and what I saw and what I did," Willard said. "Never a day in all of these years."

JOHN DELMERICO
78th Infantry Division
Past President Chapter XXX
Hometown: Valparaiso, Indiana

John Delmerico served as Vice President and President of the Northern Indiana Chapter XXX of the Veterans of the Battle of the Bulge, and even after completing his term as president, continued in the role of advisor, confidant, and more importantly, friend to the members of the Chapter. John passed away on April 15, 2002. His wisdom, New England humor and friendship are qualities that the members of Chapter XXX will always miss.

John married Iris French on August 15, 1944. They had two children, a daughter Katherine Anne, and son, John Michael. Katherine and her husband David Ludwig have given them two grandchildren, Sarah and Matthew.

At age 18, John entered the service and spent some time as an Air Corps Aviation Cadet and also with the 293rd Combat Engineers before being assigned to the 78th Infantry Division in April 1944.

He was discharged as a Pfc. at Halloran General Hospital, Staten Island, New York, on November 15, 1945.

As in the case with all Bulge veterans, John had chilling memories of the deep snow and bitter sub-zero temperatures. He also remembered the now-famous crossing of the Remagan Bridge over the Rhine River at 2 a.m. on March 8, 1945.

John was wounded twice and was awarded a Purple Heart with an Oak Leaf Cluster, a Presidential Unit Citation, Bronze Star, Combat Infantryman's Badge, European Theatre Medal with three Bronze Stars for combat in the Ardennes, Rhineland and Central Europe, and the Good Conduct Medal.

The following is a eulogy presented by past president, Bill Tuley at the visitation in Merrillville, Ind., which was well attended by members of Chapter XXX.

Eulogy for John Delmerico

I met John Delmerico for the first time when I joined the Veterans of the Battle of the Bulge in 1995. There was an immediate attraction to him. Perhaps it was his smile, but we became fast and firm and close friends and he will always remain in my memory.

On August 15, 1944, John married Iris French and then went off to war. He was 18 years old.

He was eventually assigned to the 78th Infantry Division. He endured the bitter cold and snow in the Battle of the Bulge – snow sometimes knee deep and temperatures below zero. The battle remains to this day, the biggest battle ever fought by the United States Army, lasting from Dec. 16, 1944 to Jan. 25, 1945. In crude terms, it was "41 days in hell," and John was there.

In later years, he remembers the crossing of the famous Remagan Bridge over the Rhine River at 2 a.m. on March 8, 1945. The Germans tried desperately to hold the bridge and finally decided to blow it up in order to keep American troops from crossing the Rhine River. John and his fellow 78th Division members made it across, wondering if they would make it before the Germans blew it sky high.

In the war, John's 78th Division had 1,625 men killed and 6,103 men were wounded—a total of 7,728 casualties.

John was wounded twice, and has a Purple Heart with an Oak Leaf Cluster. He was also awarded a Presidential Unit Citation, the Bronze Star for bravery, Combat Infantry Badge, awarded only to those infantrymen who have undergone enemy fire and in turn have fired on the enemy. He was also awarded the European Theater Medal with three campaign stars for combat in the Bulge, Rhineland and Central Europe, and the Good Conduct Medal. He was a hero among heroes.

John was discharged from Halloran General Hospital at Staten Island, New York on November 15, 1945. He returned home to Iris and took advantage of the GI Bill to further his education at Norwich University in Vermont, receiving a BS degree in Mechanical Engineering. He then went on to Columbia University in New York City where he received his Masters Degree in Mechanical Engineering.

In 1950, he joined the management team at Bethlehem Steel, retiring from his position after 33 ½ years. He then joined Indiana Technical College as Academic Chairperson, retiring from that position in 1993.

John was a charter member of our Northern Indiana Chapter XXX of the Veterans of the Battle of the Bulge. He has been a very active member of the Chapter and worked very hard to make it a successful chapter. He served as vice president and then as president of the chapter.

According to government figures, more than 1,500 WWII veterans are passing away EVERYDAY.

John Delmerico, our friend, our hero, our brother, has gone to join his fellow heroes. We will miss him, but be assured that we will NEVER, NEVER forget him. John Delmerico will remain in our hearts and memories forever.

RICHARD H. DAVIES
90th Infantry Division, 357th Inf. Reg. Co. B
Hometown: Gary, Indiana

Richard Davies has an old steel key hidden among the memorabilia that he keeps stored at his home in Gary, Indiana. It resembles a skeleton key of the past; one that is seldom used in the twenty-first century. Richard's steel key is one of only three that unlocked the cells of the most infamous war criminals of modern, if not all, time. He carried that key as a young man to gain access to the men in confinement awaiting the judgment against them at the end of World War II.

Richard also has many stories about the men who were incarcerated behind the walls of the historic Palace of Justice in Nuremberg, Germany, tales known by only the few who were there, for he was a Sergeant of the Guard during the Nuremberg War Crimes trial in 1945.

In addition to the key, narrative, and a lifetime of memories, Richard also compiled a scrapbook filled with photos, newspaper clippings, and most interesting of all, autographs of 17 of the 21 Nazi leaders held in captivity during the trial that the world watched with more than a just passing interest.

The 21 men on trial were the highest ranking leaders of the Nazi effort to dominate Europe, and perhaps the rest of the world some day, and were also accused of being the architects of the incarceration and eventual murder of millions of Jews in Europe. These men on trial were the brain trust behind one of the darker periods of mankind, and gave new meaning to the phrase, *Man's inhumanity to man.*

The main person missing from the trial in 1945 was Adolf Hitler, and in this story there is an eerie assessment of the Fuhrer's destiny by one of the prisoners in the Nuremberg cellblock awaiting his own fate. Most of the world believed Hitler had committed suicide as the Allies stormed Berlin during the closing days of the war. But did he?

You decide.

When WWII ended in 1945, leaders of Nazi Germany were accused of crimes against international law. Some of the defendants were charged with causing World War II deliberately, and with waging aggressive wars of conquest. Nearly all were charged with murder, enslavement, looting and other atrocities against soldiers and civilians of occupied countries. Some were also charged with responsibility for the persecution of Jews and other racial and national groups. For the first time in history, the leaders of a government were brought to trial on the charge of starting an aggressive war.[19]

The following is a list of the men captured, the charges against them, and the sentences they received.

On November 20, 1945, twenty-one Nazi defendants filed into the dock at the Palace of Justice in Nuremberg to stand trial for war crimes. Another defendant, Martin Bormann, was believed dead.

Karl Doenitz – Supreme Commander of the Navy; in Hitler's last will and testament he was made Third Reich President and Supreme Commander of the Armed Forces. Sentenced to 10 years in prison.

Hans Frank – Governor-General of occupied Poland. Sentenced to hang.

Wilhelm Frick – Minister of the Interior. Sentenced to hang.

Hans Fritzsche – Ministerial Director and head of the radio division in the Propaganda Ministry. Acquitted.

Walther Funk – President of the Reichsbank. Sentenced to life in prison.

Hermann Goering – Reichsmarschall, Chief of the Air Force. Sentenced to hang, but committed suicide in his cell.

Rudolf Hess – Deputy to Hitler. Sentenced to life in prison.

Alfred Jodl – Chief of Army Operations. Sentenced to hang.

Ernst Kaltenbrunner – Chief of Reich Main Security Office whose departments included the Gestapo and SS. Sentenced to hang.

Wilhelm Keitel – Chief of Staff of the High Command of the Armed Forces. Sentenced to hang.

Erich Raeder – Grand Admiral of the Navy. Sentenced to life in prison.

Alfred Rosenberg – Minister of the Occupied Eastern Territories. Sentenced to hang.

Fritz Sauckel – Labor leader. Sentenced to hang.

Hjalmar Schacht – Minister of the Economics. Acquitted.

Arthur Seyss-Inquart – Commisar of the Netherlands. Sentenced to hang.

Albert Speer – Minister of Armaments and War Production. Sentenced to 20 years in prison.

Julius Streicher – Editor of the newspaper Der Sturmer, Director of the Central Committee for the Defense against Jewish Atrocity and Boycott Propaganda. Sentenced to hang.

Constantin von Neurath – Protector of Bohemia and Moravia. Sentenced to 15 years in prison.

Franz von Papen – One-time Chancellor of Germany. Acquitted.

Joachim von Ribbentrop – Minister of Foreign Affairs. Sentenced to hang.

Baldur von Schirach – Reich Youth Leader. Sentenced to 20 years in prison.[20]

Staff Sergeant Richard Davies had fought the Nazis as a front line infantry soldier for many months during WWII, but when the fighting finally ended and the leaders of the Third Reich were being rounded up awaiting trial for their atrocities, he did not have enough points to be eligible to return to the States. He was transferred to the First Division, ordered to Nuremberg, and assigned to duty as Sergeant of the Guard at the Palace of Justice, where the Nazi leaders were imprisoned awaiting trial for their actions.

Richard's story of his involvement in WWII was told to a visitor at his home in Gary, Indiana, while the world prepared for the Christmas season.

Each December, as the birth of Christ is celebrated, the thoughts of the men who fought in the Battle of the Bulge are seldom far from that cold, snowy Christmas in 1944, and Richard's mind-set was firmly on those days and nights in the Bulge as he related his story.

The events of those winter days are forever imprinted in the memory of those soldiers who suffered through the difficulty they encountered in Belgium and France during what some refer to as the coldest, and others would argue, the bloodiest December in Europe in modern history. Sometimes, relating the incidents to a stranger who wasn't in the battle and didn't witness the death and destruction they did, is difficult for the aged veterans, and for Richard, it was especially so.

Richard and his wife were both born in England, he in 1918. Richard moved to the United States in 1930, following his dad who came to America six years earlier to find work. A 1937 graduate of Emerson High School in Gary, Richard went to work for the EJ&E Railroad at U.S. Steel Corp. in Gary after completing high school. In 1940 he married his wife Vera, and by the time Richard enlisted in the military in the spring of 1944, he was the father of a three-year-old daughter, Judith Ann.

"I felt like I owed America something after coming here from another country," Richard said. "I was willing to join the service and fight the Germans for the freedom we all enjoy here, and God willing, after the fighting ended, I would make it back home to my wife and family."

His Basic Training took place at Fort Blanding, Florida, where Richard trained in the swamps and desert heat of the south, and then it was on to Camp Kilmer, New Jersey, for advanced infantry training.

"I was trained in heavy weapons, but that basically meant I was familiar with all the weapons that an infantry outfit would have available to them, including a machine gun."

After advanced training was completed, Richard sailed out of New York harbor, along with 20,000 other soldiers, on board the *Queen Elizabeth*.

"We didn't have an escort while crossing the ocean because we were assured the QE could outrun any enemy submarine lurking in the water. Even still, we were a little uneasy about not having any protection while crossing an ocean that had German U-Boats in it looking for easy targets to sink."

"The crossing of the Atlantic Ocean was okay," Richard said. "I didn't get seasick, but a lot of the other guys did. The QE was so big that we didn't have the type of movement that can cause seasickness that a lot of the smaller troop carrying ships did. Still, it was a long time to spend onboard a ship at sea."

When their ship arrived at its destination in South Hampton, England, it scraped bottom because of the extremely heavy weight and had to be pulled out of the harbor by tugs. The QE then traveled to Glasgow, Scotland, where the troops disembarked and were moved by train to South Hampton. There they were placed on a battleship and moved out into the English Channel awaiting orders to go ashore in France.

"We sat out in the middle of the English Channel for a few days until the orders finally came for us to go ashore. Finally, the LSTs pulled up alongside our ship and we all went over the side into the landing vessels that moved us as close to shore as possible, and then dropped us off in deep water where we waded to shore somewhere in France."

Hoping to find a hot meal, the men made their way to a tent area where a kitchen crew was serving food.

"We got a hot meal alright – served in mess kits in the rain. By the time we got to eat it, it was nothing but soup—typical Army."

The next day, Richard was shipped to the 357th Infantry Regiment of the 90th Division in an area somewhere beyond Paris.

The letters T-O of the insignia (of the 90th Division) actually stand for Texas and Oklahoma, being a carryover from World War I, when the 90th, made up of men from these states, fought at St. Mihiel and Meuse-Argonne. The Tough 'Ombres of this war hail from everywhere in America.

The division was reactivated at Camp Barkeley, Tex, Mar 25, 1942 and after training there went to the Louisiana and California-Arizona Maneuver Areas before sailing for England on Mar 23, 1944.[21]

"That's where we discovered there was a war," Richard said. "We were trucked to an outfit that had taken heavy casualties. One sergeant told us that he had 28 men two days ago. 'Now I have five,' he said. It took us a day to get all of the replacements into the units where they were needed, and then it was off to the front lines."

"As we neared the sights and sounds of combat, I was scared to death. After about two hours on the move to the front, we could hear small arms fire. I was one of the oldest men in the outfit, and I had made friends with an 18-year old. He was just a kid to me. As we started taking fire, our sergeant yelled out, 'All right you guys, now we're going to kick some ass.' About that time, all hell broke loose. The Germans started shelling us with everything they had. I thought the world was coming to an end. When the dust finally settled, I looked for my little buddy. He was gone – killed."

"When you're in combat, you remember the things you were taught in Basic Training – the survival techniques—and you apply that to the situation you find yourself in. We remembered how to creep and crawl and stay out of sight of the enemy, and how important it was to keep your weapon fully loaded and in perfect working order at all times. And we did those things almost automatically. Every act in combat was different, and we had to adjust accordingly. You had to constantly stay on your toes, and expect the unexpected, as the enemy also had a desire to survive and attempt to win the war. According to the history books, our division, the 90th, spent more time on the front lines during WWII than any other outfit. I stayed with the 90th until the war ended."

"As time moved on, a lot of young officers that we called "90-day wonders" joined our ranks and were placed in charge of our actions, but they had a lot to learn. Many of them were proud of their rank and had a desire to show off their authority," Richard remembered. "A shiny piece of brass displayed on their uniforms disturbed us so we would ask them to either remove or cover up their insignia as the enemy always looked for that type of target to shoot at."

"After you spend some time in combat, you realize it's sometimes the little things that you have to remember in order to survive. You had to learn how to adjust to situations. If you attacked the enemy one way today, tomorrow you better think of a different way to do it because the Germans learned from what you previously did. The element of surprise was the best weapon we had. Sometimes we would run out of ammo on the battlefield during a fire fight, and we would take rifles and ammunition off the bodies of dead GIs. We never wasted ammunition. Sometimes one bullet could make the difference in living and dying."

Richard, like all the veterans interviewed, said it was the infamous SS soldiers that gave them the hardest fight.

"The men of the SS were trained killers. We could tell the difference during a battle. If we were in action against them, we knew we were going to have a heck of a fight on our hands."

"Enlisted men seldom saw a map – maybe that was a good thing. If we would have seen what we were going up against, it probably would have scared the hell out of us. We'd ask, 'What's our objective? And what's between us and the objective?' The answer usually was, 'Don't know. Guess we'll find out.'"

"It seems now like there was never any time to rest. We would take an objective, take a small breather, and then it was on to the next town, the next objective. Once, after a successful engagement, replacements came and gave us a chance to go to the rear for hot food and a rest. While at our rest area, the change of diet caused many of us to be infected with dysentery and we asked to be allowed to return to the front lines where we felt safer fighting the enemy than from those soldiers preparing and serving our meals.

"I'll never forget the city of Reims, France. It was called the champagne capitol of the world. We had a blast in Reims. We found a lot of wine cellars and loaded up on champagne. Our CO got drunk there and stayed drunk for about two weeks after that. The time we were there, we had a good company commander. He let the NCOs run the company."

"I actually got to meet General George Patton several times," Richard said. "One time we had to cross a river while in France and there weren't any bridges, so we had to cut down trees and make rafts to cross on. We were in the woods cutting down some trees when one of the men said, 'The hell with it. I've had enough of this.' He sat down and wasn't helping us at all. Suddenly, we heard someone yell, 'Get off your ass and get back to work.' We turned around to see who had spoken and there was General Patton, sleeves rolled up helping us cut down trees. We didn't even know he was in the area until then. Another time, in a combat situation, Patton ordered us to remove our bayonets. He said if we let the Germans get that close to us, we deserved to be shot."

"We finally made it across the river on our home made rafts and then discovered we were by ourselves and stranded. The Germans could have wiped us out if they had realized our situation. We were almost out of ammo after a few weeks and lived on water and candy bars for two weeks. Finally, other GIs made it across the river with supplies for us, and we were able to move out."

Later, Richard would see Patton south of Bastogne. "We were hiking down the road one day, and here comes this Jeep with Patton in it. I saluted him, and he saluted back. General Patton was okay in my book."

"One time, somewhere along the Siegfried Line, I was in a foxhole with this guy from Minnesota named Slim. He was about six feet tall. Our orders were to hold the line. We were trapped in that foxhole for two days because a sniper had us pinned down and we couldn't leave – not even to go to the bathroom. I got diarrhea and ended up going in my pants for two days. It was awful. I smelled so bad, that after two days of that, Slim told me that I either left the foxhole or he was going to shoot me. I climbed out of the foxhole, and as I was running to the rear lines, saw an American Jeep going down a road close to me. I hitched a ride to the back of the lines, but they made me ride on the hood of the Jeep because I smelled so badly. My clothes were in such a mess they had to cut them off of me. I cleaned up, got new clothes on and was sent back to the front lines. In the meantime, Slim had been shot and he told the Medics that he thought I had been killed after leaving his foxhole, because I never came back. The Army sent a telegram home to my wife telling her that I was missing in action and presumed dead. A few days later, she received a letter from me that was mailed after the date the Army said they thought I had been killed. I'm certain those were some trying days for her before she received my letter."

"Another event that I will never forget was the time after we had received new officers and soon after we had captured a small village. We were still under heavy bombardment when one of the new officers said, 'Sergeant, those Germans are really intent on taking back this area.'"

"I told him that those shells weren't coming from German guns – they were coming from our own. He asked how I knew that, and I told him that after awhile, you could tell by the sounds and the smell of the shells that were coming our way if they were being fired by German artillery or ours. We decided to attempt to contact our leaders and advise them of the suspected situation. Since the side of the road where we were standing appeared to be taking most of the shelling, we decided to run to the other side of the road as it appeared to be a much safer position. I suggested that we make a run for it, find a more secure position, and call our higher command advising them of what we thought was taking place. There was a barn on the other side of the road and we took off running towards it. When we got to the barn, we dove in head first to stay out of sight, not knowing that the barn floor was deep in fresh manure. What a pleasant landing."

Richard's unit came under friendly fire because orders had become confused, sending the 359th Regiment in one direction, the 357th in another, both firing at each other without realizing the error until much later.

"Our outfit fought the Germans all the way into Czechoslovakia, and if Patton would have had his way, we would have gone farther. But the orders were that we would hold our position and wait for the arrival of the Russian army. Patton was still intent on moving forward and to stop his movement, our supplies were shut off."

"The Russian troops finally arrived and their first move was to start up the small brewery that was in this village, and as soon as it was operating, they proceeded to indulge. They were rough and tough troops, and I'm glad that we didn't start any trouble with them."

"On the day that we moved into the village, we heard an uprising in a far section of the community. When we arrived at the scene of the noise, we saw the body of a local woman hanging from a tree branch. She had been Hitler's representative and mistress of the town, and controlled it with an iron fist. After we liberated the village, the residents captured her, hung her in this tree, and beat her with branches and clubs until she died."

"It was mostly women and children in the village when we arrived – the men were gone. For the first time in a long, long, time, we had an opportunity to sleep in beds, and we did that night. When we awoke in the morning, all of our uniforms were gone. We thought, 'Boy, we're going to be in trouble now.' But the local women had taken our clothes, washed and ironed our uniforms and brought them back to us. They were spic and span clean."

"The women asked us for our shovels and when we gave the shovels to them, they went out and dug up food they had hidden. They used the once-hidden food to prepare meals for us. They were really good to us, because they were afraid of the Russian soldiers and felt that we could help keep them safe from the Russians. We were there when the Russians came and took over the town. I don't have any idea what happened to the people in town then because we were pulled out of there."

"I remember when we passed through the town of St. Lo. That place was practically leveled, but I remember seeing one building that had only one wall still standing. When we went by, we could see a mantle on that only-standing wall, and it had a plate on it that had not been disturbed. I'll never forget that. The whole town had been destroyed except for one piece of china sitting precariously on a shelf."

Richard proudly displayed a small Bible that he still owns. "I carried this Bible with me throughout the war," he said. "We were told that the Germans didn't believe in God, but the first house I entered in Germany had a picture of Christ hanging from the wall."

"There are so many stories from my time in combat," he said. "A GI by the name of John Doe (this name was changed to protect the privacy of the soldier in the story) and I were running for a foxhole while being shot at. I made it safely to the foxhole, and as John was about to jump in, he was shot between the legs. A bullet passed through both his penis and his thigh. But they were able to repair it and he survived and later was married and had children."

"Another time, we noticed two German soldiers running into a barn. We ran after them, and just as I got to the barn, the door flew open, and out they came, riding a motorcycle. They actually hit me with it, before taking off. They didn't get far though. They were eliminated."

When the war ended, Richard was assigned to the Army of Occupation, transferred to the 1st Division, and received orders to report to Nuremberg, Germany, to be a Sergeant of the Guard at the Nuremberg War Crimes Trial.

"Presiding over government leaders accused of war crimes, was something new to the Army," Richard said. "There were 21 prisoners, and they were under our watch 24-hours-a-day, seven days a week with a guard on every cell door. In charge of our detachment were one American Lieutenant and one American Colonel by the name of Andrus. The English and Russian governments also provided guards. The Nazis were always glad to see the American guards come on duty. Most of the prisoners spoke pretty good English."

During his tenure as Sergeant of the Guard in Nuremberg, Richard would come to know most of the prisoners.

"Julius Streicher was a nasty, bitter human being. Frick and Keitel were neurotic and acted like idiots. Hess wouldn't talk to anyone. We took them out for walks in the courtyard every other day. They were handcuffed at those times and they weren't even allowed to bend over to tie their shoes, for fear they might pick up a small piece of glass or something and later try to commit suicide with it. After their walk, they were strip searched."

"I saw all of them in different moods. Sometimes, some of them would be crying in their cells. Most of them insisted they were forced to commit the crimes they were accused of doing. Albert Speer told me when asked why he joined the Nazis, that he wanted to live a longer life. Herman Goering said that he thought hanging was inappropriate sentencing for a man of his position. He said he preferred to be shot. He would later commit suicide by taking cyanide, a day before he was scheduled to be hung. We don't know for certain where he got the cyanide pill from, but I remember he had an incision under his belly. He might have had the pill hidden in that incision and retrieved it by cutting the wound open with his fingernail."

"Albert Speer also told me that the Nazis had made plans for the next 100 years, and that someday the schools and businesses in the United States would be invaded by people of another color – that was in 1945. He also told me when I commented that it was too bad that Hitler had committed suicide, that his leader hadn't died in Berlin. 'Hitler did not commit suicide,' Speer said. 'He left for South America before the Allies arrived in Berlin.'"

Richard arrived back in the United States in 1946. "By the time I arrived home, I had learned to hate war," he said. "We are so fortunate in this country to have the freedoms we enjoy. The ordinary German people were suppressed. They were scared to speak out against the government."

"I docked in New York harbor, the same place we sailed from, on March 10, 1946. It was my daughter's fifth birthday. As soon as we got off the ship and were debriefed, I called home to wish my daughter a happy birthday. It was a birthday I'll always remember."

Richard returned to work at the railroad from where he would eventually retire. In addition to his daughter, he would also have one son, Richard W. Davies. Richard and his wife continue living in Gary, Indiana.

ROBERT ANDERS
94th Infantry Division, 376th Inf. Reg. Co L
Hometown: Dolton, Illinois

Bob and his wife were both born and raised in Dolton, Illinois, moving to Crown Point, Indiana, in October 1993.

"Despite living in Crown Point for the past 10 years, we've always felt that Dolton has been our real hometown," Bob said.

Bob graduated from high school in June 1943, and then attended college in Ames, Iowa, for the summer semester. Because his birthday is on July 2, Bob had to register for the draft while in Iowa. When he received his draft notice, Bob requested to be drafted from his hometown of Dolton, which was not an uncommon request at that time. Bob's father was the chairman of the Thorton Township Draft Board, a position he held from the beginning of the draft until the end of 1946, so one could say that Bob's dad was responsible for drafting him. The Thorton Township Draft Board had 5,776 men registered for the draft during WWII, and actually drafted 1,617. Many of the men registered for the draft enlisted into other branches of the service after registering. The rest were deferred.

Bob was inducted into the service of his country on Sept. 23, 1943. America was already at war. He was single at the time, and remembers the day well.

"A busload of draftees left the draft board in Lansing, Illinois, and was taken to Union Station in Chicago. Other busloads of draftees had also arrived there, and we all boarded a train and were sent to Camp Grant, which was in Rockford, Illinois," Bob remembered.

From Rockford, Bob was sent to Fort Benning, Georgia, where he attended 15 weeks of Basic Training. He was in the Seventh Company, Fifth Training Regiment at Fort Benning until Feb. 5, 1944. He was a Private in the U.S. Army, earning $21 a month.

"I was in the Army's ASTP (Army Specialized Training Program) in Basic Training, which most of us qualified for while in High School," Bob said. "After completing a much regimented Basic Training, we were to be sent to various colleges and universities throughout the United States so that we could complete a college degree. I was assigned to Pomona College in California, but before leaving for the Golden State, we learned that the Army had cancelled the entire ASTP program, and that we would all be going into advanced training for combat."

Bob, along with other men who had completed Basic Training at Fort Benning, were then sent by troop train to Camp McCain, Mississippi.

"The 94th Division was at Camp McCain, but they were not up to division strength yet," Bob remembered. "We were sent to Camp McCain to bring them up to full strength. Before we arrived, a lot of men from the Division, after completing maneuvers in Tennessee, were sent to other outfits, mostly as replacements."

Bob was assigned to L Company of the 376th Regiment of the 94th Division.

"The camp was laid out to hold a division of Infantrymen," Bob said. "We were housed in tar paper barracks. The barracks were separated by company units. Each company had five or six barracks, each platoon their own barracks. A platoon consisted of about 40 men. Inside each building were two small coal burning stoves."

"Each day we were at Camp McCain, we trained for combat. We completed a lot of target shooting, not only with rifles and machine guns, but also with mortars. We went on a lot of speed marches, completing four miles in one hour while carrying light packs and rifles. Other times we would go on 25-mile hikes while carrying a full pack and rifle, and had to complete those marches in eight hours. We sometimes went out on overnight training missions as well so we could learn how to navigate terrain in the dark, and become familiar with the use of compasses. Then there was the obstacle course."

"The obstacle course was laid out so there were hills to navigate, wooden walls to climb, ditches with barbed wire that we had to crawl under while machine guns fired live ammunition over our heads. We were told not to stand up while the bullets were flying overhead, and we didn't. Eventually, the entire division went on maneuvers in the Holly Springs area for approximately a week or so, simulating real combat situations the entire time we were in the field away from civilization."

When Bob left Camp McCain, he did so with the rest of the Division.

"We were loaded onboard trains and had no idea where we were going," Bob said. "After a couple of days, the train we were on finally arrived at Camp Shanks, New York. When we stopped in New York, we figured we would be going to the war in Europe somewhere."

Most of the men with Bob were able to obtain a pass that day, allowing them to go into New York City for an afternoon, but the next day, they were all loaded onto the *Queen Elizabeth*, preparing to cross the Atlantic Ocean.

"We didn't know what ship we would be sailing on until we arrived at the harbor and saw the QE. That ship was so big that our entire division of 16,000 men was loaded on it for the trip to Europe, and I believe that a few thousand other soldiers went along with us."

The cruise ship turned troop carrier left New York Harbor loaded with the men of the 94th Division on August 6, 1944. It crossed the ocean in just five days and docked in Scotland. It made the trip in five days despite sailing a zigzag course to avoid possible contact with enemy submarines. The ship had no escort as it sailed through the waters of the Atlantic Ocean.

After disembarking the QE, the men were then transported by train to somewhere in southern England.

"After arriving in England, we stayed in tents," Bob said. "There were maybe as many as 10-12 men in each tent. I remember that it rained most of the time we were there. We kept in good fighting shape by taking long hikes in the countryside."

When it was time for the 94th to enter the arena of combat, they crossed the English Channel on landing crafts. It took the ships all day to cross the Channel and land in France. It was September 8, 1944 – D-Day plus 94.

"We landed at dusk on Utah Beach and walked and walked until we were told to stop and set up our pup tents. After bedding down for the night, we awoke the next morning to the sounds of military trucks pulling up to our site. We boarded the troop-carrying trucks and were driven to an area on the east coast of France known as Lorient and St. Nazaire. We were told that there was a pocket of about 60,000 German soldiers who had been bypassed during the initial invasion on June 6, 1944, and our job was to contain them."

The 94th inflicted over 2,700 casualties on the enemy and took 566 prisoners before being relieved on New Year's Day 1945.[22]

"Our units were assigned areas of responsibility, and we dug foxholes among the infamous hedgerows to protect ourselves from enemy fire. There was constant patrolling by German soldiers while we were there, but they didn't try very hard to get away from us," Bob said. "We watched them, and they watched us, and we kept trying to get closer to where they were at, so that meant moving forward, and then digging more foxholes. There was a lot of artillery being fired, both at the Germans, and by the Germans at us."

"The areas where we were at were close to a German submarine base. They had "pens" made of thick cement that protected the submarines. The concrete was six to eight feet thick and couldn't be penetrated by aerial bombardment. The German soldiers were protecting those pens so that their navy could use the port to get their submarines in and out."

"We fought in that area for a long time, and every week or two, we were relieved from the front lines so we could go to the rear and clean up."

"The 66th Division was on a troop ship crossing the English Channel to prepare to deploy to the field of battle when they were torpedoed and sank," Bob remembered. "They were on the Leopoldville, one of the largest ships we were using at the time, on Christmas Eve, 1944, when they came into the crosshairs of a German U-Boat. They lost more than 800 of their men as a result of the ship sinking, and that caused the Command to change their minds about sending that division to the Battle of the Bulge, which had begun on December 16. So, the 94th Division was sent to that area to replace them."

"We were loaded in 40x8 railcars (Boxcars designed to hold 40 men or eight animals) on New Year's Eve and sent to General Patton's Third Army, which was already engaged in the Battle of the Bulge. It was so cold at the time – zero degrees or colder, and the snow was about knee deep in places. As we moved into combat, we would occasionally find bombed-out houses that we could use for shelter, but as soon as we took one town from the enemy, we would be on the move to another."

Moving west, the Division took positions in the Saar-Moselle triangle facing the Siegfried Switch Line on January 7 and shifted to the offensive, seizing Tettingen and Butzdorf that day. The following day, the NenningBerg-Weis area was wrestled from the enemy, but severe counterattacks followed, and Butzdorf, Berg, and most of Nenning changed hands several times before being finally secured.[23]

"One morning, as we were attacking an enemy position, we found ourselves in a mine field. We lost many men to those mines – some killed, others had their feet or legs blown off."

"Next, we spent a few days maneuvering in and a round the Ardennes Forest. Again, it was snowing and the temperatures hovered around zero. We were being shelled by both German artillery and mortar fire. We lost many, many men to the shelling we took in the Ardennes. Then, because of the weather and the fact that we didn't have proper footwear, we had to deal with frozen feet and trench foot. I was pulled off the front lines on January 30, and sent to the rear lines because I had trench foot," Bob said. "All the GIs who were suffering with similar feet problems were kept in an old school building in Thionville, France, that had been turned into a hospital where we were treated for our ailments. I couldn't even walk for two weeks, per the Doctor's orders."

"I've always said that trench foot saved my life, but it wasn't fair for the other men who had to stay on the front lines."

"I believe it was the middle of March before I was sent back to my Company. When I rejoined my old outfit, I discovered that the Company Commander and many of my friends had been killed while attempting to cross the Saar River. The Division was moving pretty good by the time I rejoined them, and we took the city of Trier from the Germans – that was a big deal. We kept advancing though, until about the second or third week of April."

By 2 March 1945, the Division stretched over a 10-mile front, from Hocker Hill on the Saar through Zwef, and Lampaden to Ollmuth. A heavy German attack near Lampaden achieved penetrations, but the line was shortly restored, and on 13 March, spearheading the XX Corps, the 94th broke out of the bridgehead and drove to the Rhine, reaching the river on 21 March.[24]

By May, the hostilities had ended, but not the work Bob and the men of the 94th had to perform.

"After V-E Day, we were again shipped by railcars, this time to Vodnany, Czechoslovakia, where we were housed in a well constructed school. It was springtime, and the weather had turned nice. There was a guard house on a road that separated the Russian Army from the American forces, and our responsibility was to man that post. It was like a no-man zone and neither side was supposed to be able to cross to the other side. But the Russians would come storming through the gate at night time and go into town where there were American soldiers. It was about that time that General Patton made two trips through our guard post to speak with the Russian officers about their soldiers' activities. I actually saw Patton on three different occasions," Bob said.

Bob would continue with the assignment in Czechoslovakia until Thanksgiving, 1945, when he began his long trip back to the States. Before leaving there though, he took part in a celebration that was reported in his hometown newspaper, *The Pointer.*

Sgt. Robert J. Anders of the 376th Regiment, 94th Infantry Division, had the honor of being one of the few Americans to participate in the celebration of the independence of Czechoslovakia.

A composite company from the 376th Regiment and the 94th's 35- piece band marched in Prague with troops from the British, French, Russian and Czech nations.

President Benes delivered the address of the day and received the applause and cheers of the thousands of people who thronged into the large modern stadium to commemorate the 27th anniversary of the Czech's birth of freedom. He inspected the troops of the different nations which were represented, as they passed in review before him.

Czechoslovakia declared its independence on October 21, 1918. Almost six years of oppression and death were meted out to the Czechs by the Nazis during the occupation but the Czechs were not discouraged and are now rebuilding their country and establishing policies of government and law. October 21, 1945, was an important day in the history of their country. President Truman of the United States sent a message of congratulations.

After the ceremony in the stadium the troops paraded for several hours through the streets of Prague. An elaborate banquet climaxed the day of celebration.

A great many pictures were taken which will soon be released in the newsreels in the United States.

"That parade day in Prague was so outstanding because everyone treated us like we were all generals. After the parade, they had a formal dinner for us in the finest hotel that included more food, more white table cloths and more silverware than any of us had ever seen before."

After a stopover in London for New Year's Eve, on January 7, 1946, Bob sailed for New York on board the *Lake Champlain*, an aircraft carrier turned into a troop carrier attached to the 80th Division for the trip across the ocean. After docking in New York Harbor, he took a train to Camp Grant, Illinois, where he was discharged from on Jan. 23, 1946.

"I'm like most of the rest of the guys who served in WWII," Bob said. "I'm glad that I was able to serve my country and do my part in the war effort, but I wouldn't want to ever do it again. The month of January 1945, is a time in my life that I will never forget. It was nothing but snow, cold, more snow, more cold, and all the while we were fighting to take small towns while being shelled by the German 88s."

Bob was awarded the European-African-Middle Eastern Ribbon with four Bronze Battle Stars, two Overseas Service Bars, the Good Conduct Medal, the WWII Victory Medal, the Expert Infantry Badge, the coveted Combat Infantryman Badge, and the Bronze Star.

When he returned home, Bob's father turned over the operation of their grocery store business to him. He would run the business for 11 years. He then took a position as a teller with the Riverdale Bank in Riverdale, Illinois. On July 1, 1988, Bob retired as Vice President, Commercial Banking. He remained on the Board of Directors at the bank until 1996.

PAUL GRAHAM
99th Infantry Division, 395th Infantry Regiment, HQ Co.
Past Director, Chaplain, Chapter XXX
Hometown: LaPorte, Indiana

L ooking at the photograph taken more than fifty years ago, I see three young men sitting at a table filled with beer bottles and glasses. They are obviously enjoying themselves. And as I look into the eyes of the one with the pensive look, I recognize that he is the same handsome man I interviewed recently at his home in LaPorte, Indiana. Facial features may change over a half a century of aging, but eyes seldom do. The eyes in the photograph are of a man, like many others that I have interviewed, who has witnessed much pain and sorrow in his life time, maybe more than men should have to see. Despite that, he seems at peace with himself each time that we have met and was this day as well, even though a war is being waged in a desert in Iraq and the sights and sounds of that engagement brings the horror of World War II closer to the surface.

We talked for hours and I am amazed at both his ability to remember events that occurred so many years ago, and at his eagerness to discuss the strategy of the battle that brought us together to chat about his time spent in Europe in the 1940s. As we talked about the largest battle ever fought by the United States Army, one phrase kept popping up in our conversation – "Luck enters into so much of what happened." If I didn't believe that in the past, after speaking with so many veterans who narrowly missed serious injury or worse in battle, it has become increasingly clear that luck, does in fact, play a major role in the outcome of one's life. Especially one who has been in combat for any length of time.

Paul Graham is 80 years old and neither looks it or acts like it. That is not to say that he is the same 19-year old boy he was when Uncle Sam beckoned in the 1940s, but he is both spry and articulate, and takes pleasure in sharing a good story. We enjoy our time together, first at lunch, and then in his comfortable home in the middle of the city that is the County seat.

Paul didn't start out wanting to be a soldier in the U.S. Army.

"I remember trying on a Navy pea coat one time and thinking that I liked the look and feel of that coat," Paul said. "I must have decided then that I wanted to be in the Navy." More precisely, he wanted to be on a naval carrier, so he attempted to enlist in the Naval Air Corps. Traveling with a friend from Michigan City, Indiana, to Chicago, they started their day at the Navy recruiting office located in a Post Office downtown.

"The first thing we had to do was take a test to determine if we were color blind. They had a table with a lot of dots on it," Paul remembered. "They asked me, 'What numbers do you see in those dots?' I didn't see any number. The recruiter said if you don't see any numbers in those dots you are color blind and we won't accept you in the Navy. So, I faked it and told him the numbers that I thought might be there. That didn't work! So, because I failed that first test, they wouldn't take me in the Navy. I was crushed but went down the hallway to the Marine recruiters' office. I was determined to get into the service. They asked if I had been turned down by any other branch of the military. I told them the truth and they said they wouldn't accept me either."

As fate would have it, the U.S. Army wasn't nearly as critical about color blindness and on December 11, 1942, Paul was on his way from Fort Benjamin Harrison in Indianapolis to Camp Van Dorn in Mississippi to begin Basic Training.

"Van Dorn is three miles from Centerville, and that's three miles from nowhere." Paul was assigned to Headquarters Company, 395th Infantry Regiment of the 99th Infantry Division.

"We didn't have toilets or shower facilities in the tar paper shacks they called barracks," he remembered. "Those facilities were located in another building. And, we didn't even have sheets on our cots. We slept on mattress covers." To make matters worse, their meals were served in mess kits because there wasn't any dishes for the trainees to eat on. "Our camp was so bad that even Walter Winchell, the famous radio broadcaster, talked about it on one of his radio broadcasts."

The men at the camp actually built the first PX and when it was completed, it too, lacked basic needs. And when a Recreation Center was built later in the camp, it was struck by lightning and burnt to the ground. Paul does not have many good memories about his time spent in Mississippi.

Long hikes of 25-30 miles were not uncommon while at Camp Van Dorn, and in August and September 1943, Paul's outfit participated in "D" Series maneuvers in Louisiana with members of the 84th, 102nd and 103rd Divisions. The maneuvers went so well that on November 15, they ended up in Texas at Camp Maxey.

"We thought we were ready to go overseas and fight," Paul said.

About that time, there had been so many American casualties in the combat being waged in Italy against the Axis forces that there was a need for replacements.

"On our last bivouac in Texas, men with certain job classifications were taken out of training and shipped overseas – not whole divisions or companies of men, only certain classifications of soldiers left."

Prior to this time, the U.S. Army had a program that allowed men who had attained high scores on their initial tests to attend college while still in the service. They were referred to as ASTP soldiers. When the casualty count in battle became high, the Army stopped that program and sent all of those men to the divisions who ranks had been depleted. Most of the ASTP men had little training, so they had to start from the beginning with Basic Training, which some attended at the same Camp where Paul was trained.

On September 12, 1944, the division left Texas for Boston, Massachusetts. Upon arriving there, the men just "waited around" until September 29 when they shipped out for Europe. The war for Paul was merely an ocean voyage away, and they were en route there. Soldiers from Paul's division made landings in Scotland, Ireland and Plymouth,

England, where Paul's outfit moved by train to South Hampton. From South Hampton, they boarded another ship for Le Havre, France. When they arrived on November 5, 1944, outside of France, they disembarked via rope ladders thrown over the side of the ship and four days later they had replaced the 9th Division on the line. The 9th was moved to Monschau, Germany, on their left.

"I remember thinking at the time that if I make it through the war that I would like to come back to Monschau," Paul said. "It was beautiful while we were there. I could only imagine how nice it could be in peacetime." Many years later, his dream to return to the scenic town in Germany came true and he was able to return to the area and visit without fear of being hit by a stray bullet.

The 2nd Division had been on their right flank when they arrived on the line on December 13, but were sent back around the 99th to attack the Roer River Dams and pill boxes. Paul's regiment, the 395th, was to protect the right flank of the 2nd Division. They were still in that position on December 16 when the intense artillery barrage that signaled the beginning of the Battle of the Bulge began. The men of the 393rd and the 394th Infantry Regiments took the brunt of that artillery fire, while Paul's regiment was not called back from this attack until later.

According to an on-line article from the 28th Infantry Division Association that talked about the dams, *At the end of November, vital targets, dams along the Roer River, the importance of which were not realized until late in the fighting in the Battle of the Hurtgen Forest, were still in German hands. Had the First Army gone for the Roer River Dams early in the fighting, there would have been no Battle of Hurtgen Forest. That men must die in battle is accepted, and some fighting will always be more miserable and difficult than others. If there had been a push directly from the south to take the Roer River Dams, the loss of lives could have been just as costly. However, if that had been done, at least the objective would have been clear and accepted as important. Those who fought in the Battle of the Hurtgen Forest fought a misconceived and basically fruitless battle that could have, and should have, been avoided.*[25] The dams were never taken.

On December 12, Paul was in the Huertgen Forest, south of Monschau.

"The Huertgen Forest was an eerie, eerie place," Paul said. "The forest lies south of the town of Aachen and the trees there were so tall and so thick it seems like it was dark in there all the time. There were short days and long nights while we waited in our foxholes for the word to advance."

Three regiments from the 99th Division, the 393rd, 394th and the 395th took up positions. They protected the flank of the 2nd Division which was next to them.

"The weather was miserable. It was zero or below, and it would alternate between sleeting and snowing, and when it wasn't doing that, it was foggy. And we didn't have the proper footwear such as rubber boots – that was all stored in trucks someplace. We also didn't have any intelligence about what the Germans were up to. It was reported by some that the Germans were active because you could hear their tanks, and even troops moving around, but no one believed that it meant there was an attack imminent."

On December 16, at 5:30 in the morning, beginning with an artillery attack that lasted approximately an hour, three powerful German armies advanced into the Ardennes region of eastern Belgium and northern Luxembourg. History would tell us later that 500,000 German soldiers took part in the offensive. Attempting to stop them was a thinly-spread line of three American Divisions and a part of a fourth, while a fifth was making local attacks and a sixth was being held in reserve. Division sectors were more than double the width of normal, defensive fronts.[26]

"We were fortunate that we were situated where we were," Paul said, his fingers spread wide. "We were like the thumb of a hand, away from where the main thrust came through. Our sister regiments really caught a lot of what the Germans were doing."

According to author Stephen Ambrose, *holding the battle's north shoulder did not simply delay the German advance but stopped it along its critical path – Elsenborn Ridge. The Germans were stunned at the courage and might of the young, new recruits of the 99th Division. They thought they were striking at a weak link in the American defense. Baron Hasso Von Manteuffel, Commander General of the Fifth Panzer Army, stated after the Bulge: 'We failed because our right flank, near Monschau (north shoulder) ran its head against a wall.' John Eisenhower wrote, 'The action of the 2nd and 99th Divisions on the north shoulder could well be considered the most decisive battle of the Ardennes campaign.*[27]

"The battle was bitter, with the Germans trying again and again to penetrate our lines and push us back. During the first two days there were 17 different attempts to break through. I don't think the Germans knew at the time that there were two divisions of Americans on the line. They thought there was only the 99th. Eventually, we were ordered to pull back, and pulling back actually put us right in the thick of things. The 2nd Division and the 14th Cav. had already turned around and broke off the engagement with the enemy. Our immediate right flank was now open and the Germans were pouring through."

As the 99th fell back they fought a delaying action battle to keep the Germans from overrunning them.

"Actually, the positions we occupied prior to the battle were referred to as a winter camp. In other words, it was late in the war, the enemy seemed to be on the run and I think the Army believed they would put our divisions up on this line to give us a break after the Hurtgen Forest battle. That's why there were so few of us spread so thin. No one was expecting a major offensive."

Looking at a map of the area, the most obvious feature that stands out is a lack of roads.

"We had too many support people and too many trucks up front," Paul said. "And as we started to fall back during the battle, it was chaos. The roads were nothing but knee- or hip-deep mud with broken men and stuck trucks and artillery pieces attempting to use them at the same time. It was a real mess. And it was still cold – freezing cold!"

By December 18, two days after the battle began, General Dwight D. Eisenhower, realizing that there was a major German push coming across the lines, sent the 1st and 82nd Divisions to help repel the enemy forces.

"As the other two divisions arrived, they were trying to use the same roads that we were trying to use to get out. It was total chaos for awhile. We didn't think we would ever get out of harms way. We thought we were all doomed." It was about that time that the 99th, along with the 2nd Division, were ordered to Elsenborn Ridge.

"That ridge was some of the highest ground around, it gave us a good field of fire. It was also a straight line from there to Antwerp." The men tried to dig foxholes for protection but the ground was so frozen it became almost a waste of time. Behind them the American artillery opened up on the enemy forces trying to take the ridge.

"Thank God for the artillery," Paul said. "They just pounded the

German forces trying to break through the lines. We had the 1st Division on our right then, and the 82nd was all along the lines plugging gaps. The Germans tried frontal assaults on our lines four or five times, but we held. The 1st and 82nd Divisions really, really fought like the devil. The Germans just kept coming at them. The artillery fire was relentless. If the Germans would have gotten to Elsenborn first, or would have broken through when they first attempted, the outcome of that battle could have been much different."

While at the Elsenborn Ridge, the building where Paul was at was hit by enemy artillery fire three different times. They were finally ordered to vacate the building.

"You know," Paul said. "It wouldn't have mattered what outfit was on the front lines in that battle, they were going to get overran. All of our guys put up a valiant fight, but we were just overwhelmed by the amount of enemy soldiers coming across the lines. The Germans thought if they could overrun us, they would take our gasoline and use it to keep going. We had lost so many men and so much equipment we weren't able to fight as a division. We had to wait for replacements and that took about three weeks."

Everyone in combat handles the possibility of dying differently and Paul said he saw a lot of different emotions displayed by the men around him.

"We had a burly Irishman who wasn't afraid of anyone, but when the artillery fire started, he shook so bad you didn't think he would ever stop."

On one mission undertaken by Paul's platoon, they had to return to a house where American troops had left some maps. The men found the house, retrieved the maps, and as they were leaving, saw a German tank coming down the road.

"We left the road through the 10 foot high hedge rows that lined the road, and took a different route back to Elsenborn. It took us two days to get back to our unit. If we would have stayed on that road, we would have been seen and probably killed."

The Allies launched a counteroffensive two days before the New Year. This counteroffensive involved the U.S. Third Army striking to the north while the U.S. First Army pushed to the south. They were supposed to meet at the village of Houffalize to trap all German forces.

The Germans did not go easily, however, and the Americans had a tough time.

On January 8, Hitler ordered his troops to withdraw from the tip of the Bulge. This indicated that he realized his offensive had failed. By January 16, the Third and First Army had joined at Houffalize. The Allies now controlled the original front. On January 23, Saint Vith was retaken. Finally, on January 28, the Battle of the Bulge was officially over.[28]

When the war in Europe ended, some of the men from the 99th Division, as well as the 2nd Division, were put on ships heading to Japan. The war in Asia wasn't over yet and there were plans for the invasion of Japan.

"Fortunately, I was one of the men sent to another outfit and didn't board a ship headed for more combat." Paul, along with most of the men from the 395th HQ Company, was sent to the 1st Division in Bamberg, Germany, for reassignment.

The war officially ended for Paul Graham on New Years Eve, 1945. After arriving in Chicago from Indianapolis where he was discharged, Paul rode a South Shore Train to Michigan City. He hadn't told anyone that he was coming home so there wasn't anyone there to greet him.

"I walked out of the train station at 11th Street in Michigan City and decided to celebrate the New Year and the fact that I survived the war. I saw a bar across the street called the Silver Inn. Leaving my duffel bag, which had a German Luger pistol inside, lying on the sidewalk outside the train station, I walked across the street to have a drink." People inside were strangers that Paul didn't recognize. No one spoke to him as he entered and ordered a draft beer. "I toasted myself," he said. "I lifted my glass and said here's to you Paul Graham. You made it." Paul left and walked home. He didn't wake his parents when he arrived home so he waited for the morning to surprise them. "It was late and I just wanted to get into my old bed and sleep."

Reminiscing about the battle that he took part in – The Battle of the Bulge – Paul asked and then answered his own question, "What caused the front to collapse?"

"I believe there were a number of reasons," he said. "First, there was an intelligence failure. Someone should have been able to recognize that there were a half million men and equipment massing across the front from us. Secondly, there weren't enough troops to repel the assault and we were poorly placed and spread too thin. There were too many non-Infantry men too far forward, and the Cavalry shouldn't have been on the front lines with us. Next, we didn't have the proper winter clothing for the weather we were fighting in. And lastly, we shouldn't have attacked the dams. That was poor strategy that took men away from the front lines."

"I'm no hero," Paul said. "But I'm glad I was there and did what I had to do."

When Stew McDonnell convened the first meeting in Michigan City in December 1993 to determine if there was enough interest to form a local chapter of the Veterans of the Battle of the Bulge, Paul Graham was one of the veterans in attendance.

"I listened with great attention to Stew and what he wanted to accomplish with a local chapter. But I thought to myself, 'We're old men.' So I asked Stew, 'Why do you want to do this now?' I'll never forget his response. 'If not now, when?' Stew answered."

From that initial meeting at the VFW in Michigan City, the chapter was formed and the membership has grown to more than 100. Paul Graham has been a part of the chapter since its inception, holding positions of Director and Chaplin.

"It's been good for us veterans," he remarked. "Where else can we go and rehash events of more than fifty years ago? Maybe no one else would be interested in hearing us relive the trials and tribulations of that cold winter in Europe when we stopped the Nazis in their final push. But to those of us who were there, it gives us a chance to talk about those days and our deeds. It's been good."

THE MEN OF THE AIRBORNE DIVISIONS:

The 101st Airborne Division

The 82nd Airborne Division

RALPH DUENAS
101st Airborne Division
FRANK HERIDIA
82nd Airborne Division
Hometowns: Gary, Indiana

They were young men when they first met in Gary, Indiana, in 1940. Sixty-plus years later, their friendship has endured the horrors of WWII and is still going strong. At a recent Battle of the Bulge membership meeting in Michigan City, Ralph and Frank talked about their experiences during the Battle of the Bulge.

"We both joined the paratroopers during the war," Ralph remembered. "I was in the 101st Airborne Division and Frank was in the 82nd Airborne Division."

Fate would have both of those airborne units involved in combat over enemy held territory, with Ralph and Frank taking part in combat jumps.

"I was about 20 years old at the time I enlisted," Ralph said. "I was sent to Fort Sill, Oklahoma, and while I was there, one of the guys I was stationed with talked me into joining the paratroopers. I thought, 'Why not.' I was young and adventurous."

Ralph would make about 24 training jumps in preparation for the combat jump that he eventually made over Holland. That combat jump over enemy territory is forever etched in his memory.

"Some of the guys on the plane heading to Holland were pretty scared. Actually, we were all scared, but some of the guys were throwing up on the plane. I remember we passed a bucket around for them to vomit in."

As the planes loaded with Army paratroopers approached the drop zone, the Germans began firing at them, with bursts of ack-ack exploding near the planes.

"I give those pilots a lot of credit," Ralph said. "That stuff was exploding all around us and they kept the planes flying pretty level."

Soon the commands to, "Stand-up, hook-up, check equipment and stand at the door," were given, and Ralph was next in line waiting to jump out. Just then, a shell exploded not far from the plane he was in and Ralph was thrown in the air heading for enemy territory below him.

"We missed the drop zone by five miles and we had to hike back to where we were supposed to rendezvous. But, all things considered, the jump was pretty good. Some of the guys called it a playground jump because it was so easy," Ralph remembered.

Frank's combat jump with the 82nd Airborne took place over Normandy at night.

"Actually," Frank recalled, "night jumps are better because the air temperature is different at night – better for parachuting."

Besides, the darkness does hide the paratroopers from enemy bullets.

"We were pretty low when we jumped, so we weren't in the air very long. It seemed like we no more than jumped and we were on the ground. We were all scared though, and as soon as we hit the ground, we were right in the middle of combat."

On one of his many missions after he landed, Frank was on a patrol with another GI looking for signs of enemy tanks.

"We heard what we thought were tanks and then saw German soldiers. We took off running for the rest of our outfit when we realized that the Germans had seen us and they were running after us. What they didn't know was that we were taking them back to our lines. Our guys ended up shooting and capturing a lot of German soldiers in that skirmish."

The closest Ralph came to being wounded during the war was while he was on his way to a forward observation post. He was with another GI when they heard incoming artillery shells.

"I dove for cover and made it inside a ravine that completely sheltered me. My friend wasn't as lucky, only getting partially inside the ground cover. Shrapnel from the shells hit him, tearing off the top of his head. I was covered in his blood."

Both Frank and Ralph suffered from frozen feet during the Battle of the Bulge. Frank was in a makeshift hospital suffering from frostbite when the word came that the Germans were close to overtaking the area.

"We were told that anyone who could walk needed to get out of there as soon as possible. I left, despite the condition of my feet. I figured that even frozen feet would be better than being shot by the Germans."

When the war ended and the two friends returned to civilian life, they both went to work at U.S. Steel in Gary, Indiana. Ralph worked at the #5 Open Hearth and Frank at Gary Screw and Bolt Works. They both retired from U.S. Steel many years later.

What both men remember most about arriving home from the war was that it was a long time before either of them could sleep in a bed.

"I tried sleeping in a bed," Ralph recalled. "But usually, before the night was over, I would end up sleeping on the floor."

After years of sleeping on anything they could find, a mattress was too comfortable for either of the two ex-GIs.

Frank and Ralph continue to live in Gary with their families.

TOM EVANS
101st Airborne Division, 502nd Parachute Inf. Reg.
Hometown: Portage, Indiana

Twenty-one dollars is not a lot of money in 2004, and it wasn't much in 1940 either, but that's the total that Tom was paid per month as a Private in the United States Army. But he wasn't alone, as thousands of other young GIs at that time were paid the same amount for the privilege of serving their country. Little did they realize in 1940, however, just what they would have to give in return for that monthly paycheck, as World War II had not yet begun.

Tom, considering the Army as a career, enlisted in the military service on August 23, 1940, and along with a group of other young men, was sent by bus to Fort Benjamin Harrison in Indiana, to begin his training. He stayed at that location for three days, during which time he was housed in wooden barracks and learned about Army chow in a mess hall.

"Actually," Tom reported, "the food there was good." It would prove to be infinitely better than the chow he would eat during combat.

While the new recruits weren't issued any weapons at Fort Benjamin Harrison, they were issued Army clothing, such as woolen kakis. Later, like many other GIs, he would carry an M-1 into combat. At least, after being issued Army clothing, the new recruits were beginning to look like soldiers.

Three days later, on August 26, Tom was sent to Camp Walters, Texas, where he began his 13 weeks of Basic Training. He would remain in Texas until he was sent to Fort Bragg, North Carolina, to join the 101st Airborne Division.

"I enjoyed Jump School at Fort Bragg," Tom said. "I didn't have any problems there, and fortunately, later on, I never had to make a combat jump."

Tom was sent overseas on a troop ship to England, and would remain in Europe for two years, serving there from September 1943 to September 1945. Before engaging in the arena of combat, Tom and the men in his unit were billeted in Quonset huts. They were close enough to civilization, however, that they were able to walk or take a bus to town.

As a member of the 101st Airborne, Tom was one of those unfortunate soldiers who found themselves surrounded in the town of Bastogne.

By December 21 (1944) Bastogne was completely surrounded. Captain William Roberts' three teams from the 10th Armored Division had fought off the first furious German attacks. Team O'Hara still held a sector southeast of Bastogne and was almost intact. But the other two teams had been badly mauled. Team Cherry had tried to stem the main German attack in front of the town and had been ambushed. Only a few men survived. Team Desobry had valiantly defended a village five miles north of Bastogne until forced to withdraw after two days of bitter fighting.

Now it was up to the 101st Airborne Division – sent to the Ardennes as a result of Hodges' urgent plea to Eisenhower – to withstand the brunt of the German attacks.

But nobody could predict how long the defenders of Bastogne could hold out against the increasing German attacks from all sides. With every hour the enemy pressure grew heavier.[29]

History books tell us that the siege of Bastogne wasn't lifted until December 26, when Patton's Third Army was able to break through the German lines. During the period that the Americans were surrounded in that small Belgium town close to the country of Luxembourg though, there was much suffering, and Tom was one of those unfortunate soldiers who suffered the effects of prolonged exposure to the weather without proper protection.

"While in Bastogne, I was with a unit of men from Service Headquarters Company in a chateau just outside of town," Tom recalled. "It was so cold, and the snow so deep, that we were all pretty miserable. To make matters worse, the soles of our boots had worn so thin that we looked for anything we could find to put inside our boots for warmth and protection. We used cardboard, paper, rags, or anything else we could find to fill in the holes in our boots."

Those actions might have helped stave off frozen feet for some, but not for Tom. He became one of many casualties whose fighting days ended as a result of frozen feet. Somewhere during this period of time, Tom even found a pair of boots that had belonged to a German soldier that were brand new. Unfortunately, the boots didn't fit Tom's feet, and he had to make do with his makeshift, worn-through pair of GI-issued Army boots.

It has been almost fifty-nine years since Tom was discharged from the U.S. Army at Camp Atterbury, Indiana. In the years since then, he has suffered the results of having frozen feet during the Battle of the Bulge, undergoing four or five surgeries on his legs because of poor circulation problems, and as of this writing, having to have his right leg amputated above the knee.

Tom was discharged from military service as a T-5 Corporal. He received the American Defense Medal, the WWII Victory Medal, the Belgian Forrageire, European-African Middle Eastern Campaign Medal with four Bronze Service Stars, one Bronze Arrowhead, the Purple Heart, the Bronze Star Medal, and a Distinguished Unit Citation with one oak leaf cluster.

Before WWII ended, Tom and five of his six brothers would all serve in the military – one brother in the Navy, and the other four brothers served in the U.S. Army in the Pacific Theater.

One of Tom's memories of his time in Europe is about time spent at the end of the war.

"Our unit was transported by truck to the town of Berchtesgaden, in the Alps, for R& R (rest and recuperation). This area was known as the "Eagle's Nest" because it was used as a mountaintop home during the war by Adolf Hitler. The 101st Airborne had captured Hitler's retreat in Berchtesgaden, and immediately after the war ended, sent a number of units there for R&R. There was a lake nearby, and several of us decided to go there for a swim. We quickly changed our minds though, after getting waist deep into the water. It was freezing cold! Later in the day, some of our boys found a boat and they took it out onto the middle of the lake to do a little fishing. They used dynamite caps instead of fishing poles, but they were successful, and we had a fish dinner that night in the mess hall."

In closing, Tom remarked, "As a 101ster, I'll say, 'Airborne All the Way!'"

MY MEMORIES OF THE BATTLE OF THE BULGE
By Cipriano Gamez, Director, Chapter XXX
82nd Airborne
Hometown: Highland, Indiana

(All veterans remember their Army serial number as if it has been permanently engrained in their being. Cipriano is no exception and began his story of World War II with his address and Army Serial Number –35583421.)

On December 7, 1941, I was at my buddy Tony's house listening to Xavier Cugat's band. Abbey Lane was singing. The program was interrupted by President Roosevelt who announced that Pearl Harbor had been attacked and that we were at war. I turned to Tony and told him that I was going to volunteer. He told me that he was going to wait and that I should do the same.

When I got home that night, I told my parents of my intentions. Mom became very emotional and asked me not to do so. I then asked my Dad, but all he said was, "Listen to your mother, son." I knew that meant no! The next morning I went to my girlfriends' house and told her what happened. She said that she was glad that my parents had said no. Of course, I still had to register for the draft.

In mid-January, 1943, I received my notice to report to the corner of Michigan Ave. and Guthery Street where there would be several busses to take me and a large group of guys to Ft. Benjamin Harrison, Indiana, for induction. The ride was hilarious, with everyone joking, singing and laughing – all of us wondering what the future held.

On the 27th of January, after four days of exams and tests, a group of us were shipped to Camp Grant in Illinois, which turned out to be a medical basic training camp. This was a big disappointment to me because I did not like the idea of being a Medic who would be shot at and not able to shoot back. I went to the Captain and told him that I wanted to transfer to an Infantry unit. I told him why I wanted the transfer. The Captain said that the Army was in dire need of Medics therefore he was denying my request.

Camp Grant was the cleanest camp that I was ever in. The camp was immaculate and the food terrific. The only bad part about it was we had to do everything at the sound of a whistle. The camp was about a two-hour trip to Chicago, which was about an hour away from my home.

At the time, I was a Private, drawing $50 a month.

After 13 weeks of Basic Training, we were getting ready to ship out, when teams of paratroopers came to the camp looking for volunteers. This appeared to be my chance to be a rifleman, so I approached the officer in charge and told him that I would volunteer only if I could be a rifleman. His response was, "No problem, soldier. Sign here." That is how I became a paratrooper and a rifleman. There were eleven of us who volunteered – some as medics, some as riflemen.

We left Camp Grant and were taken to Ft. Benning, Georgia, for paratrooper training. Little did we know what was in store for us. We soon learned.

The officers and non-commissioned officers were tough and hard on us. Everywhere that we went was at double-time. The training itself was so rigorous that it bordered on being brutal. It seemed as if the instructors enjoyed their work. More than anything else, the heat was the hardest on me. The first week of training was all calisthenics, followed by a week of learning how to pack our own parachutes. We were then introduced to the mock towers and then finally to the 250' towers. An awesome sight! This training was all for the purpose of learning how to jump out of airplanes and how to tumble after landing.

The last week of training we had to pack our own chutes. Then we were taken up in planes and were required to jump. What an experience!

After jump school, a group of us were shipped out to Camp McCall in North Carolina, where I became a member of the third squad, third platoon, "C" Company, 508th P.I.R. I would be apart of that outfit from August 1943 until March 17, 1945.

Camp McCall was a new camp. The streets were dirt, and when it rained, they turned to mud. The barracks were more like wooden huts. There were no trees, no grass, but plenty of dust, especially when the wind blew. This called for what the Army likes to refer to as, "Beautify the area." After an intense effort on everyone's part, the camp began to look real nice.

We then began intense training in small arms fire. Everyone had to have a working knowledge of all the weapons used by the Infantry. Trips to the firing range became a daily routine. We then studied tactics, and engaged in long marches with full equipment, and as the Army says, "Carried the load of a mule with the speed of a prairie fox," all on a canteen of water. After this intense training and several practice jumps, we had a month of maneuvers. Finally, we were considered ready for combat.

On December 19, 1943, we received word that we would be shipping out. On the 20th we were at Camp Shanks, and on the 27th we were on our way overseas aboard a liberty ship by the name of the *James Parker*. After eleven days at sea, we landed in Ireland. We boarded trains there and left for Camp Cromare, where we underwent more hard training and had our first experience with Nissen huts, which were corrugated steel buildings that looked like a half a barrel. Finally, on the 10th of March, we were on the move again – first to Belfast, then to Scotland by boat, then to Nottingham, England by train. That would be our base camp. This would be our final training phase. We were now combat ready.

I took part in the invasion of France on D-Day, June 6, 1944. I was a member of one of the Pathfinder teams. My war began at 12:30 a.m. The Airborne invasion started at 2:15 a.m. The mission of the Pathfinders was to jump in ahead of the main force, then set up a radar unit and a series of lights to help guide the planes in.

The 508th P.I.R. was in France from the 6th of June to the 13th of July. I was now a Private First Class. About this time, all airborne units and troop carrier outfits were placed under a single command.

My next experience was the invasion of Holland, called Operation

Market Garden. We jumped at 1 p.m. on the 17th of September. That night, about 10 p.m. while I was out on the point, I ran into a German patrol. During the exchange of gunfire, I was wounded in the elbow. I ended up spending two weeks in a hospital recovering from my injuries.

On December 15th, my birthday, I was 22 years old and a Sergeant. The next day, we received the news of the German breakthrough in Belgium. On the 18th, we were on our way to Belgium. We were there for almost two months. I've never been colder in my life than I was during those two months. On February 20th, my regiment was pulled out of combat and returned to base camp in Sissone, France.

My stay with the 508th P.I.R. lasted another month when I got screwed and sent to the 86th Infantry Division. I fought with the 86th until the end of the war. We were informed that we would be going to the Pacific Theater of Operations to prepare for the invasion of Japan. We were saved from the invasion by the dropping of the A Bomb. By then, I had enough points to return home.

I returned to the United States in November 1945. I was discharged at Camp Atterbury, Ind. and was home in time for Christmas.

For my service, I earned four Bronze Stars, a Presidential Unit Citation, the French, Belgium and Holland Forrageire, the Purple Heart and several other medals.

The friendships forged during a war are like brotherly love, something never to be forgotten. I keep in touch with some of my buddies from that time, and once a year, we have a re-union. We talk about old times and how we won the war. We talk about how tough our sergeants were, but how glad we were that they did teach us how to survive. We talk about how the youth of today doesn't know about World War II, how they don't seem to be as patriotic as we are. We talk about our lives after the war – some seem to have had a hard time adjusting to civilian life. It is good to be home looking forward to a long and peaceful life.

(A practice I established when I first began working on this book is to send a hard copy of a draft of what I have written to each veteran. I ask them to review the draft and make any changes that they feel need to be made. Some make suggestions or spot errors that I have made in telling their stories, others haven't. The following is a note I received from Cipriano after he received the draft from me.)

I am very pleased with this condensed version of my report. I wish that I had the ability to write like you. Thank you so very much.

It has taken me a very long time to come to grips with the good and the bad memories — my emotions surface all to (sic) quickly. I choke up and at times tears come to my eyes. My wife criticizes me and encourages me to be stronger. She feels that I should talk more about my experiences to my boys and my grandchildren — to release my feelings — my emotions so that I can be more at ease with myself.

Thanks again! Cip

Thank you Cipriano, for letting us share your story with the world.

MARION SHAGDAI
82nd Airborne Division, 504th Parachute Reg.
Hometown: Michigan City, Indiana

Marion "Shag" Shagdai is a United States Army veteran, having fought in the Battle of the Bulge during World War II, even though at the time he was drafted, he wasn't a United States citizen.

It didn't matter to Shag that he wasn't a citizen of the USA. He felt he was as much an American as any soldier that would be fighting alongside him. With a war raging in Europe, warm bodies were much more important to the draft board than the technicalities of citizenship.

"I was born in a small town in Russia. My father was Russian and my mother was Polish. My parents immigrated to this country after I was born, and after initially spending time in Grand Rapids, Michigan, we moved to Herminie, Pennsylvania."

The area in Pennsylvania where Shag resided as a child was coal mining country, and his father worked in a coal mine.

"Neither one of my parents ever obtained their American citizenship papers," Shag said. "And I didn't get mine until after I was drafted."

Prior to the draft, the young man from Herminie spent two years working in the Civilian Conservation Corps, then went to work in one of the many steel mills that populated the Pittsburgh area at the time.

"I was the oldest of five children, and had to help my family financially, so I started working at an early age."

After Shag was drafted, but prior to reporting to the service, he underwent instruction with 300 others to obtain naturalized citizenship papers.

"One of the people in that class with me turned out to be a pretty important man," Shag recalled. "His name was Henry Alfred Kissinger."

The Kissinger family fled Germany to avoid persecution by the Nazis, and after becoming a U.S. citizen with Shag in 1943, Henry also served in the U.S. Army. He would go on to become one of this country's most influential foreign policy advisors to two American presidents – Richard Nixon and Gerald Ford—and was secretary of state from 1973 to 1977.

Shag's first assignment in the Army was at Camp Croft, South Carolina, where he undertook 17 weeks of Basic Training. An additional 17 weeks of training at the same location awaited him after Basic Training, during which time he continued preparing for combat in Europe. By then, Shag had been promoted to Corporal, and was itching to, "go fight."

While in South Carolina, members of the 82nd Airborne Division came to the base looking for men who would be willing to be paratroopers.

"A couple of us guys, who had been listening to their spiel, decided that the paratroopers sounded pretty exciting to us, so we volunteered," Shag remembered. "We didn't undergo training in that field until we reached England. Once there, I undertook paratrooper training and made the mandatory six jumps to qualify for my wings. Jumping out of an airplane is really exciting. It's almost like being in heaven. After you jump, there isn't any sound, except for the wind, as you make your way to the ground. It's something. Even today, I wish I could make one more jump."

On December 17, 1944, the day after the Battle of the Bulge began, Shag's outfit departed Sissone, France, onboard trucks. The military trucks maneuvered through war-torn France and Belgium on their way to the front lines.

"We saw an awful lot of destruction along the way. The 106th really took a beating. There were burning trucks and equipment both on the road and alongside it. We knew we were going to see lots of combat when we arrived on the front lines. As we passed Bastogne, we got off the trucks and started walking down the road. We had men on both sides of the road and we walked for about four or five miles. Then we were ordered to dig in. We started digging foxholes on each side of the road when all of a sudden we heard this loud bang. Everyone scrambled for cover and waited. Then we heard one of our guys screaming for help."

The GI they heard calling for help had been digging out a foxhole when a grenade fell out of his pocket, the safety pin coming loose as it fell, and it detonated, sending hot shrapnel into the man in the foxhole.

"After that happened, we took black tape and wrapped it around our hand grenades so the pin couldn't accidentally fall out. I don't know what happened to the guy who was wounded. They took him away in a truck and we never saw him again."

Later that day, sometime around noon, their lieutenant led the men toward the town of Chenaux.

"We were told that the Germans had some of their best troops in and around that town," Shag said.

About half way to the town, the lieutenant ordered the men to take off their heavy, cumbersome overcoats and leave them in a pile.

"We'll come back and get them later," he told the men. They never did.

"We walked a few more miles until we got to the edge of town," Shag said. By then it was about 8 p.m. The lieutenant told me to take one man, go to the left in the woods, and check out the area. He said if we were to hear or see anything, we should report back to him."

Not long after Shag and the other GI entered the woods, they heard men talking and the sounds of shovels digging.

"I told the kid that was with me to go back to the lieutenant and tell him what we've discovered. Then I crawled a little further to investigate additionally. Crawling on my belly, I finally got close enough that I could hear the conversations of men, but I wasn't sure if they were speaking German or English. So I called out, 'Who's there?' There wasn't any answer, but there wasn't any more talking either."

Fires in the buildings in town lit up the sky enough so that when Shag saw a figure of a man crawl out of one hole and head towards another, he recognized the distinctive German helmet on his head.

"I was carrying a Thompson sub-machine gun and I fired 8-10 rounds from my gun. I saw the man go down. Then I sprayed about 30 more rounds in the area where I saw the man crawling to, and afterwards heard the moans of wounded men. I knew I was really in harms way by then, as I was sure there were more Germans around and that very soon they would be firing at me, so I crawled out of the woods and into a plowed field and lie down in the furrows of the field. I reached for a grenade to throw in their direction and couldn't get the tape off the pin that I had put on to keep the pin from accidentally falling off. I finally unwrapped the tape and lobbed the grenade towards where I thought the enemy soldiers were at. I heard more moans. I threw a second grenade. By then the Germans were firing their weapons at me. I could feel and see dirt kicking up all around me. I felt dirt kicked up from bullets hitting my helmet and boots. I crawled about 50 yards and then got up and ran like hell."

Shag wouldn't realize the extent of the damage he inflicted on the Germans until later when they were able to survey the area. He would be awarded the Silver Star, the nation's second highest award for his actions that night. His award reads:

HEADQUARTERS 82nd AIRBORNE DIVISION
Office of the Division Commander
22 May 1945
Subject: Award of the Silver Star Medal.
To: Staff Sergeant Marion Shagdai, 504th Parachute Infantry.

Under the provisions of AR 600-45, as amended, and pursuant to authority contained in letter 200.6 (AG) Headquarters XVIII Corps Airborne, dated 31 August 1944, the Silver Star Medal is awarded to the following named individual:

MARION SHAGDAI, 33690098, Staff Sergeant, 504th Parachute Infantry, for gallantry in action on 21 December 1944 near CHENAUX, BELGIUM. During a night assault the platoon of which Staff Sergeant SHAGDAI was a member became pinned down by intense crossfire from two enemy machine guns. Staff Sergeant SHAGDAI made a lone assault on the enemy gun positions. With utter disrespect for the enemy fire focused upon him, he crawled close to the first gun, threw two hand grenades and fired upon the crew with his sub-machine gun, killing them all. The second gun immediately turned its fire upon him, but Staff Sergeant SHAGDAI coolly and courageously stood his ground and forced the crew of the second gun to flee. Staff Sergeant SHAGDAI's courage and unflinching devotion to duty enabled his platoon to proceed without further delay. Entered military service from HERMINE, PENNSYLVANIA.

JAMES GAVIN
Major General, U.S. Army,
Commanding

"When I made it back to my platoon, my lieutenant said he thought I was a goner," Shag remembered. "I told him what happened and the lieutenant got the platoon together to go after the remainder of the Germans."

The GIs started across the field around midnight to the area where Shag had returned from.

"We sent six men into the woods to the left; another six went to the right. I stayed and covered for them. When they arrived at the spot where I had thrown the two grenades, they found two foxholes with dead bodies in them. Each had three to four dead enemy soldiers in them."

As the platoon advanced further into the woods, the enemy started firing at them.

"Two of our guys got hit right away – one in the stomach, the other took a bullet in the ankle. I dragged the one who was hit in the ankle up a little hill."

The enemy continued firing at the GIs as they withdrew to the town behind them.

"I quickly dug a foxhole close to the top of the hill I was on. From there we could see the town in the near distance and could see lots of German soldiers in the town. There was a haystack nearby and we tried shooting it in an attempt to ignite it so we could see the enemy better, but we weren't able to. I borrowed an M-1 rifle from one of the guys in the platoon, set the sights as far up as they would go and fired a round at one of the German soldiers in town. He must have been at least 1,000 yard away. I didn't hit him, but the bullet must have come close to him because he ran like hell after that."

Shag downplayed the incident in the woods and the award he received as he related the story, but it was a tremendously heroic action he undertook. The incident may have possibly saved the lives of many of the men in his platoon, for if the two machine gun positions had not been wiped out that night, they would have undoubtedly wrecked havoc on the GIs the next morning.

The next day, Shag's platoon entered the town and found that the

Germans had left. They conducted a house-to-house search, but the town was devoid of any enemy soldiers. The following day it began snowing and didn't stop until there was more than foot of fresh snow on the ground. And somewhere, many miles behind them, their winter coats were sitting in a pile alongside a road.

"It was so cold. We were trying to make our way through snowdrifts, the wind was howling and it was freezing. We walked about six or seven miles when the lieutenant said we'd stop for a five minute break. I was a squad leader at the time. Two of the guys in our platoon said that they had enough and they were going to surrender to the Germans. They took off all of their combat gear and said they were just going to walk until they found someone to surrender to. I took my .45 pistol out of its holster, pointed it at them and told them to pick up their gear and get going. No one from my squad was going to surrender just because they were cold."

The platoon got back on the road and started walking again. Shag heard a noise and turned to find the man behind him had been shot through his neck.

"I never heard the shot, but the guy was spewing blood all over the place."

The ground, covered with freshly fallen snow, was now turning bright red. The men looked around to see where the shot came from and suddenly, another GI was shot, this one in the stomach.

"We realized there must be a sniper in the building ahead of us, so we all ducked for cover. The lieutenant told me to take two men and get the sniper."

The men approached the building where the enemy gunman hid and after a few minutes a German soldier came out with his hands in the air.

"The guy had a smile on his face, like he was happy at what he had done," Shag said. "His eyes had a glazed look to them like he was on drugs or something.

"During my time in combat, I saw so many men wounded and killed, but I was lucky. I never got hit."

Luck! So many of the men in Chapter XXX have remarked during interviews that the ones who survived combat did so because they were lucky.

One time as Shag's outfit was on the Siegfried Line, a chain of steel forts and concrete tank barriers Hitler had built on the border between Germany and France, something quite unusual happened.

"There were two American tanks on the road this one day and the tankers asked us if we wanted to move forward with them. We said, 'Yea. We'll go with you.' So, we started walking in their direction. We were walking through this field, and had gone maybe 100 yards or so, when we heard music. We recognized it as the song, *Lillie Marlene,* a popular song in Germany. I said, 'Where the heck is that coming from?' We fanned out and started walking towards the music. We came upon a pipe, about four inches in diameter, sticking out of the ground. Putting our ears to the pipe, we could hear music and men talking in German. I took four hand grenades, pulled the pins and dropped them down the pipe. After they exploded, we heard the sounds of men moaning, and we started looking for the entrance to the underground bunker. We finally found the entrance, broke down the door by shooting rounds into it from my Tommy gun and went inside. There were three dead German soldiers – two by their cots and another one a little further away."

Another incident Shag remembers began with a jammed Tommy gun at night.

"I had a spent shell lodged in my gun and I couldn't get it to eject," Shag said. The gun was useless until the shell could be dislodged. "I tried for a long time to get it out, even asking the lieutenant and other guys if they had anything that I could use. No one had anything that was of any use, so I saw this old barn and walked over to it thinking I could find something I could use as a tool there. I didn't have a flashlight and there weren't any lights in the barn, so I just felt my way around the walls until I finally came across a hoop from a wooden barrel. Using that, I was able to pry the shell out of the chamber of the gun. By the time I left the barn, my platoon was out of sight. As I was walking in the direction of where I believed the men had gone, I saw this building on my left and heard music. I walked over to it and heard German male voices and the voices of women laughing and having a good time. I kicked the door in and fired rounds from my now functioning Tommy gun into the ceiling. There were eight German soldiers and four or five women inside. I told them to 'Raus,' and they all walked outside with their hands on their heads. I walked the prisoners down the road until we came to some other American units and I turned the captives over to them. They didn't put up any fight and I think they were just waiting to be taken."

On another occasion, Shag's outfit captured some 30 Germans who had been hiding in their foxholes in a field and were camouflaged by fallen snow.

"It didn't take much for them to surrender," Shag said. "Of the 30, one of them was an officer. He had a pair of binoculars and a Kodak camera. I took them both and brought them home. I still have the camera."

As the war came to a close, Shag's outfit met with Russian soldiers for a little celebration.

"When we met the Russians towards the end of the war, we had some good times with them. I couldn't speak their language, but we could understand what they were saying. We drank their Vodka, sang and danced the polka with women who were bigger than the Russian men," Shag said.

"But, the Russian soldiers were real cocky. They had their own type of sub-machine gun and they thought theirs was better than our Tommy guns. So, this one Russian puts a target on a tree one day and tells me to fire at it. I fired 10 rounds and hit the target three times. The Russian soldier thought he could do better, but when he went to fire his weapon, the gun wouldn't fire. He tried again. It still wouldn't fire. He was so mad he took the gun and banged it against the tree until the whole thing fell apart. They were mean people, those Russians. At night time we could hear the screams of women in town that they were raping."

In Berlin, Shag met "good people," and along with about 100 other paratroopers, made a jump to demonstrate their capabilities for the Russians.

"What I remember most about the Battle of the Bulge is how cold it was. At times there was up to two feet of snow on the ground and it was very, very cold. I remember one time when we were in the Ardennes, I saw two dead German soldiers whose guns had frozen and they couldn't fire them. It happened to us too, but when our guns froze up, we peed on them. That loosened them up enough for us to fire them."

When Shag was discharged from the Army, he was a Tech Sergeant. He was married in 1947 to Carolyn and they have a daughter, Patricia. Shag worked for U.S. Steel in Dravosburg, Pennsylvania, before moving to Michigan City, Indiana.

In the basement of his home in Michigan City, a wall is covered with the mementoes of Shag's time in Europe – certificates, photographs and awards—and he proudly displays the Silver Medal he earned during the Battle of the Bulge.

JOHN TROWBRIDGE
101st Airborne Div. 501st Parachute Infantry
Hometown: Valparaiso, Indiana

John enlisted in the U.S. Army on November 19, 1942. He was single at the time, and was inducted into the service at Indianapolis, Indiana. John remembers that a Private at the time was making fifty dollars a month, but after completing parachute training and getting his wings, a paratrooper made one hundred dollars each month – enough of a difference in pay to motivate some men, if given a choice, into the airborne divisions.

John was sent to Camp Tacoa in Georgia for Basic Training, and soon discovered that the living quarters there consisted of tarpaper shacks, each holding one platoon of men – approximately 36 GIs. The building where they lived was heated by a potbellied stove. The men at the camp ate their meals in an Army Mess Hall.

"The food the Army served us in Basic Training was mostly of low quality, and it was poorly prepared by unskilled cooks who were simply chosen from the ranks of the men who were drafted or enlisted in Uncle Sam's Army," John remembered. "A normal breakfast sometimes consisted of green, scorched scrambled eggs with half-cooked fatty bacon, or cold, heavy pancakes. Lunch was often nothing more than a bologna sandwich and coffee, and dinner was almost invariably lamb stew and rubbery Jell-O."

John described life at this location as, "Hectic at best. It seemed to be the duty of all the officers we encountered there to weed out the weak of heart. A man would get in trouble for any infraction of a rule, but a second violation would cause that person to be transferred out of there."

John soon discovered that Basic Training for paratroopers was somewhat different than the typical training other recruits received.

"This phase of our training was a little more intense than the typical 13-week Basic Training. Except for when we were marching in close-order drill, we weren't allowed to walk anywhere. We double-timed everywhere we went. And if we yawned during an Orientation class, we would be given 50 push-ups."

The obstacle course in Basic Training is a phase of Army life all of the men in Chapter XXX remembered, and John did as well, referring to it as, "God-awful."

"While we were in this phase of our training, we were assigned to platoons such as machine gun, mortar and communications. Although our weapons consisted of 30 cal air-cooled light machine guns and 81mm mortars, we were the Heavy Weapons Company. Because the crews of these weapons must have their hands free of rifles, we carried as side-arms, folding stock carbines, either in scabbards or holsters on our belts."

There wasn't much leisure time for the men while they were in training, but as John said, "If there wasn't any training scheduled for the weekend, and we had no gigs during the week, we could obtain a pass at noon on Saturdays, which would allow us to be off-base until 6 a.m. on Monday."

John remained at Camp Tacoa from December 1942, until March 15, 1943, when he was sent to his next duty assignment at Fort Benning, Georgia. While at Fort Benning, John would be trained in the three stages of Jump Training.

"Actually," John remembered, "there were four stages, as the last stage was the real thing. First, the A Stage was what we called the muscle-building stage."

"During the A Stage, the Army used mock-up planes to demonstrate, and for the men to practice proper inside-the-plane procedures and the method used to exit an aircraft. Landing trainers were used to give us safe landing instructions, such as the right tumble or the left tumble. During all phases of this training, we were also taught demolition tactics and the art of Judo."

During the next phase of Jump School, high-tower trainers were used to assist the paratroopers-to-be.

"During the next phase we were taught how to slip or guide a parachute," John said. "That would be a very important maneuver later during combat jumps. The towers were 250-feet high and definitely presented a challenge to a man's courage. The most frightening of the tests we had to take during this phase was one called the shock harness. It was absolutely terrifying!"

The instructors in Jump School all held the rank of Staff Sergeant, and they had full authority over all trainees—officers and enlisted men alike.

"During the B and C stages, the instructors loved to pull rank on, not only the enlisted men, but Lieutenants, Captains and even Colonels as well. They would embarrass, berate and even punish them for infractions of rules such as spitting in the sawdust or for putting their hands in their pockets."

When the trainees finished the first three stages of Jump School, it was time for their first jump out of an airborne airplane.

"It was time for the real thing," John remembered. "We were finally going to take that important step from a plane in flight. I jumped out of that damn plane and when I hit the ground, I dislocated my left shoulder. I had to undergo 10 weeks of therapy before I could make my last four jumps. Jumping out of an airplane, reaching the ground, and being alive was euphoric! You say to yourself, 'See what I did – I jumped out of that damn plane!'"

Shortly after John's arrival at Ft. Benning, in the spring of 1943, he received a telegram informing him of the death of his sister-in-law in Indianapolis, Indiana. He was granted a 10-day furlough so that he could return home for the funeral. It would not be until he returned home from the Normandy Campaign in July 1944, that he would be granted another leave, which he spent at what he described as the "beautiful resort of Bournmouth, on the English coast."

By the end of his first year in the military, John was at Camp Macan, North Carolina, and was a Pfc.

In January 1944, John sailed on a liberty ship in a convoy across the Atlantic Ocean. The trip took 13 days.

"My first overseas duty station was in the village of Lamborn, England. While we were there, we were billeted in horse stables. Our training for the four and-a-half months I was there consisted mainly of dealing with night problems, and it made us realize that we would probably be jumping into combat at night. We completed two actual night jumps in England, in addition to mock jumps from the tailgate of moving trucks. There were also live firing exercises on the Salisbury Plains."

"We had occasional passes into London," John said. "I discovered that if I shined my boots and polished the buttons on my uniform in preparation for guard duty, I could get the Number 1 Post, which was the main gate to Battalion Headquarters. Anyone who was chosen for that post received an automatic pass to London. We also discovered that there were dances in Oxford, Newbury, and other towns, and we soon found local pubs where there was piano playing and group singing."

John's recollection of combat, in particular his jump on D-Day, is vivid.

"Finally, our plane was on the runway and beginning to roll. With engines roaring, rivets rattling, and trees flashing by, we were airborne at last. It was still daylight and we wouldn't be jumping until well past midnight.

"Some of the men slept, while others made their peace with God. Many times I have wished I would have spent more of those moments seeking His blessing. As we passed over the English Channel, some of the men became excited over the amount of ships in the Channel; some had become air sick. We were all getting pretty restless when the jumpmaster shouted, 'We're over France. Stand up and hook up!'

"Then all hell broke loose! Guns were firing at our plane. That was the first time anyone had ever tried to kill me. A cold shiver took over my whole body. I would experience that feeling many more times after that. When were we going to jump? Where's the green light? I wanted out of that plane.

"Stand in the door", yelled the jumpmaster. Then "Go!" Men were jumping out, but just as John got to the door, the pilot made a quick dodging maneuver, causing the plane to lurch to one side, and causing him to slip in vomit on the floor and slide all the way across the cabin. The jumpmaster helped him back to the door and then it was out the door and into the inferno waiting below.

"I came down in a tree that was just tall enough so that I couldn't get my feet planted solidly enough to unfasten the harness. I finally had to cut my way out of the chute. An enemy machinegun was firing about two fields off to my right, but not in my direction. A few mortar shells landed also, but not dangerously close to me.

"I hid in a nearby hedgerow and waited for others from my outfit to arrive. I loaded my carbine and waited, but eventually fell asleep. When I awoke, I saw the air battle over the beach taking place. A B-26 exploded in mid-air, and a wing came off a P-38 and it spun into the ground. I watched as two P-47s were taking out a bridge by the Douve River. The first one went in and dropped a delayed-fuse bomb. He was followed by the second plane, which arrived over the target just as the first bomb went off, sending the poor guy in the second plane tumbling end-over-end to the ground in a huge fireball. People were dying all around me.

"Soon afterward, a group of men from our mortar platoon came along and I joined them as we walked toward the town of Addelville."

He had survived his first combat jump.

"After our return to England from Normandy, we lived in a tent city near Newbury. The entire regiment was together there, and we spent the next two months integrating replacements into our units."

"Twice we were alerted for combat jumps, but twice we stood down. General Patton outran us. On Sunday, Sept. 19, we spearheaded the invasion of Holland. During the fourth day of battle, on Sept. 21, I got that million dollar wound and was sent back to a hospital in England to heal.

"My departure from Holland was via an ambulance, having taken a bullet in my right thigh during First Battalion's night attack on Schijndel on September 21."

"The entire division, including my unit, was in Mormulon, France near Rheims, when I rejoined them in late November. By Dec. 19, we were in Bastogne, Belgium.

"Very early in the morning on December 19, 1944, we marched through the pre-dawn darkness in an eastward direction out of town. We made good progress, despite the confusion created by the disorganized withdrawal of several units that had faced the enemy onslaught from the very direction we were heading.

"I hadn't noticed the fog as we walked through town, but most of the countryside was invisible. Perhaps that's why our entire First Battalion veered to the right at the fork in the road and headed toward the town of Marvie.

"Soon, our squad found itself about 100 yards or so behind the forward elements and we began to receive fire from the direction of Neffe. That was the first enemy fire I had experienced since being wounded in Holland.

"There was a grove of trees on the ridge about 100 yards to our left which we assumed was under the control of A Company, but we were getting small arms fire and a great deal of shelling from that area.

"Someone ordered a machine gun up there to clear out the trees, and I knew it would be our machinegun crew that would be sent. We started up the slope on our bellies when the Germans opened up on us with machine gun fire. We slid back down much faster than we went up. I don't know who took over that grove after we tried, but that night an enemy patrol came within 50 yards of our position. We challenged them, and when they didn't know the password, fired at them. Next morning we found one dead enemy soldier and we heard that another one had been captured.

"One foggy night, while we were on outpost, Fred Rasmussen and I were on the machine gun. He was asleep and snoring pretty loudly. I'm trying to keep him quiet when all of a sudden, out of the fog, comes an enemy patrol with a scout on their right front. They're about 150 yards away and coming right at us. I shook Fred awake, pointed at the patrol, and we began firing. We kept firing until the fog closed in again. He never snored again the rest of the night."

On Jan. 3, 1945, my fighting days ended. The remainder of my military life was spent in hospitals."

"About noon on January 3, the Third Battalion crossed a set of railroad tracks and immediately came under heavy enemy fire. We pulled back to a clearing at the edge of the woods when shells began exploding all around us. As we ducked into the woods, I saw a shallow trench and made a dive for it. I landed in the ditch with my back toward the clearing, and was immediately hit, with what seemed like 10 pounds of searing hot shrapnel, all along my exposed left side. Most of the larger pieces hit me in my chest cavity, although I had been hit from head to toe with shrapnel. I heard someone yell for a Medic, then saw them take off running. I knew the war was over for me, and I suspected that it was just a matter of time before I died. I asked a man close to me for a shot of morphine and told him and Rasmussen to get the hell out of there. Instead, they set up the machine gun and began returning fire at the enemy about 500 yards away from us. The enemy stopped their advance then, but the gun became jammed. Rasmussen and the other man went for help. I realized that enemy soldiers were moving into the adjoining woods, 60 yards away from where I was at.

"I soon heard the crunch of footsteps in the snow and wasn't too surprised to see a Kraut looking down the barrel of his machine pistol at me. I thought it was over. But then, the German soldier got into a nearby abandoned Jeep with another soldier and left. In the meantime, my two friends had reported my position to an evacuation team and sent them in my direction. By the time they found me, the afternoon was fading fast."

"We were truly blessed with leaders," John remarked. "When bullets were zipping by and shells were bursting all around us, they were up front, and we were following. I've shed many a tear for the beautiful, brave leaders that were killed or wounded in combat."

"Once, while we were fighting in France, we took a group of German soldiers as prisoners. One of the frightened prisoners said to me, 'me no German, me white Russian.' I felt like blowing the S.O.B. away. In Holland, a German officer that we had captured demanded to surrender to an American officer. I laughed in his face. I think he understood when I told him that he was lucky to be alive. Another time, after being wounded in Bastogne, I was evacuated to Liege, Belgium. I was unconscious all the way, but I came to long enough to realize that I was being carried into the hospital by German soldiers."

"Late March or early April 1945, I arrived at Wakeman General Hospital at Camp Atterbury, Indiana. I was astonished to see German POWs working in the wards. Little did I know at the time how the Germans were treating our POWs in the Fatherland, but we sure treated the German POWs well. How sad."

John was discharged from the military on Feb. 21, 1946. His unit, the 501ˢᵗ PIR, received its first Presidential Unit Citation for action taken in combat. Later the entire division received the citation, allowing John to wear the ribbon with an oak leaf cluster. The countries of France, Holland, and Belgium awarded the 101ˢᵗ with Croix De Guere- Orange Lanyard, and another Croix De Guere. John also received an ETO Campaign ribbon with two arrowheads, denoting spearheading invasions, and one battle star. He also was awarded the Purple Heart with one oak leaf cluster for being wounded twice, and the Bronze Star.

John actually saw a number of prominent people while he was in the service. He saw President Roosevelt and Gen. George Marshall while he was stationed at Fort Benning; saw Gen. Dwight Eisenhower and Winston Churchill while he served overseas; and marched in a parade for Gen. Charles De Gaulle when he toured the base in North Carolina.

When he was finally discharged from the military in 1946, John, like most other veterans interviewed, said it was somewhat, "although not too," difficult to adjust to civilian life again.

LARRY TANBER
705th Tank Destroyer BN, (Recon Co.)
Attached to 101st Airborne Div.
Hometown: Michigan City, Indiana

Surrounded by a roomful of World War II memorabilia that aids in the telling of a story of a war fought so many years ago, Larry Tanber is seemingly at peace with the world. He has worked hard since returning home from Europe in the 1940s, even waiting until he was 74 years old to marry for the first time, and he obviously enjoys the manifestation of his hard work. Bring up the subject of war, however, especially the current situation in Iraq, and a visitor will get a glimpse of how the battles he fought during the "last, just war," have shaped his psyche.

"During World War II, I believe it was necessary for us to intervene in what was occurring in Europe," Larry said. "What Hitler was trying to do was unjust and inhumane. He was committing atrocities against the countries the Nazis conquered in Europe, and even against Germans. It was necessary for us to be there to help liberate Europe. I believe it was a good cause at the time."

The conflicts and wars Americans have fought since then though are another issue in Larry's mind.

"I don't know if there has ever been another just war since the one we fought in. I believe all the wars we've fought since then have been unnecessary. There's just too much suffering during a war. Diplomacy has failed. Politics and greed have taken over the world. And it's all done in the name of money and power."

The war Larry fought in was brutal and left lasting scars on all of the men who are part of the Northern Indiana Chapter of the Veterans of the Battle of the Bulge. The physical scars have healed over time, almost 60 years now since the battle began on December 16, 1944, while emotional scars still lie beneath the surface for most of the men who saw more than 80,000 of their comrades killed, wounded or captured, all in forty-one days. How could anyone forget those terrifying events that have since brought them together many years later? They haven't.

Their stories can be told now, and even though the facts are a half century or more in the past, they are still vivid—permanently etched memories waiting for a chance to be retold.

On a hot summer day, relaxing in the coolness of his beautiful home alongside a fairway in the Pottawattomie Country Club area of Michigan City, Larry talked about his time in the military.

"I was drafted in October 1943," Larry remembered. "I was 19 at the time. Before leaving for the service, I was working at Dwyer Products in Michigan City. At the time, the company was making ammo boxes for the Navy and gas tanks for the Army."

At the end of the war, Dwyer was still making products for the military, creating galleys for Navy patrol planes as well as 40mm ammo boxes.

"Everything built for the military had to be meticulously designed and produced," Larry said. "The Navy had inspectors that came to our plant and checked the quality of what we were making for them."

Larry's first military assignment in 1943 was at Fort Sill, an Artillery Training Facility in Oklahoma, where he took Basic Training.

"I was at Fort Sill during the winter months and I can remember it was windy and very cold there."

At the end of his 16 weeks at Fort Sill, Larry was qualified to train other military people for occupational duties. He was accepted into the ASTP program, the Army Specialized Training Program that would create a pool of college educated personnel for various military duties, but before reporting to duty, the assignment was cancelled. First there was a war that had to be won. At the time, Larry was an Acting Corporal.

Nine men were sent from Fort Sill to Fort Lewis, Washington, after Basic Training. Larry was one of the nine.

"I had no idea what was awaiting us at Fort Lewis."

The 705th Tank Destroyer outfit that Larry was sent to had been a National Guard unit prior to the war. Now, they were preparing for their mission overseas. Larry was assigned to Recon Company within the 705th.

"The main vehicle in our outfit was called an M18 Tank Destroyer. It was a track vehicle armed with a 76mm gun. I was a gunner on an M8 Armored Car, which was a six-wheel vehicle. The armament on that vehicle was a 30 cal. machine gun and a 37mm cannon."

"We were all pretty hot to get into combat. We had trained for our mission and were ready to go overseas."

The call for deployment to the European theater for the 705th came on April 10, 1944. They were on their way.

The 705th deployment included men and all of their equipment and was a five-day train trip from Fort Lewis to Camp Shanks, New Jersey. The train passed through Chicago around midnight and eventually through Michigan City, but Larry had fallen asleep by then, missing an opportunity to see his hometown.

"I had met another fellow from Michigan City by the name of Bernard Kutch while I was at Fort Lewis. He had a lot of problems dealing with being so close to home when the train passed through town. We all knew where we were heading once we arrived at Camp Shanks."

On April 18, the men boarded a ferry that took them to Pier #53 and the awaiting *Queen Elizabeth*. The cruise-ship-turned-troop-carrier, loaded with 10,000 soldiers began a five-day trip to Greenock, Scotland. The ship followed a zigzag course across the ocean. At the time, the ship was fitted with 5 inch guns and 40mm Anti-aircraft guns. No enemy action was encountered during the trip.

"While on board the *Queen Elizabeth* crossing the ocean, I saw ammo boxes that had been made at our plant in Michigan City. That made me pretty proud. "

Larry also discovered that while on the ship, all KP assignments were to be handled by the men of the 705th.

On April 25, the men boarded a train in Scotland and headed for England. Once there, they underwent additional training while being attached to the 3rd Army. They didn't know it at the time, but D-Day was being planned for June 6, 1944.

"On D-Day, the sky was full of airplanes flying overhead. There were gliders being towed by C-47s, and there was a constant roar of planes all day long. We listened to Ike's (General Dwight D. Eisenhower) speech on the

radio that day, and we learned what was occurring and what we were soon to be part of."

On July 16, the men of the 705th started their journey across the English Channel on their way to the combat awaiting them. They boarded their transportation near Weymouth, a small town on the Southern Coast of England.

"We crossed the Channel on LSTs, large landing craft that transported both men and equipment to a combat zone. It took us two days. Barrage balloons were suspended by cable about 700 feet above us. The balloons acted as a deterrent to any enemy plane that might try to strafe or bomb the ships crossing the English Channel."

They landed on Utah Beach and headed inland.

"We set up camp in France, and on August 1, General George Patton visited our outfit, met with our commander, Col. Clifford Templeton, and spoke to the men. His speech got everyone pretty fired up."

At the time, Larry was assigned to Task Force "A".

"As we moved into combat, my crew was assigned to escort General Herbert L. Ernest across northern France to the Brest Peninsula."

"We had many encounters with the enemy as we moved across northern France," Larry remembered.

By September 21, one of the toughest battles fought in France was nearing an end – the fight at the Brest Peninsula.

Brest is a seaport city on the northwest coast of France. It currently is a base for France's nuclear submarine fleet, but during WWII, the Germans captured the harbor city and used it as a major submarine base. Brest and Lorient were beleaguered cities that the Germans didn't give up easily.

On September 22, the 705th moved to Rennes for R&R, and on October 11, drove through the streets of Paris.

"As we drove through the City of Lights, I had to look back to see the Eiffel Tower – what a sight!"

By December 18th, two days after the official beginning of the Battle of the Bulge, Larry's outfit was stationed in Kohlscheid, Germany, a town next to Aachen, attached to the 9th Army.

"We were kind of a renegade outfit," Larry said.

"During our deployment in Kohlscheid, we would scout the surrounding country looking for German paratroopers who may have dropped in during the previous night."

"On the evening of Dec. 18, 1944, Colonel Templeton received marching orders form Ninth Army Headquarters to take the battalion to Neufchateau, Belgium, and report to General Troy Middleton, VII Corps Commander. Middleton had recently withdrawn his headquarters from Bastogne to Neufchateau, approximately 10 miles southwest of Bastogne."

"The 705th left Kohlscheid at 2240 hours (10:40 p.m.) on Dec. 18. At the time, the Germans were firing "Buzz Bombs" along our route. Our column stopped in Liege, Belgium, after midnight while the city was being bombed and lit up with flares. We could hear the rocket engines cut-out, and we awaited the ensuing explosions with trepidation. We didn't know where they would land. Luck was with us, though, as they all missed us."

"The battalion could not proceed to our destination, Neufchateau, by the shortest route, Liege-Houffalize-Bastogne, because the enemy was already around the town of Houffalize. The Germans had switched road signs during the night all along the route to confuse the troops who were en route. The column of the 705th, therefore, moved by way of Laroche where it assumed a defensive position along the heights six miles south of the town on Dec. 19, at 0915 hours (9:15 a.m.)."

"Col. Templeton looked Laroche over and was alarmed at what he saw. American units were in confusion along the road, blocking traffic and making no attempts to set up a defensive position."

By mid-morning, Colonel Templeton sent two platoons with four M18 tank destroyers to set up a roadblock to the north of town. The remainder of the battalion was to stay in the area until further notice.

Leaving the town, he went on to Neufchateau, where VIII Corps Headquarters was established. His was escorted by a lead jeep that had a three-man crew and a 30 cal. machine gun. The Colonel's command vehicle had a three-man crew and a 50 cal. machine gun, and were accompanied by an M8 armored car with a four-man crew that had a 30 cal. machine gun and a 37mm cannon. The gunner was Larry Tanber.

"Leaving Laroche, we went on to Neufchateau. Along the route, engineers were mining bridges and setting dynamite charges around large trees to be blown later. Col. Templeton reported to Gen. Middletown and was given orders to make contact with Gen. Anthony McAuliffe in Bastogne where the 101st Airborne Division was being deployed."

"Gen. McAuliffe ordered Col. Templeton to go back north to Laroche and bring the 705th back into Bastogne. At about 1400 hours (2 p.m.), our three vehicles, with full crews, left Bastogne on the mission. At the time, troops from the 101st were being trucked into Bastogne, along the same route we were using. The airborne guys were happy they didn't have to jump into this battle. Jump casualties usually amounted to 10 percent."

"As our vehicles moved to the north, Col. Templeton told us to keep our eyes open for signs of the enemy, as we were in no-man's land. It was an eerie silence, with no guns being fired and no artillery shells falling around us. We traveled about six miles when we came around a curve in the road and came face-to-face with elements of the German 116th Panzer Division who had set up a roadblock."

All hell broke loose.

"The lead jeep was the first thing hit by enemy fire, killing the driver and forcing the remaining crewmen to dismount and seek cover. Colonel Templeton's command vehicle was disabled forcing him and the crew to dismount. One of the assistant gunners was taken prisoners as he got out of the turret of his vehicle and was left behind. His name was Benny Chambliss – I think he was from Cleveland."

Chaos was everywhere as the GIs scrambled to get out of harm's way.

"Our driver was able to maneuver the vehicle between the ditches and head to higher ground where we had a chance to return fire on the enemy."

An enemy machine gun located on the left flank had opened fire at the American convoy and, until Larry's vehicle got to higher ground, they were unable to return fire because the withdrawing crews were in the immediate line of sight.

"I fired two rounds from the 37mm cannon destroying the machine gun emplacement, and our vehicle turned around while taking heavy fire from other enemy gun emplacements."

The road the men were on was narrow, approximately 27 feet wide, and it was difficult to turn the armored car around, but they were finally able to, and picked up the men of the two withdrawing crews, including Col. Templeton, and withdrew several hundred yards. All the while, Larry was firing rounds from the cannon in the direction of the ambush to cover their withdrawal.

"All you do in that situation is react," Larry said. "Survival is utmost in your mind. All the training you had to prepare you for combat comes to the forefront, whether you realize it or not, and you just try to survive."

The action lasted approximately 20 minutes. Later, Larry would discover 14 machine gun slugs in the tires of his armored vehicle. Col. Templeton radioed from the armored car to the Battalion that they should expect the German roadblock at Bertogne. The 705th reached Bastogne at 2030 hours (8:30 p.m.) on December 19 by taking the Laroche-Champlon-Bastogne route.

For his bravery that day, Larry was awarded the Silver Star Medal, one of our nation's highest combat awards. The award reads: *Technician Fifth Grade Lawrence T. Tanber, 35897108, Field Artillery, Reconnaissance Company, 776th Tank Destroyer Battalion, United States Army. For gallantry in action in the vicinity of Bertogne, Belgium, on 19 December 1944. On the afternoon of 19 December 1944, as a motorized reconnaissance patrol of the 705th Tank Destroyer Battalion, led by the Battalion Commander, proceeded along the road near Bertogne, they came under intense hostile tank, machine gun and small arms fire and casualties were inflicted on the patrol. Although the entire party left their vehicles to seek nearby positions of cover, Technician Fifth Grade Tanber, then a 705th Tank Destroyer Battalion gunner, courageously ignored the hail of fire, remaining in his M8 armored car and, bringing his 37mm gun to bear on a strategically located enemy machine gun, fired two rounds accurately at the automatic weapons emplacement, completely wiping out the nest and crew. Then, traversing his gun, Technician Fifth Grade Tanber brought withering fire on the rest of the enemy positions, silencing their weapons and enabling his commanding officer and his comrades to withdraw from the ambush. His outstanding courage under fire, strong initiative and loyal devotion to duty reflect the highest credit upon Fifth Grade Tanber and the armed forces of the United States.*

"We finally made it into the town of Bastogne, but we had no idea what was awaiting us there."

Bastogne was besieged for eight days during December 1944, ending the night after Christmas. The Germans had broken through American defenses, isolating the 101st Airborne Division, Combat Command B of the 10th Armored Division, and the 705th Tank-Destroyer Battalion – the only troops available for defense of the strategic road-junction town in the Ardennes.[30]

"The importance of Bastogne was the seven roadways that led to the town," Larry said. "That made the town of strategic importance to the Germans. The rest of our outfit was left at the La Roche area. There was mass confusion as we prepared for an all-out assault on our positions."

During the Battle of the Bulge, Larry's Battalion lost every Company Commander to an enemy's action. Battlefield commissions saw Sergeants becoming Second Lieutenants as fast as they could be made.

"We were completely surrounded and we knew it. Supplies started getting low, but on December 22, C-47s dropped much-needed supplies such as ammunition and food, over our area."

A few minutes before noon, the first of 241 C-47 cargo carriers droned over the drop zone. Red, blue and yellow parachutes billowed like fantastic Christmas ornaments, floating downward with priceless gifts of ammunition, medical supplies and food. Not all of the planes made it; some were hit by flak as they flew over the German lines, wobbled along, trailing smoke as their pilots tried desperately to deliver their loads before their craft broke into flames and fell.

The exhilarated men of Bastogne rushed out to drag the heavy Para packs back through the snow. They discovered a few foul-ups, including some shells for guns they did not have. But, nobody complained. More than 95 percent of the 144 tons of material in 1,446 packages was recovered and put to use. As an added dividend, the 82 Thunderbolt fighter-bombers that had convoyed the cargo planes to Bastogne turned to hammer the German ring around the town, flashing in low with napalm, fragmentation bombs and machine gun fire.[31]

"It was so cold in Bastogne, and the men were in bad shape. Frozen feet and trench foot were prevalent."

Larry avoided real trouble with his feet by being somewhat ingenious.

"I cut out corrugated cardboard the size of the insides of my boots and used it for innersoles. When they got wet, I simply replaced them with other cardboard. I believe that helped keep my feet somewhat dry and thereby avoiding trench foot or worse."

Food was scarce during the battle and Larry can remember only one hot meal – pancakes.

The food supply was dwindling fast – except for tons of flour that had been found in a Bastogne granary. The flour made good flapjacks, and the men ate flapjacks until they were sick of them.[32]

"We were running out of food during the battle. On Christmas Day, I had a can of cheese for dinner."

"I remember looking for smoke lockers in the town of Champs, Belgium, where there might be some food. Occasionally, we would find raw bacon and ham – we ate what we found."

The snow was getting deep – knee-deep in most places and it kept snowing.

"To get to our outposts we had to wade through the deep snow, but it's probably good that there was as much snow and cold weather as there was, because it masked a lot of death. I remember seeing a German soldier who had been run over by a tank. The body was frozen and flat as a piece of cardboard."

"During the battle, one night around 4 a.m., some 400 German Infantrymen and tanks attacked our positions in Champs. We had one tank destroyer and it nailed the first German tank. Our vehicle, a six wheel armored car, got knocked out of commission, and we ended up on foot. I remember seeing a T.D. shell go past us and as I turned to look where it was heading, I saw it hit a tank behind us, and I watched in amazement as the driver of the tank was blown skyward. His head had been blown off. When that battle finally ended, there were bodies of dead German soldiers all over the place. We wiped out those 400 soldiers and tanks."

Men and tanks of the 4th Armored Division broke though into Bastogne on the 25th and 26th of December.

"It was a great sight," Larry said.

A few days earlier, on the 22nd of December, the Germans demanded that the Americans surrender. General A.C. McAuliffe was the Division Commander of the 101st Airborne in Bastogne. Larry has a copy of the newsletter containing the surrender demand from the enemy.

The note from the German Commander on December 22, 1944, read;

To the U.S.A. Commander of the encircled town of Bastogne.

The fortune of war is changing. This time the U.S.A. forces in and near Bastogne have been encircled by strong German armored units. More German armored units have crossed the river Ourthe near Ortheuville, have taken Marche and reached St. Hubert by passing through Hompres-Sibret-Tillst. Libramont is in German hands.

There is only one possibility to save the encircled U.S.A. Troops from total annihilation that is the honorable surrender of the encircled town. In order to think it over a term of two hours will be granted beginning with the presentation of this note.

If this proposal should be rejected one German Artillery Corps and six heavy A.A. Battalions are ready to annihilate the U.S.A. Troops in and near Bastogne. The order for firing will be given immediately after this two hour's term.

All the serious civilian losses caused by this Artillery fire would not correspond with the well known American humanity.

The German Commander

The German Commander received the following reply:

22 December 1944

To the German Commander:

N U T S!

The American Commander

Larry's outfit remained throughout the siege and stayed on the front lines until they were relieved on the 18th of January when they were sent to 8th Corps.

In March of that year, Larry was attached to the 11th Armored Division and remembers the day Col. Templeton was at an outpost when one German shell hit the position and, "Clobbered it!" The Colonel was killed.

As the war began to wind down, one incident stands out in Larry's mind.

"We had captured a German searchlight battalion on May 7th, 1945. Actually, it was the day after the war officially ended. One of the guys in our outfit was Jewish and he took four of the captured German soldiers into the woods, lined them up and killed them with a 50 cal. machine gun. I suppose that was his way of getting even for the atrocities the Nazis' committed against the Jewish people. But, it was a real mess. I don't know if he was ever disciplined for that or not."

Larry remained in the Army of Occupation after the war ended until November 1. He would return to the States and be discharged from Camp Patrick Henry, Virginia, in January 1946.

Returning home, Larry attended Purdue North Central (PNC) on the GI Bill at night while continuing his employment at Dwyer Products in Michigan City. It would take him five years of night school to get his degree. He worked at Dwyer for 48 years and for 24 of those years, taught Engineering classes at PNC as well.

Reminiscing about all of the action he was part of in Europe, Larry recalled one incident where a tank he was standing next to was hit by a shell that didn't explode. The shell hit the tank, warped the steel, but didn't go off. No one was hurt. That was as close he came to being wounded in action.

Larry closed by saying, "The fact that we survived is reward enough.

THE MEN OF THE ARMORED DIVISIONS:

The 4th Armored Division

The 7th Armored Division

FRANK DUDASH
4th Armored Division
President of Chapter XXX
Hometown: Crown Point, Indiana

They've all seen death, some more than others. Anyone who has fought in combat has come face to face with the consequences of war – it is inevitable. The men of Chapter XXX were no exception.

Frank Dudash, however, may have seen more death than the rest of the men in the Northern Indiana Chapter of the Veterans of the Battle of the Bulge combined.

On the fourth of April, 1945, as a member of the Fourth Armored Division, Frank's tank crew rolled into the town of Ohrdruf, Germany, believing it was a Nazi communications center. Instead of finding radio equipment though, they found a concentration camp filled with prisoners who were near death, along with some 4,000 bodies of those who hadn't survived the brutality of the Nazi regime.

"Until we actually saw the camp and the awfulness that was there, we didn't know those places existed," Frank said. "We sure weren't expecting what we saw when we arrived. We didn't know what to do. Our men just walked around the camp in a daze, not knowing what we could do to help those who were still alive."

The camp was devoid of the German SS guards who had been there guarding and brutalizing those prisoners in their custody – they fled when they heard the Allies were near. Even some of the prisoners, those who could still walk, left the camp when they heard and saw the Americans because they didn't know what their intentions were.

"Some of our men broke down when they saw the stacks of dead bodies with lime thrown over them; others wanted to go out and kill every German they could find. Headquarters was notified and eventually Generals George Patton, Dwight Eisenhower and Omar Bradley arrived to see the evidence for themselves. Patton threw up twice while viewing the camp. The smell of burning flesh and death was present the entire time. It was horrible! I'll never forget it. Those who were still alive looked like they were from another planet. Their eyes had a blank stare to them. They didn't look like anything or anyone I'd ever seen before in my lifetime. We were afraid to offer them food," Frank continued. "We didn't know if we would be doing them any good, or possibly harming them by giving them something to eat."

The day that they arrived at the camp and saw the devastation awaiting them, the officers in the tank division went into the town of Ohrdruf and found the mayor and his family. They made them accompany the soldiers back to the camp and look at the death and carnage that was there so that they couldn't later disavow any knowledge of what took place in the concentration camp.

"The mayor and his wife walked through the camp and acted as if nothing was wrong," Frank said. "Their children kind of peeked through their fingers covering their faces, but the adults didn't look at anything. Later that night the couple went home and hung themselves. Maybe they thought they, too, would be prosecuted for war crimes."

Ohrdruf had been a labor camp, its inmates forced to dig vast caverns that housed underground headquarters and transportation. As many as 10,000 men had lived and slaved at Ohrdruf; very few survived. In its last days, with the arrival of the Americans imminent, the SS had either marched most of the prisoners to other camps or killed them. Small in comparison to other camps, without the sophisticated equipment of death and torture found elsewhere, it was in fact a minor sub-camp of Buchenwald. Yet its significance lay in the fact that it was the first remains of a camp to be discovered by either the British or American armies that actually contained prisoners and corpses, and as such was a revelation.[33]

Later, Frank's outfit made a stop in Buchenwald, another concentration camp that would become infamous by the brutality that occurred there.

"I dismounted my tank in Buchenwald and walked inside one of the many buildings there. Again, the smell of burning flesh was everywhere. Inside the building, human hair was in a pile in one corner of the building, from the floor to the ceiling; in another, eyeglasses; another, gold teeth. And one room was filled with baby shoes. I can't even explain what I was feeling at that time. What I was seeing and experiencing was almost incomprehensible. How could people commit those kinds of atrocities against other human beings?"

The Nazis built Buchenwald as a camp for political prisoners (mostly German Communists and Social Democrats), certain classes of incorrigible criminals, and – as the government stepped up its anti-Semitic campaign in 1937-38—for Jews. The site they chose had as its centerpiece the so-called Goethe oak, a tree stump that marked the poet's favorite spot in the woods. This stroke of Nazi black humor had behind it a more sinister purpose; the hidden, forbidding woods so close to Weimar provided a perfect setting for a camp that must remain a mystery yet be ever present in the minds of those who contemplated opposition to the regime.[34]

By the time Frank saw the devastation at Ohrdruf, near the end of World War II, it seemed like he had been in the Army forever. It was four years earlier, though, that Frank's military career had begun.

Frank, as a young man from Gary, Ind., began his military career, along with two of his good friends, when he enlisted in the United States Army in May, 1941. It wasn't the money that appealed to them, as a Private's monthly pay at that time was a mere $21.

"I knew I was going to be drafted sooner or later," Frank said. "So, I enlisted. At the time, I thought I would only be in the service for one year, and then I would be out."

Driving to Indianapolis, where they would undergo physical examinations and upon passing, be sworn in as soldiers, the three men decided to stop in the little Indiana town of Monon.

"We bought some booze in town and celebrated our last day as civilians. By the time we arrived in Indy, we were drunk."

After passing their physicals the next day and being sworn in as privates in the United States Army, the men were sent to a base being constructed in Watertown, New York, that would be the training ground for the Fourth Armored Division. Frank was going to be in a tank division.

(A tank is an armored combat vehicle. Most travel on caterpillar tracks. They carry weapons such as cannons, machine guns, and today, missile launchers. In most tanks, the weapons are mounted on a revolving structure called a turret. They are used to attack other armored vehicles, infantry, and various ground targets; and to fire on aircraft.)

A tank crew during World War II was comprised of five men; a driver who sat on the left side of the vehicle and steered the tank; an assistant driver (called a bog) sitting next to the driver; the gunner and the loader who were more or less in the center of the tank, and a tank commander who stood behind the gunner. Today's Army tanks, such as the M60A1, are operated by a crew of four.

"The tanks we operated used two different types of ammunition. We either fired H.E (high explosive) rounds or A.P. (armor piercing) rounds. The gunner fired both the cannon and the machine gun by stepping on a floor-mounted foot-activated button." Every fifth round from the machine guns was a tracer shell, meaning that the gunner could see where the rounds were going, and could correct his fire by either aiming higher or lower.

"We had maneuvers in New York while we were there – it was so cold – and despite the fact we were in an Armored Division, there weren't any tanks there when we arrived. Eventually, two tanks (called Mae West because they had double turrets and to some, resembled a woman's breasts) were sent to us from Fort Knox, Kentucky, so we had something to practice with."

Later, the men would become familiar with a medium, 26-ton vehicle called the General Grant – a tank that was equipped with a 37mm small gun in the turret, and a 75mm cannon in the spouse. This was the type of tank that America gave to the British General Montgomery who was fighting the Nazis in the desert of Egypt. The 4th Armored Division's main fighting vehicle, however, would be the Sherman, a heavy tank with a 75mm cannon and a 30 caliber machine gun. The tanks were air-cooled, which means the engines didn't need water.

"There were times while we were in training in New York that the temperature got down to 35 degrees below zero. But, it helped us learn how to dress for cold weather, which we eventually encountered in Europe, and taught us how to fight in snow and inclement weather."

It was about that time that Frank learned he would be in the service of Uncle Sam, not for the one year he had believed when he enlisted, but for two and a half years. His pay was increased to $50 per month.

"I was in a Radio Technician School at Fort Knox, Kentucky, on December 7, 1941. That was the day the Japanese attacked Pearl Harbor and plunged our country into war. I wondered what was going to happen next, and if I would be part of whatever war effort America was planning."

It wouldn't be long before he had an answer to his musings. During the months of August, September, and October 1942, Frank's outfit took part in maneuvers around the Murfreesboro area of Tennessee. Once, during a maneuver Frank participated in, his outfit of tanks had to cross the Cumberland River on a pontoon bridge.

"We were told by some of the locals who were watching the maneuvers that we were the first damn Yankees to cross the Cumberland River. That was a feat not even accomplished during the Civil War."

On another maneuver there, this one at night, Frank's tank threw a track, rendering it immobile. They waited for a Tank Recovery Vehicle (a piece of equipment that resembles a big tow truck) to pick them up, and while waiting saw a local man in bib overalls carrying a rifle watching them.

"Finally, the man came over to us and asked us what the tank was. He had never even heard of a tank, let alone seen one. He said, 'Golly! What is that thing?' He didn't even know that we were at war," Frank said. "He asked us if we had anything to eat, and when we said that we didn't, he took the whole tank crew to his house where he killed some chickens and his wife made us breakfast."

While in the state of Tennessee, the men also discovered that moonshine was a tree stump away.

"I don't know who brought the booze, or even when it arrived, but we found out that if we wanted some 'shine' there was a particular tree stump, where by laying a $10 bill on it in the evening, a five-gallon can of whiskey would be there in its place the next morning. No questions asked – no answers given."

After spending time in the South, Frank's outfit was sent to the

Mojave Desert in California for desert training. They were in the area for Thanksgiving, 1942.

"It was so hot inside those tanks in the desert," Frank remembered. "Once, we were caught in a sandstorm that lasted all day. We were miserable. I can appreciate what our tank divisions encountered in Iraq when they were fighting there."

The men were close enough to Los Angeles that they were able to go into both L.A. and Las Vegas on the weekends. On one visit to L.A., the men were in a bar called the Waldorf Cellar and the bartender was a man by the name of Pete Coss. He was from Gary, Ind. It truly is a small world. After spending six months in the desert, it was time to move on again, and this time they ended up in Texas at Camp Bowie.

"Camp Bowie was halfway between Dallas and Fort Worth, and it was in a dry county, which meant no booze. But we had booze at the camp. One of the radio evangelists found out about it and on his radio show referred to the 4th Armored Division as "evil" because we had alcohol in a county that was dry. We might have been evil, but we weren't thirsty."

Promoted to "Buck" Sergeant (a three-striper), Frank's outfit left Texas headed for overseas. Traveling by troop train through Chicago, the train passed Frank's girlfriend's house en route to Boston, Massachusetts, and then on New Year's Day, the men boarded the ship, the *Santa Rosa*, and headed for Europe.

"We became part of one of the largest convoys to ever leave the United States, and right in the middle of the convoy was the Battleship New Jersey, at the time one of the largest battleships in the world."

The convoy landed at Cardiff, Wales, and the men disembarked and traveled to a town called Diviese, England, which was about 30 miles west of London.

"We trained at Diviese for a few months and then went to the southern section of the Salisbury Plains in England," Frank remembered. "We were getting tired of all the training, but on D-Day, June 6, 1944, we saw and heard the Allied planes flying overhead on their way to assist the landing at Normandy, and we knew that, we too, would soon be part of the action."

And then on July 4th, it was the men of the 4th Armored Division's turn. Only the noise and sights they encountered that day were considerably different than any previous Fourth of July celebration they might have participated in.

Tracing the route marked in red ink on a table-size map in his comfortable home in Crown Point, Ind., Frank said, "We landed on Utah Beach—the infantry was already there. We pushed hard during the next few weeks to make advances – we fought battles at St. Lo and St. Pierre. We pounded the Germans in those towns, finally breaking through at Avaranches, France."

"The Germans counterattacked at Avaranches with lots of tanks and men. We finally backed off about four or five miles before receiving orders to go back into the town. When we did, we started picking off their tanks like they were sitting ducks. We knocked out a lot of them, but the Germans didn't surrender. We were new to the game of combat and we were all scared. I saw this young GI who I befriended get killed, and once that happened, I didn't have any problems killing Germans."

It was on the 25th of July at the breakthrough that Patton's 3rd Army originated.

"That was the first time I saw Patton. He came to our area and made a speech to us about our roles and the job we were doing. He carried a swagger stick and saluted with it when someone saluted him. He was really something to see."

Frank continued pointing out battles on the big, 1945-issued map.

"We moved fast and furiously. Both the 4th and 6th Armored Divisions turned and headed to the Atlantic coast. There was a submarine base at a coastal town called Laurent and when we arrived there all of the German submarines from the Atlantic area must have been there, so we didn't attack. Instead, we turned and moved east across the country of France."

"There was a big battle in Orleans – we hit quickly then left. And in Troyes—that was one hell of a fight—we lost one whole battalion of tanks. A battalion consists of four companies – A, B, C, and D. The first three each had 17 tanks with D Company having less. That's a lot of tanks to lose in one battle! And in the triangular area of Nancy, Metz and Luneville, there were really some big battles in December. Armor was really making a difference in the fighting."

The Germans and other American outfits had names for the 4th Armored Division and not all of them were complimentary.

"We were called Roosevelt's Butchers, the Elite Tank Division, Patton's Panzers, Patton's Best, and the Breakthrough Boys."

And while other Armored Divisions had nicknames on their patches, the 4th Armored Division's was simply, "We shall be known by our deeds alone." The battle cry of the men in that division became, "They got us surrounded again – the poor bastards."

"We were told we would be going on a rest break in December and we had no more than unpacked our gear out of the tanks when there was a rumor going around that something really big was happening up north," Frank said.

On December 19, 1944, the rumor came true and about one-third of the 4th Armored Division's tanks and men headed north. They drove for 22 hours, utilizing black-out conditions, which meant they drove with their lights out during the hours of darkness. Later it was said that former President Richard Nixon called that 22-hour drive, "the greatest movement made in the history of the U.S. Army."

"Those of us who went north were attached to the 1st Army. We made up a task force known as Ezell. The task force had a company of medium tanks, an infantry regiment from the 10th Infantry, a battalion of artillery and some supply transportation vehicles. We were heading to the beleaguered town of Bastogne."

Bastogne was a small town occupied by men of the 101st Airborne, and they were surrounded by German forces.

The stage was set on December 22nd. The Germans had surrounded the 101st Airborne Division two days earlier in their final great offensive. On December 19th, a pocket of over 7,000 Americans had capitulated to the Germans in the Eifel. Gen. d. Pztrp. Heinreich Freiherr von Luttwitz, who was in charge of the force responsible for the capture of Bastogne, hoped that such a negotiated surrender might help to avoid a costly battle to pry the stubborn American troops out of the town. The fighting there had already cost the Baron many casualties.[35]

"We made it all the way into Bastogne with the Task Force," Frank said. "We saw lots of German soldiers, some dead, most of them alive, but we made it there and reported to a Col. in the 10th Armored Division. We were told to leave because of the seriousness of the situation there, and we did. On our way back to our lines we saw tank tracks in the snow and then we came across deserted American 155mm Howitzers. Our officers said they always wanted to have artillery pieces in our outfit, so we hitched those big guns to the back of our tanks and took off." Later, they would be ordered to return the guns to the Artillery. And they reluctantly did.

"During the sub-zero temperatures that we encountered at Bastogne, we had a procedure for changing our socks that prevented frostbite or frozen feet," Frank remembered. "I kept two pair of socks next to my body – one pair under my arms pits, the other flat against my stomach. When we changed our socks, we took off one boot at a time and slipped on a dry sock that had been next to our body. We took the sock that had been on our feet, rolled it in the snow, getting it wet, then wrung it out and put it next to our body for the next change."

There was also a procedure for cleaning one's teeth.

"We used small rounded rocks the size of small marbles. We would roll them around in our mouths to get off the plaque, and then we rubbed the rocks on our clothes and stuck them in our pockets to save for our next opportunity to use them."

It would be in a town called Chaumont that Frank would be wounded.

"An enemy airburst exploded nearby sending shrapnel down around us and pieces of it hit me in the head. My wounds were wrapped by some fellows who were nearby and I was put on the back of a tank and taken to the rear lines. Five days later, my wounds were healed well enough that I was ready to go back into combat."

"I got back to my outfit in Luxembourg and we started crossing Germany. We were in one battle where the German soldiers began attacking us with fixed bayonets. We mowed them down with machine gun fire. After the battle ended, we checked the bodies and discovered that the soldiers weren't any older than 16 and their canteens were filled with wine. Somebody got those kids high on alcohol and sent them out to die."

On March 15, 1945, Frank was a Staff Sergeant assigned to the 3rd Platoon as a Platoon Leader.

"There were only two officers left in the Company," Frank remembered. "One was Captain Fishler and the other, Fist Lieutenant Warner. At the time, we only had two platoons, the first and third.

"The situation called for Lt. Warner to lead the column of tanks on one day, and then I would lead the CCB Column every other day."

Frank would lead the platoon as a Staff Sergeant for the next two months – all the way to Czechoslovakia.

"We learned to shoot with armored piercing shells at every hay stack we saw," Frank Said. "A majority of the time, the shells would bounce off the stacks because inside the hay was either a German tank or pillbox. We also knocked down every church steeple in every town because they were ideal places for snipers to hide."

Frank was offered a battlefield commission but refused the promotion because at the time the Army had a point system that allowed anyone with 88 accumulated points to return home at the end of the war, and Frank had already earned 99 points. Going home was much more desirable than a battlefield commission.

It was during this period of combat that Frank received a citation while leading a column of tanks from Jena, Germany to Chemnitz, Germany.

Detailed description of incident on 1ˢᵗ Sgt. Frank W. Dudash 35159917 Co. A 8ᵗʰ Tank Battalion APO United States Army:

1ˢᵗ Sgt. Frank Dudash (then s/sgt.) has acted as a platoon leader of the 3ʳᵈ Platoon Co A 8ᵗʰ Tk. Bn.; from March 17, 1945 until the present – and shown himself to be a leader of great ability. He took the platoon over at a time when there was a shortage of officers in the company and handle it with skill and combativeness that would be hard handle in a commissioned officer. He has on numerous occasions been the lead tank of the whole division column, and his drive and aggressive leadership have often been enabled the column to make great strides.

As an example on April 14, 1945, 1ˢᵗ Sgt. Dudash led the combat column from the vicinity of Jena, Germany to Waldenberg, Germany where he secured a bridge across the Zwick-Mulde River, a total distance of fifty-seven miles. His calmness under fire and in the most hazardous situations. His ability to make quick decisions, and his driving leadership have made him one of the best platoon leaders this organization has ever had. His conduct compares with the highest standards in the Army.

Leonard H. Kieley
Captain, Infantry
Commanding "A" Co.

F.W.D.
Bronze Star Medal
When the war officially ended on May 8, 1945, Frank was still

in Europe, in a town called Pisek, and his outfit had more than one encounter with Russian soldiers.

"We moved into Strakonice, which is a small town in Czechoslovakia not far from the German border. We entered from one direction; the Russians came in from another. The civilians in town were really afraid of what the Russians might do to them, so we spent the night sleeping in a gymnasium filled with civilians and Russian soldiers. We slept right in the middle of both groups, keeping them separated. Thankfully, there weren't any incidents."

Frank's unit occupied the town for two days and it wasn't long before refugees began pouring into the area.

"They were returning home any way they could. Some walked back into town; others were riding bicycles or oxen. Some of them rode in charcoal-burning trucks. Eventually, more than 4,000 people showed up and we directed them to a field and turned them over to Czech patriots. And then the Russians came and took control of the prisoners from the patriots. They raped the women there and we were helpless to do anything about it."

A few days after the official end of the war, while in the Czech village, a Russian lieutenant invited Frank and his tank crew to join him for a celebration.

"We met the Russian in an open area – he laid a blanket on the ground and we began drinking this rot gut that was supposed to be Vodka, but tasted more like gasoline. I drank more than 3 canteen cups of this stuff, but my crew was smart – they dumped their drinks on the ground."

What happened next is what his tank crew members told Frank later, because he doesn't remember anything after drinking the Vodka.

"They said I got into an argument with the Russian soldier and I pulled my .45 pistol out of its holster and stuck it in his stomach. The Russian stuck his hands in the air and I fired three rounds into the air. When the Russian brought his hands down, I again stuck the pistol in his stomach and when he raised his hands, I again fired three shots in the air. My crew told me I repeated this three times before my driver got behind me, pinned my arms back and got me out of there. I almost started WWIII in those woods. The next day I was summoned to the C.P. to talk to the Commanding Officer. I thought I was in real trouble, but instead, I was promoted to First Sergeant and told that I would be running the Company. I never told him about the incident in the woods."

That promotion made Frank the top NCO of his outfit and he actually ran the company from May until his discharge in October, 1945.

Before returning to the States, Frank was transferred to the 9th Armored Division and was told he would have to remove his 4th AD patch and replace it with the new division patch.

"I wouldn't do it," he said. "That patch had too many memories and too much meaning for me to discard it."

Instead of replacing the 4th A.D. patch, Frank put the patch on his right sleeve, and the new 9th A.D. patch on his left.

Coming home on a liberty ship, Frank remembered, "We hit every damn wave in the ocean."

First Sergeant Frank Dudash was discharged from the service of his country on Oct. 26, 1945. During his ten months of combat, he served in the Normandy, Northern France, Ardennes, Rhineland, and Central Europe campaigns. He received the Presidential Distinguished Unit Citation, the French Croix De Guerre, and the French Forrageire Citations.

A month later he was back to work at U.S. Steel in Gary, Ind., in the Open Hearth Process where he would retire from after 45 years of service. He would meet his wife Ethel, or "Toots," as he always called her, in Crown Point, Ind., and they would marry in 1946. They would have three children – one became a Catholic priest and is currently the Pastor of St. Helen's Church in Hebron. Another son would become a naval pilot and spend 22 years in the military before retiring. A daughter works for an investment firm and is single. Ethel would die after 46 years, six months and 20 days of marriage.

Frank has served as a volunteer at St. Anthony Hospital in Crown Point since September 1993. He is currently the president of the Auxiliary there – the first male president. During the last five years, Frank has served on a panel with a survivor of the Holocaust and a French Freedom Fighter. Together they have helped educate grade school kids at Taft Jr. High about their experiences. For the past two years, Frank has spoken with 8th graders at Notre Dame School in Michigan City about his time in Europe.

"These kids are hungry for information about WWII," Frank said.

Reminiscing about the best of times, Frank said it would have to be the times spent in the small towns of France and Belgium.

"It made your heart feel so good knowing that you were helping to free these people from the evil that had overtaken them. Little girls wanted to hug and kiss us when we liberated them – a good feeling. Then there was the time we went swimming in a pool in Nancy, France. It was like being in a YMCA pool."

"The 4th A.D. was so outstanding because of the quality of troops we had," Frank said. Our soldiers were dedicated, experienced professionals from top to bottom, and we had the leadership of Gen. John Wood who was known as 'The Rommel of the American Army.' Our training had so much to do with our success. We fought the blizzards of New York, the rivers and valleys of Tennessee, the sands of the Mojave Desert and had the great firing range of Camp Bowie, Texas. The final tune-up for combat on the Salisbury Plains in England helped as well. No unit was more ready for combat than the men of the 4th Armored Division. Being in the 3rd Army under the command of the daring, imaginative and visionary Gen. Patton meant a lot also. Patton once said that to be successful in combat, you have to have the right tools, and he found that in the men of the 4th A.D. Patton was cocky, reckless and aggressive, but he had confidence and discipline, and the will to fight."

The worst of times memories included seeing his best buddies killed- some instantly, and one who bled to death after having his leg shot off; and getting caught in a shoot-out with the Krauts that ended with six American tanks being lost in the battle.

"I have no regrets though. It was one hell of an experience; and it was worth it, because we were fighting for freedom. If I was younger, I'd do it again!"

The Fourth Armored Division lost 1,519 men killed in combat in Europe during World War II.

FRANK G. MIDKIFF
7th Armored Division, 77th Armored Med Battalion, Co C
Hometown: Chicago, Illinois

Frank was in the Illinois National Guard when, in March 1941, the unit was activated. He was 23 years old and single at the time. Upon entering the service, he was a private making $21 a month. Like all men and women who have served in the military, he remembers his service serial number – 20618673.

Frank was sent to Tullahoma, Tennessee, for training at Camp Forrest. While there, he was housed in the standard Army barracks of the time, and ate his meals in the camp's mess hall. He would remain in Tennessee from March 1941 to November 1942 when he was sent to Officer Candidate School (OCS) at Camp Barkley, Texas. While there, he trained for receipt of a commission – second lieutenant.

Before departing for duty overseas, Frank served at Camp Polk, Louisiana in the 77th Armored Medical Battalion, Company C.

When he sailed for the European Theater, he did so onboard the *Queen Mary*, a luxury ship-turned-troop-carrier. It took a week at sea to make the crossing to the other side of the Atlantic Ocean. He would serve in Europe from 1944 to 1945.

At the war's end in 1945, Frank was in Germany assisting in the occupation of the country.

When he returned to the United States in 1945, Frank was discharged at Camp Grant, Illinois. He was awarded the following decorations: the Bronze Star, the American Defense Medal, the Western Defense Medal, the EAME Medal with four battle stars, the Victory Medal, and the Occupation Medal.

THE ARTILLERYMEN:

31st AAA Group, 113th Gun Battery

188th Field Artillery Group, 957th FA Battalion

190th Field Artillery Battalion

977th ACH, 3rd Army

JAMES W. ALDRICH
977th ACH, 3rd Army, 1301st Engineer Reg.
Hometown: Mishawaka, Indiana

J ames was inducted into the military service in Niles, Michigan, on July 8, 1943. The next day, history books will show, U.S. and British airborne troops began being dropped in Sicily as a prelude to a full scale invasion. On July 10 Sicily was invaded by elements of the U.S. Seventh and the British Eighth armies—about 12 divisions altogether. In the first day, some 160,000 Allied soldiers were put ashore. The war in Europe was heating up, and fresh troops were going to be needed.

James, along with a group of other new recruits from the Wolverine State, was sent to Fort Custer, Michigan, where he remained for three days. He traveled to Fort Custer on board a passenger train that left its military-bound passengers at the train station in Battle Creek, Michigan, where they were picked up and delivered to the military post.

During his time at his first military post, James was issued Army clothing such as shoes, overseas hat, khakis, sun tans (uniform color), ODs (good old olive drabs), and long sleeve shirts.

"Basically, we spent the short time we were there getting organized," James reported. "We also discovered the meaning of K.P. and Guard Duty."

From Fort Custer, James was sent to Camp McCoy in Wisconsin, where he spent time at the rifle range, took part in close order drills, and again pulled guard duty – typical Basic Training instruction.

James would spend approximately one year in the States undergoing training and preparing for combat before being shipped overseas.

Traveling on a troop ship by the name of the *Sequel,* James arrived in England after 11 days at sea on April 5, 1944. He was a Pfc at the time. In England, the men of James's outfit slept in tents and some civilian buildings that were used to accommodate the influx of American soldiers there. When the invasion of France began on June 6, 1944, James was pulling guard duty at a warehouse where the maps of the invasion were kept.

Later in France, James's outfit was guarding a bridge at Point of Musan on the Muse River.

"The Germans tried to bomb that bridge," James remembered, "and they missed both the bridge and those of us who were guarding it."

Assigned to the Third Army, the men of the 1301, 1303, as well as two other Engineering Regiments, built a wooden bridge across the Rhine River that allowed Allied troops and equipment to speed towards their final destinations inside of Nazi Germany.

The Great German retreat was on. At last there was no doubt. For several days Dietrich's Sixth Panzer Army had led the way back to Germany. Now (after the defeat at the Battle of the Bulge) Manteuffel's army joined the full retreat.

Everyone was in retreat except a few picked infantrymen left behind in shattered buildings or lonely foxholes to slow down the rampaging Americans. These men of the rear guard were picked because they were very young or very old. They fought gallantly, in lonely hopelessness. They knew they had been abandoned so that the best fighting men could escape behind the Siegfried Line. Boys of fourteen were found with rifles frozen to their hands.

Rivers of men and machines flowed back toward the Fatherland. Great lines of trucks, tanks, and self-propelled guns rumbled east over icy roads and trails clogged with snowdrifts. Long lines of discouraged infantrymen trudged in the powdery snow.

"Watch on the Rhine" was crawling back to the Fatherland like a great wounded beast. The will of the German soldier was broken. No one who survived the retreat believed there was a chance of German victory. Three and a half months later, on May 7 (1945), Germany surrendered.[36]

The war may have ended in Europe on May 7, 1945, and many of those American GIs who had accumulated enough points were discharged from military life. But James hadn't amassed the needed points and was sent to the Philippines to work as a carpenter until the war against Japan ended. He was sitting on a troop ship in the Pacific Ocean when hostilities against the Japanese finally put an end to his military obligation.

James was discharged from the Army at Fort Sheridan, Illinois in 1945. He was awarded the Victory Medal, the European-African-Middle Eastern Theater Ribbon with four bronze Battle Stars, three Overseas Service bars, the Good Conduct Medal, the Meritorious Unit Award, the American Theater Award, the Philippine Liberation Medal and a Pacific Campaign Ribbon.

(Included in the information sent back to me by James Aldrich is a small photo of him taken in 1943, and his personal immunization register. It shows that he received a smallpox vaccine, a triple typhoid vaccine, a tetanus toxoid, and others from 1943 until 1945.)

ROBERT J. GALGAN
31ˢᵗ AAA Group, 113ᵗʰ Gun Battalion, Btry C
Hometown: Palos Heights, Illinois

B ob entered the service of his country in late 1942 or early 1943 after requesting an end to the deferment that had kept him out of the military.

A 2A deferment, based on the technical skills Bob possessed at the time – he was proficient at wiring electric motors, had kept him from the list the draft board used to send out draft notices.

"I knew I must get into the service, and one day I made up my mind to enlist," Bob remembered. "I went to the draft board and asked them to end my deferment and put me on the list, and they did. A short time later, I received my induction papers. So, theoretically, I both enlisted and was drafted."

Inducted into the military in Chicago, Illinois, along with 1,000 other young men, Bob was sent, first to Camp Grant, Illinois, then to Fort Bliss, Texas. His pay as a private in the United States Army was $21 a month.

While stationed at Fort Bliss, Bob lived in four-man huts and ate chow in a mess hall. He described the food there as, "Bad! Especially while on bivouac." While stationed at Fort Bliss, Bob said they were quarantined to the post and that the discipline there was severe.

Bob left Fort Bliss on board a train – destination unknown.

"The train actually started towards the West Coast," Bob said. "And then somewhere along the way, it made a big sweeping curve and we were heading east. I don't know if that was done to confuse anyone who might have been watching troop movements, or what the reason was for that maneuver."

When the troop-carrying train arrived in Chicago on its way east, it stopped in the freight yards for approximately three to four hours.

"Some of the men who lived close by were able to get off the train and call their families to tell them where they were at. Pretty soon, there were a lot of people at the freight yards meeting with their sons or husbands, not knowing when, or if, they would ever see them again. That was a pretty moving scene. Unfortunately, I wasn't able to meet with any of my family members."

The train finally made its way to Camp Kilmer, New Jersey, where the men knew they would soon be boarding a ship to cross the Atlantic Ocean and the war awaiting them on the other side.

"The Army actually handed out passes for anyone wanting to go into New York City the evening that we arrived in New Jersey, but the following day, all passes were cancelled. Some of the guys did get to go into the city, even though I didn't."

The day after the passes were cancelled, the entire outfit from Fort Bliss boarded the ship, the S .S. *Monterey,* and headed for North Africa. The trip across the ocean took seven days.

"It seems like were always standing in the chow line while were at sea. We were served two meals a day, and there were long, long, lines to get to the mess hall. So, by the time we would finish one meal, it was time to get back in line for the next one," Bob remembered.

Sleeping arrangements on the ship were bad as they were double-loaded.

"One night we would get to sleep in bunks inside the ship, the next night we slept on the deck. One time, because the ship was rolling with the seas, some of the men were tossed out of their bunks. Along came this young lieutenant, who, I guess, was pretty impressed with himself, and he pulled his .45 pistol on the guys and told them to get back into their bunks."

Because of the intense heat inside the ship from the constant cooking, it was more than a little uncomfortable for the men aboard.

"A lot of us ended up with a heat rash before the trip ended," Bob said.

When he arrived in North Africa, his artillery unit supported the

34th Infantry Division, which was made up of National Guardsmen from Iowa and Nebraska.

"We paid a big price to learn how to fight. We faced combat situations for the first time while in North Africa, and that is where we learned how to use our weapons. The men of the 34th, at first under a British Command, took a brutal beating at the hands of the Germans, but we eventually won out."

Bob was in an artillery outfit that fired 90mm weapons.

"Those big guns were designed to outmatch the German 88s," Bob said. "But for the most part, they were underutilized. We discovered they were good weapons to use against German armor, and when the Army learned that, the 90mms became a dual-rated weapon, and we began using them for ground support."

Bob remembered traveling in railcars that were known as 40x8, which meant they were designed to hold 40 men or eight horses. Later, the weather in Europe during the Battle of the Bulge was some of the worst on record.

"Soldiers for the most part fight and live outside," Bob said. "We had to endure the bitter cold and snow and ice of the winter of 1944-45. It was terrible. We were sleeping in foxholes, dugouts, or occasionally in bombed-out buildings. I'll never forget the wind during that period of time," he said. "It was brutal. It would have been bad enough living outside just trying to survive the weather, but we had enemy forces that were trying to kill us as well. So, we were actually fighting two enemies – the weather and the Germans."

During the Battle of the Bulge, Bob's outfit supported several Infantry Divisions with artillery fire.

"Some time around Christmas 1944, we were surrounded by the Germans, and things were not looking very good," Bob said.

The men had been in a convoy going down one of the roads east of St. Vith when they came face to face with a German roadblock.

"Before we could react, the Germans opened fire on the convoy," Bob remembered. "We were driving single file on the road when the shooting began. At first, we didn't know what the heck was happening. The Captain and his driver in the lead Jeep were killed right away, but most of the rest of the convoy was able to get out of harm's way even though we were taking withering fire from the enemy guns. We fell back and drove on to another location. We holed up there throughout the Battle of the Bulge because most of our vehicles had been destroyed."

There would be other close calls for Bob and his artillery unit during the battle. At one time, they were sure their positions would be overrun.

"Around noon on that day, all of the officers and NCOs gathered together and were told the severity of our situation," Bob said. "We were instructed that if the situation didn't improve by three o'clock that afternoon that we were to blowup our artillery pieces and move out as infantry soldiers. We began preparing the charges that would breach our weapons so that the Germans wouldn't be able to use them if we did have to leave them behind."

The infantry held. The guns weren't breached. The battle continued.

"Sometime after Christmas, the German thrust turned north toward Liege. We had patrols out checking to determine where the enemy was, and we were able to locate some of their positions. One day an Air Force lieutenant showed up and called in American air power to help ward off enemy concentrations of troops and armor that were still in the area around us. Four P-47s flew over the German positions and dropped 500-lb bombs on the German tanks. They kept dropping their bombs until they ran out of targets. They did a wonderful job."

"One of the really bad things that were experienced during the Battle of the Bulge was wounded men freezing to death before help could get to them. If the enemy had an outfit pinned down by fire, there wasn't any way to get to a wounded man to help him, and it was so cold that it didn't take long for the weather conditions to turn against a helplessly wounded soldier. One time, we were walking down this road and the wind was blowing snow into drifts along side of the road. I saw something that the snow was piling against and went to investigate, and it was the frozen bodies of four dead GIs. I don't think I will ever forget that sight."

"The Nazi SS troops were the worst," Bob remembered. "They were brutal, and I hated them with a passion. If I ran across a man today that was in the SS during the war, I'm not certain how I would react toward him. Most of the typical German soldiers were just doing what they were told to do, but the SS Troopers were a much different breed of soldier."

"A tactic the Germans used was to mine ditches alongside of a road, so if artillery fire started pounding American GIs walking down that road, and they jumped into a ditch for protection, there was a possibility that they would be wounded or killed by the land mines the Germans had placed there."

Bob also remarked that a lot of packages from home for besieged American soldiers during the battle were interdicted by the Germans, and the food eaten by them.

Bob was a sergeant when discharged from the Army in 1945 at Camp Grant, Illinois. He remembers seeing Generals Bradley, Patton and Hodges. He also had an opportunity to see Bob Hope and Glenn Miller while they were entertaining the troops overseas.

Ask Bob today about the Battle of the Bulge and the offensive in the Huertgen Forest, and you will get an honest, brutal assessment of what he thought of the campaigns.

"My artillery unit was sent to the Huertgen Forest," Bob said. We pulled into the assembly area during a torrential rainfall that created mud as bad as I've ever seen. After spending two days there, it was decided that artillery was of little use there and we were pulled out and sent to Aachen, Germany, the first German town to fall into the hands of the Allies. Aachen and Duren were defended bitterly by the Germans – we were on their soil for the first time."

"First Army commander Hodges, and 12th Army group commander Bradley, made the decision to fight in the hellhole known as the Huertgen Forest in the autumn of 1944. They were obviously ignorant of the conditions that would be encountered in such deep pine growths. Anyone who had spent anytime in the forests of America would know that each pine tree in a forest is a veritable candle, filled with pitch and explosive upon contact with heat. It was estimated there were 50 miles of forest within the Huertgen. Those leaders should have known there would be horrible casualties if we fought in that forest. We fought there anyway because Hodges, it was stated, said that we needed to protect our flank. Before the battle in the Huertgen Forest ended, there were 35,000 American casualties. Proud, experienced divisions were decimated."

"The survivors became a thinly spread line of defense from Monschau to the Luxembourg Dutchy that would later take the brunt of the German Ardennes Offensive (The Battle of the Bulge). Placing the decimated divisions along that line was an invitation for disaster, and the Germans gladly seized the opportunity."

"One must recognize that military leaders carry the responsibility for the lives of their troops. Commanders must use every initiative to obtain information, including personal inspections of the area where their men will fight. Nothing less can be accepted. If the commanders respected the lives of the soldiers who were committed to carrying out their orders, under threat of court martial or death, then they should have found other, superior ways to accomplish their objectives. They didn't. The lives and futures of thousands of American men were wantonly thrown away," Bob said.

Bob was discharged from the Army in 1945 at Camp Grant, Illinois. He remained in the active reserve for eleven more years before retiring as a First Lieutenant.

WARREN GOODLAD
957ʰ Field Artillery Battalion
Past President Chapter XXX
Hometown: La Grange, Illinois

Warren Goodlad is an intelligent and introspective man. His demeanor suggests that in his working lifetime he might have been a banker, accountant, or some other handler of money. In fact, he was an industrial engineer. But, at eighteen years old, like many other eighteen-year-olds in the 1940s, he was a soldier engaged in war.

On June 10, 1943, the day he graduated from high school, Warren received his draft notice. The notice didn't congratulate him on his pending graduation from high school, but rather it announced that he was to report for induction in the military in one month.

"I actually tried to get into the Air Force in late February 1943," Warren said. "But they were only taking enlistments of seventeen-year-olds at the time, and I would turn eighteen on March 4. However, in the course of my enlistment process, it was discovered that I was colorblind so that scotched my career in the Air Force."

On July 9 of that year, Warren was inducted into the U.S. Army. The Army didn't have any discrimination regarding color blind candidates.

"I had taken and passed tests my senior year of high school that made me eligible for a program the military had at the time. It was called ASTP (Army Specialized Training Program). The purpose of ASTP was to provide a pool of college educated personnel for various technical and specialized assignments. Evidently, the day I was inducted, they were not taking any recruits into the ASTP program. I must not have been destined to be in that program either."

Instead, Warren was sent first to Camp Grant, near Rockford, Illinois, where he encountered his first POWs. There were a large number of Italians being held at Camp Grant. The prisoners of war there were used in different capacities, ranging from mess hall duty to maintenance work around the camp.

Upon finishing his induction process, Warren was sent to Fort Bragg, North Carolina, for Basic Training.

"The trip to Fort Bragg was by train, and that took the better part of three days and two nights to get there. I remember the ride was a hot one and all of the windows were open. By the time we arrived in North Carolina, there was a layer of cinders and dirt all over the coaches."

Warren was assigned to the Army Field Artillery Specialized Training School at Fort Bragg where he was put into a platoon that was to be trained as Instrument and Survey personnel. Also included would be training in fire direction and control.

When Warren arrived in North Carolina, he was not too impressed with the caliber of the officers and non-commissioned officers he encountered.

"I was just out of high school, and not very knowledgeable about the military, but everything I had ever heard about the Army was coming true. No one knew anything, or if they knew, they weren't sharing any information with us. I thought, 'Is this the kind of leadership we're going to have in combat?'"

Warren began a 17-week Basic Training program that entailed learning the fundamentals of surveying, and fire direction and control. Included in the rigorous training were a lot of dismounted drill practice, map reading, calisthenics, small arms orientation, cannonading, and long hikes.

Primary training involved the use of the aiming circle and transit, both of which were used to "survey in" gun positions. The aiming circle was also used to set the artillery pieces in proper position for firing missions. Basic Training also included a basic orientation on observing targets and how to relay appropriate data and information to the fire control center.

"There were map reading classes, where we were taught a lot about the basics of observation, as well as running combat courses, infiltration courses, and field exercises where we would simulate actual combat situations using live ammunition."

The training was necessary for the type of warfare that Warren would be part of when he arrived in Europe in March 1944.

A week after arriving at Fort Bragg, Warren was on KP duty one Sunday when he happened to look down the street. He saw a familiar figure. The individual he saw had a familiar gait to him and had his hands in his trouser pockets – a very unmilitary manner for a soldier, but not unusual for new recruits. It happened that the familiar figure was one of Warren's fellow inductees from back home who also had the first name of Warren.

Warren Hannas was a high school friend of Warren who had graduated the year before and had gone on to Purdue University. Hannas was assigned to a Basic Training platoon housed in a barracks in the battery adjacent to Warren. Their training cycles were one week apart, but later circumstances would keep these two GIs together in a series of remarkable coincidences.

Towards the end of their Basic Training, Warren's friend caught a case of pneumonia. Upon completing Basic Training, Warren received a "Ten Day Delay en Route," a sort of furlough which provided him an opportunity to go home before reporting to Fort Meade, Maryland, for processing for overseas assignment. At the same time, Warren's friend, Warren Hannas, was released from the hospital and went home on a recuperation furlough. Both of them were home on furlough at the same time for Thanksgiving, 1943.

Warren reported to Fort Meade early in December 1943. He knew that he would be assigned overseas duty soon and wondered where he would be going. On Christmas Day he was in Baltimore on a three-day pass. Baltimore was a popular city for GIs on a pass. While sitting in a movie theater, Warren heard his shipping number announced over the theater's public address system. He was under orders to report back to camp immediately if he heard the number announced. Warren had not been feeling well in the days preceding the holidays, and as he and his friends were going through their final inspection at their base later, Warren fainted and ended up in the hospital with pneumonia.

Following a two-week stay in the hospital, Warren was sent home on a ten-day recuperative leave.

Warren was finally sent to Camp Shanks, New York, for overseas deployment on March 14, 1944. He set sail on the ship, the *Aquitania,* with 5,000 other soldiers, arriving in Greenock, Scotland, six days later.

Warren, with the other men in his group, was then sent to Bristol, England, where they were interviewed and encouraged to consider volunteering for transfer to units such as the paratroopers, rangers, and other high risk units. Very few of the men volunteered for these kinds of assignments.

"During my stay at Fort Bragg, the 101st Airborne Division, a paratrooper outfit looking for volunteers, provided a glider ride one Sunday to see if I might be interested in joining their ranks. After that glider landed, I had no interest in jointing the paratroopers," Warred remembered.

After about a week in Bristol, Warren ended up in Heath Camp, located in Cardiff, Wales. Heath Camp was set up to house and train both Field Artillery and Tank Destroyer replacements. It was shortly after arriving at Heath Camp that the two Warrens would once again encounter each other. It would be their good fortune to stay together until they were eventually assigned to a staging facility in Yeoville, England, a short distance from the seaport of Plymouth, England.

It was while Warren was at Heath Camp that he ran into some of his Basic Training buddies and learned that the fellows that had been in his original shipping group ended up on the Anzio beachhead. Most of the men had been assigned to a Field Observation Battalion which was hit hard with casualties. Of about 15 men sent to the unit at Anzio, Warren believes about 12 were either killed in action or died later from wounds they received.

When he arrived in Britain, Warren found the weather was much milder than it had been in the states.

"It was cold in Baltimore when we left there, but in England, spring had arrived and it was nice. Many of the people there had gardens and the vegetables were already well developed."

Much of the time in England was spent on physical conditioning, map reading classes, small arms orientation and care of material. The men also did a lot of practicing aircraft recognition and enemy uniform familiarization.

"We knew that the big day was impending," Warren said. "The area where we were located was quarantined and made a secure area. The facility where we were billeted was a hospital. We figured out that they were setting up parts of unused areas as wards."

"Finally, we knew that the invasion was on. We were being sorted out and assigned to ships. That would b the last time I would see my friend Warren Hannas until January 1946. My group, all replacements, was assigned to a small troop ship which we boarded by entering the ship from a dock. Unloading the boat later would be a different story."

"As replacements, we were not part of a regular unit, but in anticipation of expected casualties, we had tentative assignments to specific units. I had been assigned to the 65th Armored Field Artillery BN. As things went, I did not end up in that unit."

The men arrived at Utah Beach and disembarked the boat in mid-afternoon. Leaving the ship entailed climbing down a cargo net while carrying full gear, and boarding a landing craft. The task was made even more difficult because of a rough sea.

"I'd estimate the waves were three to four feet high," Warren said. "Your timing had to be exact as you jumped from the net to the ship. Some of the fellows already on board the landing ship were holding the net in order to steady it and keep it close to the vessel unloading."

Upon landing on shore, the men were instructed to remove their outer clothing. They had been issued special fatigues, leggings and field jackets to wear over their regular clothing. The extra items served two purposes – the clothing had been impregnated with a material to protect them in the event of a gas attack, and it also served as a waterproofing agent to keep the men from getting too wet as they waded ashore.

After discarding the clothing, the men hiked about a half mile to a field where they were told to dig slit trenches and to bed down for the night. The field had 11 glider planes lying in it – all of them having various types of damage – from a simple broken rudder to being complete junk. Some of the gliders contained cargo such as jeeps, small trailers and even mortars. The field showed signs of a fire fight and the remnants of obvious casualties remained, both from the landing and the ensuing fight.

The replacements began to salvage the more desirable parts of the gliders to use as structures to improve the character of their slit trenches – mostly to serve as flooring or roofing.

The day after landing in Normandy, Warren was assigned to the 957th F.A. Battalion, a battalion of 155mm Howitzers, but their weapons hadn't arrived yet.

"Our Howitzers stayed on board the ships offshore until the 12th of June. They were not brought ashore for a number of reasons – weather, lack of operating space, etc. We fired our first combat rounds on June 13, near St. Marie Eglise, in support of the 9th Division.

One of Warren's scariest moments came when he accidentally walked onto a minefield.

"I had walked in this field about 40 or 50 feet when my lieutenant yelled for me to stop. He said, 'Don't move. Back out the same way you walked in.'"

"The lieutenant had noticed lumps in the dirt, and they turned out to be buried mines called Bouncing Betty's. Those mines had prongs sticking out from them, and if touched, they would jump about six feet in the air and explode, sending steel ball bearings in a 360 degree circle. They were deadly, and eventually took the lives of many soldiers. I got down on my knees, turned around, and started back to the lieutenant. He talked me back out of the minefield. I had been carrying a stick called a rod, a tool used for sighting, but I left it where I stopped, and I never went back to get it."

Before the war ended for Warren there would be another frightening incident.

"We were riding in a Jeep in northern France on our way to our gun positions when the Jeep hit a land mine. There were two men in the front seat and four of us in the back."

The blast threw Warren out the back of the vehicle into the air. He landed on his back, injuring his spine, but had no other apparent injuries. Others in the Jeep weren't as fortunate.

"Two of the men were killed, others wounded," Warren said.

On July 25, 1944, while awaiting chow from the mess hall truck in the field, a flight of American B-17 bombers flew overhead on their way to striking targets at St. Lo. An American P-47 airplane was with the flight, carrying smoke bombs that would designate targets for the bombers. One of the smoke bombs accidentally fell off the wing of the plane, landing near where the men had gathered for a meal. A bombardier onboard one of the other planes, thinking that the smoke marked a target for his bomber, dropped bombs on the men waiting in the chow line. They were decimated – wiped out. Warren was approximately 150 yards away in a foxhole and escaped unscathed.

The war continued for Warren as the 7th Corps moved south of Paris and into northern France.

"We came in contact with a German Panzer Division in Mons, Belgium. There was a heck of a battle there, but we couldn't fire at the Germans because they were too close to us to be able to use our Howitzers. The 957th FAB was assigned to the 2nd Armored Division at the time. German infantry, along with the Panzers, was advancing on our positions. Behind us was the 1st Division. They were mopping up some resistance, and their 33rd F.A. group had 105mm guns. We called on them for help and their firing on the Germans stopped the advance by the enemy. When it was all over, more than 100 Germans lay dead or wounded. We took about 50 of them prisoner."

Warren's outfit continued moving through Belgium and by early September, they were in the vicinity of Aachen, Germany. There, his outfit participated in various assignments.

"We were there about a month supporting the 1st Division. We had been in constant combat since landing at Normandy. On the 16th of December, the day the Battle of the Bulge began, I was on a 24-hour pass in Verviers, Belgium. I had left that morning about 6 a.m. and went to a Replacement Depot there. I showered, ate breakfast, and grabbed some new clothes. I was actually out on the street when the MPs came around telling all of the troops who were there that they had to report to their units. Tanks from the 2nd Armored Division started rolling into town. Our lieutenant had the truck we used to go on pass, and he left us to go to the town of Liege. Once there, he got thrown in the pokey by the MPs, so he didn't show up to take us back to our unit."

"During the day of December 16, my buddies and I were able to stay off the streets of Verviers by attending several USO shows. We saw Andre Kostalanetz and his orchestra with Lily Pons. We saw Marlene Dietrich and a movie titled *A Guy Named Joe.* That night, we approached an MP station and told them of our plight when our lieutenant failed to pick us up. The MPs told us to flop on the floor and they would give us a ride back to our unit in the morning."

"The roads were solid with troops moving somewhere, and overhead, American planes patrolled the skies providing protection."

The next day, December 18, Warren's unit pulled out, making a 90-mile trip from their base in Germany to Noiseaux, Belgium. They would support the 2nd Armored Division until the end of the battle on the 25th of January, 1945.

"During the Battle of the Bulge, our artillery pieces fired so many rounds through them that they had to take the tubes off and refurbish them," Warren remembered.

The battle was flexible with both sides gaining and losing ground during the 41 days.

"On Christmas Day, we made two strategic withdrawals, and I remember eating Christmas dinner in the basement of a Belgium schoolhouse seated next to a coal pile."

After crossing the Remagen Bridge that crossed the Rhine River, Warren's outfit ended up at the Nordhausen Concentration Camp, near Halle, Germany.

Thumbing through a small photo album containing many black and white photographs of the hundreds of dead bodies piled up at the camp, Warren said, "There is no way to prepare men for the things we saw at that concentration camp. It was a shocking experience for me and the rest of the men who were there."

When the war ended, Warren participated in occupational duty, and then in late summer of '45, he sailed from Bremmerhaven, Germany, for the states. He was going home.

"We left Germany on New Year's Day and landed at Ft. Dix, New Jersey, on either the 14th or 15th of January. I was sent to Camp Granite in Rockford, Illinois, and discharged from there, six weeks shy of my 21st birthday."

When asked about his worst of times, Warren responded, "I don't think you ever get over the shock of seeing combat deaths. It's an experience that you try to put out of your mind immediately after it happens, but if I'm an example of other veterans, as you get into your older years, those memories come back to you. You think about those people that you knew or were with that didn't make it home and you realize that they didn't have the same opportunity to live a full life like the rest of us did. Those are the things that you feel deeply and sadly about – the deprivation of life. And you recall the events that caused you to assert your manhood."

"War is an experience that no one wants, but once you're there, you take pride in your participation in it because of your love of country and the patriotism that you feel. We were trained to fight as a unit or "team." We were stripped of our individual dignity early in our training to make us "team-oriented" and by God it worked."

On January 19, 1950, Warren married Elizabeth Frisbie. They now have two daughters and three grandchildren. Warren worked for several companies as an industrial engineer, finally retiring from Calumet Steel Company in Chicago Heights, Illinois. Today, he and his wife reside in Crown Point, Indiana.

FOOTNOTE

The 957th Field Artillery Battalion was a 155mm Howitzer unit that participated in five major campaigns in Europe – Normandy, France, Rhineland, Ardennes-Alsace, and Central Europe. The unit was assigned to the VII Corps and the First Army, and provided supporting fire for the 1st, 4th, 9th, 83rd, 84th, and 104th Infantry Divisions, as well as the 2nd and 3rd Armored Divisions.

The other Warren – Warren Hannas, was assigned to the 200th Field Artillery Battalion, a 155mm "Long Tom" unit assigned to the V Corps, First Army, and participated in all five campaigns. The wives of both Warrens chose the same dish pattern when they later married and set up housekeeping.

FRANK ZOLVINSKI
190ᵗʰ Field Artillery Battalion, Battery B
Hometown: Michigan City, Indiana

The men who fought in the Battle of the Bulge came from all walks of life. They answered the call to military service from small cities, farms, large urban areas and from the Appalachians to the west coast. All of them unsure of what awaited them in Europe after they had been drafted or enlisted.

Some, like Frank, had already begun their work lives – occupations they would return to at the end of the war. Others were recent high school graduates. All had one thing in common. They were young.

More than anything else, Uncle Sam needed fresh young bodies that could tolerate intolerable conditions, continue fighting in the face of overwhelming odds, and tough it out unquestioningly when things got tough. When they returned home years later, those young men came back with enough memories to last them a lifetime, and with the conviction that they had fought in a just war.

"I'm glad I served during the war," Frank will tell a visitor when asked about his time in the service. "I saw a lot of the world, traveled to places I couldn't have imagined before being in the military, and saw how people elsewhere lived. Besides, I didn't have it that bad, not like the Infantrymen did."

Frank's journey into the chasm of World War II began with a draft notice he received while working at Weil-McLain in Michigan City. He was 23 years-old at the time.

"I received the draft notice and figured, 'What the heck. I might as well go in and get it over with.' I thought I'd only be in for one year."

At the time, despite the noise of war drums beating in Europe, a draftee only had to serve a one-year tour of duty in the military service.

"I was inducted into the Army on September 26, 1941, at Fort Benjamin Harrison in Indianapolis. From there, about 100 of us were sent to Fort Sill, Oklahoma. I stayed there until January 1942, at which time half of the men who had been sent to Fort Sill were then sent to California, the other half to Camp Shelby, Mississippi. I ended up at Camp Shelby."

The hopes of the men contemplating their discharge after one year were shattered by the Japanese attack on Pearl Harbor on December 7, 1941. The men soon learned that they were going to be in the service of their country for the "duration."

While at the artillery training facility in Mississippi, Frank was instructed in the use of 155mm "Long Toms," artillery pieces that would be of invaluable use later in combat. Frank, and the other men that accompanied him to Camp Shelby, fell right in line with the original members of the 1st Battalion, 190th FA Regiment, who had been part of the Pennsylvania National Guard before being inducted into Federal Service and ordered to the Camp in Mississippi for a one year training program.

"Being trained in the handling and firing of artillery weapons was interesting," Frank said. "I was a gunner on the crew. The sergeant on the crew did the actual firing of the weapon. There were two sections of material that were loaded into the Long Toms, the shell itself, pushed in with a long ramrod, and then the powder charge was laid in after the shell. After the shell was fired, we had to swab out the tube to ensure there weren't any hot sparks still inside that might ignite the next powder charge."

In March 1942, the men in Frank's outfit made a three-day march to Camp Sutton, North Carolina. A few months later, on July 11, Frank was married to Frances R. Foldenauer, a Michigan City girl, in a town called Monroe, North Carolina. Like many of the marriages of that era, it has withstood the separation of war and the passing of time, and continues to this day.

The battery of artillerymen was moved to Camp Kilmer, New Jersey, on the 19th and 20th of July, to await transportation to an overseas assignment. Some of the men from the nearby state of Pennsylvania were able to go home for a few days before departing the States, but the recently-married Frank Zolvinski from Indiana would soon be on his way to Europe without first visiting his hometown.

On September 1, the men of "B" Battery, 190th, boarded the *Queen Elizabeth* and embarked for Greenock, Scotland. After three and a half days at sea, they arrived in Scotland, and the next day disembarked and then sailed to Belfast, Northern Ireland. There, the men guarded "V" Corps installations while awaiting further instructions.

Four months later, Frank and his outfit left Ireland headed for a town called Devizes, England. While there, the men were served mutton, which, according to Frank, "mostly ended up in the garbage can."

"I hated the taste of that stuff," Frank recalled. "And so did most of the other men."

Before entering the arena of combat, the men of the 190th had one additional assignment – in a place called Bude, Cornwall, England. There, the men spent about two-thirds of their time in the field preparing for their initial engagement with the enemy. The call to combat came on May 18, 1944, as the men left Bude and headed for the marshalling area and the invasion that would take place on June 6, 1944, D-Day. While there, they waterproofed all of their equipment.

Left CAMPGROUND, CORNWALL, ENGLAND June 1, arrived FALMOUTH area (Hard 5) loaded on LST No. 307, 2030 hours. Weather cold and clear. – Exact morning report Battery "B", 190th FA Bn V Corps. 1 June, (D-5). [37]

After moving into convoy position, the men spent the next three days lying at anchor, awaiting orders to move out. On June 5th, the convoy slowly proceeded along the coast of England, moving like a marathon runner inching his way to the starting line before the beginning of a race.

After five days at sea, the convoy moved southeast toward the coast of France. It was then the men realized that they were going to be part of the initial invasion. At dawn's first light, the men in the convoy saw that there were literally thousands of other ships that had maneuvered into position during the night – all awaiting deployment to the coast of France and the combat awaiting them.

Initially, the 190th was expected to disembark on June 7, the day after D-Day, but as the men watched the invasion from the boats that day, they realized that lack of movement on the beach would not allow them to disembark on schedule. So they waited, and wondered. It would be June 8, after spending eight days on a LST, (Landing Ship Tank, a military landing ship capable of hauling amphibious cargo and up to 400 men), they finally headed ashore.

At 1500 hours (3 p.m.) on June 8, 1944, the men of the 190th landed on Omaha Beach, near St. Laurent-Surmer, France.

The beach was filled with mines, barbed wire entanglements, blockades and pill boxes. This explained the many damaged landing craft and still burning tanks. Here was grim evidence of the big price in lives and equipment for a small strip of land, a foothold. Our dead was piled high. The badly wounded were being given the very best of care at the already over-crowded Field Hospitals. Those not so badly wounded were more concerned about the more seriously wounded comrades and patiently waited their turn.[38]

The 190th's first combat assignment came as the men and their artillery pieces moved into Colleville-Sur-Mer. After de-waterproofing their weapons, the men awaited firing orders. The orders came the next day.

Sgt. Reeser's section had the honor of firing the first shells into the German fortified positions. After firing only 14 rounds, we had won the respect of our doughboys. As one of the doughboys came through our position in pursuit of the Krauts, he paid his respect to us by throwing his arms around the tube of the guns, kissing it, saying he was mighty happy to see our "Long Toms" in the fight. [39]

"There were four guns in each battery, and four batteries in each battalion," Frank said. "The number one gun of a battery would fire the first round for effect. There would be forward observers watching where that first shell hit, and, using instruments they had, would send deflections (a method used in the redirecting of fire) on the target. Our sergeants would use a tool called an aiming circle and they set that tool to the deflections we received from the observers. Then they would lay the guns in on the target. Our guns were pretty accurate and delivered a heck of a punch."

During that summer, the 190th engaged many targets, from Balleroy, to Rouxeville to Vire, traveling some 425 miles across France.

When they entered a combat zone in Belgium in September of that year, it was to support the 78th Infantry Division in the Huertgen Forest.

"We were actually on the edge of the forest," Frank remembered.

The forest was heavily wooded. The battles that were fought here were known to be the bloodiest of the entire war. Air activity here, and counter battery was the heaviest we had encountered. Though we did not have any personnel casualties, one of our light vehicles was damaged in a strafing attack and one of the big guns was slightly damaged when a shell landed 30 yards in front of No. 3 gun.[40]

"The closest I came to being wounded was during the Battle of the Bulge. We were in Liege, Belgium," Frank said. "A couple of shells came in and hit an empty foxhole and a kitchen that the cook had just left. The kitchen was demolished. The cook was in his pup tent and didn't get hurt."

During the Battle of the Bulge, the weather was as much an enemy as the Germans, as the men had to endure one of the coldest and snowiest winters on record for that area.

"The snow was three feet deep, and it sure made it hard to dig foxholes. And it was so cold. We were fortunate though. We almost always had a kitchen with us and that meant hot meals. There weren't many times when we had to eat C or K rations."

As the Allies finally overcame the German army and the war came to an end, Frank had an opportunity to do some sightseeing before coming home.

"We went to Hitler's retreat that was known as the Eagle's Nest. It was located in the town of Berchtesgaden in the Alps. I actually had a piece of tile taken from the kitchen there that I brought home and later donated to the Military Museum in Michigan City. I also donated other items such as Nazi insignias that I had when I returned home. While in the southern part of the country, in Garmisch, I rode a cable car to the Zugspitze, at 9,718 feet; it is the tallest mountain in the German Alps."

Before he left Europe, there would be one more assignment for the man from Michigan City – helping to set up a military government in Czechoslovakia.

"Despite the fact that we helped set up a military government in Blatna, we pretty much didn't do anything while there. We waited for our orders to come home," said Frank.

From the time the 190th landed on Omaha Beach until V-E Day, they fired a total of 21,527 rounds through their artillery pieces. The names of the divisions that the 190th supported are extensive. They include the

6th Army Group of Gen. Devers, the 21st Army Group of England's Gen. Montgomery, the 12th Army Group commanded by Gen. Bradley, Gen. Patch's Seventh, Gen. Patton's Third and Gen. Hodge's First Army. The battery was assigned to VI, VII, VIII, XIV, XV, XXI, XVII AB Corps as well as the V Corps. They supported almost every American Infantry Division as well as the 54th Scotch Highland Inf. Div. attached to the British 2nd Army. Battle honors include the Bronze, Service Arrowhead and Bronze Service Stars for Normandy, Northern France, Ardennes, Rhineland, and Central Europe Campaigns.

Returning home, four long years after leaving, the troop ship carrying Frank and other homeward-bound GIs ran into foul weather.

"It seemed like it took two weeks to get home," he said. "We ran into a bad storm that had the ocean churning. I didn't eat during the storm, because you couldn't. One man on board the ship broke his leg because the ship was being tossed around so much."

Frank was discharged at Camp Atterbury, Indiana, and returned home to his wife and job at Weil-McLain in Michigan City.

In 1972, Frank and his wife joined other veterans and their families on a trip back to the areas in Europe where he had been stationed and where combat had taken place. It was a much different trip than the one he took in the 1940s, and the scenery had changed considerably.

"We flew to London, landing at Heathrow Airport. From there we went to Devizes, where I was stationed during the war, and then we traveled to Plymouth and Bath before taking a ferry to France. The ferry landed at Le Havre. Later, we saw Paris."

The tour would eventually stop at places made famous by WWII, such as Malmedy, where American soldiers were massacred, and at Bastogne, the beleaguered town surrounded by German forces. A boat ride down the Rhine River from Cologne to Rudeshein was another highlight of the trip.

Frank has taken part in reunions of the 190th that have been held somewhere in the Keystone State of Pennsylvania each year, but recently the reunion committee decided to end the practice because of the difficultly of travel for men and women now in their 80s. That theme is becoming more prevalent among Military Divisions hosting reunions as members of the "Greatest Generation" take their place in the pages of history books.

Long may their deeds be remembered!

ORDNANCE

3519th Ordnance Company

CARROLL E. AUSTIN
3519 Ord. Co. Attached to 3rd Army
Past President Chapter **XXX**
Hometown: St. John, Indiana

C arroll was born in the town of Winchester, located in the part of Indiana that is close to the Ohio state line. He would grow up in Lynn, a town ten miles south of Winchester, where he graduated from Lynn High School. The young man from Lynn entered the service on Jan. 20, 1943, during a time when our country was at war. He was single at the time, and like a lot of Midwestern draftees during World War II, was sent to Fort Benjamin Harrison in the Hoosier state to begin his indoctrination into the military service. He traveled there with a group of about 75 other young men who were about to begin an adventure that would eventually take them into combat zones and change them forever. For that privilege, they were paid the handsome sum of $50 per month.

From Fort Benjamin Harrison, Carroll was sent to Fort Oglethorpe, Georgia, where he ate "good food" and slept in wooden barracks.

"Fort Oglethorpe was a Horse Calvary post at one time," Carroll remembered. "It had been converted to a WAC (Women's Army Corps) training facility shortly before I arrived there."

There were 2,500 soldiers and 8,000 WACs at the base in Georgia.

"Our unit was probably about one-half mile away from the WAC's barracks, but we didn't see much of them as we were confined to our barracks during the short time we were there." He did have to pull KP duty, however, once or twice a month while at Oglethorpe. Even though Carroll received some Basic Training in Georgia, it wasn't until he was shipped to Camp Sutton North Carolina, an Army base near Charlotte, that he completed Basic Training.

"While at Camp Sutton from February to September 1943, we slept in canvas tents that were on wooden frames and marched, marched, marched. There was a lot of close order drill instruction, and we went on a number of long hikes with full gear."

Later, he was transferred to Camp Stewart, Georgia.

By the end of his first year, Carroll had been promoted to a T5 (Corporal), and was still in North Carolina. Before being shipped overseas, he would attend training classes on small arms maintenance at the Army Ordnance School in Aberdeen, Maryland.

"While at small arms maintenance training, we learned how to tear down and put back together .45 caliber pistols, .30 caliber rifles, .50 caliber machine guns, as well as other machine guns – and we did it while blindfolded."

Even though class room training was extensive while in Maryland, the men did have some free time – time that was spent marching in close order drill.

"I was told that I had a strong, clear voice, so I was selected to learn how to drill other soldiers. I was scared to death! But before long, learning how to yell out drill instructions became as easy as riding a bicycle, and I believe that I could drill a military unit today without much effort."

In February 1944, Carroll was shipped to Camp Shanks in New York where he joined other soldiers in boarding the *Queen Mary* for their trip overseas. Some 22,000 troops sailed with Carroll as he departed New York for the European theatre. Some 2,500 WACs were also onboard. It took the ship, loaded with its human cargo, five days to cross the Atlantic Ocean.

"The first morning on board the ship, we went to the great dining hall for breakfast. It was an enormous room," Carroll stated. "We entered the dining room from a huge stairway. The moment we started down those stairs we got a whiff of the breakfast menu – it was kidney stew. I turned around and went out on the deck for a breath of fresh air. I never entered that dining hall again. I lived on English dark chocolate for the remainder of the trip."

"We landed in Firth of Clyde, Scotland, five days later. Once there, we boarded a train that took us to Hereford, England, where we remained until we crossed the English Channel in mid-July 1944."

Once in Europe, Carroll was housed in an old English barracks located on a horseracing course in Hereford, England.

"While I was stationed in England, I met and made friends with an English family, and that friendship endured for more than 50 years. In 1973, we went there and visited them, and two years later, they came to the States and visited us. Our families visited back and forth from 1973 to 1996. The Englishman was struck by a car and died, and his wife died a short time later. She had a son by a previous marriage and he died a few months ago. I still carry on a correspondence with the grandchildren."

After arriving on the European continent, Carroll's outfit followed the Third Army as it progressed across Europe.

"Our mission was to repair vehicles, anything from jeeps to command cars, weapons carriers, and six-bys (trucks). We didn't do any body repair, only mechanical. My special unit of six men did the repair of small arms."

"I was fortunate that I didn't actually see any combat while I was overseas," Carroll said. "And we were blessed with decent and well-respected officers."

Soon after the end of the Battle of the Bulge, Carroll was promoted to Staff Sergeant.

"When the war ended in Japan, the older members of our Company had accumulated enough points to return home – they also had all of the senior non-commissioned ranks. Sometime around September 1945, I was given the rank of Acting Master Sergeant, which meant that I had all the responsibility of that rank, but not the pay. Later, the Company Commander sent in a request to promote me to the full rank of Master Sergeant. The next day, we received orders to return home. The day after that, the request for my promotion to Master Sergeant came back denied. It would have been nice to have been discharged as a Master Sergeant, but it just didn't happen that way."

When asked if he saw any important people while in the service, Carroll remarked he saw both General George Patton and General Dwight D. Eisenhower. Carroll also mentioned that he was at the Buchenwald Concentration Camp the day after it was liberated.

Carroll was discharged on December 20, 1945, at Camp Atterbury, Indiana. He received Theatre of Operations ribbons, was proud to have served his country, and has no regrets about being in the service. Carroll was able to take advantage of the G.I. Bill of Rights, and favors compulsory military training for American youths.

THE MEN OF THE SIGNAL CORPS

303rd Signal Operation Battalion

ROBERT O. JOHNSON
303rd Signal Operation Battalion, Company B
Hometown: Lake Station, Indiana

HOME," the 1945 headline announces across the front page of the *Taylor Maid,* an "at sea" publication of the *U. S. S. Harry Taylor.*

The story under the headline reads, *Ship heads for New York:*

At 1521 Wednesday afternoon (August 16), as the U. S. S. HARRY TAYLOR, plunged westward through topic waters, the sweating men on deck were electrified by a sudden announcement from the loud speaker system: It was the voice of Captain L. B. Jaudon, Commander of the Ship, who said, "Attention all hands. Watch the shadows on the deck of the ship move as the bow of the ship turns to…" After a breathless pause, he concluded, "New York."

Men shouted and screamed, beat each other on the back, shook hands violently with the nearest person, embraced and danced about in glee. In many eyes were tears. Others stood in dazed incredulity.

The celebration and shouting continued unabated for 20 minutes or more and only then settled down to excited talk.

To a large number of men and nurses aboard, the announcement meant they were going directly to or near their home. To all it meant a return to the homeland.

The surrender of Japan the day before had been an anticlimax to what seemed a long period of waiting. This, on the other hand, was something which many had only half hoped would come true. It did.

R.O. (Robert Johnson) was going home!

The entire battalion of men from the 303rd Signal Operation Battalion had left Arles before departing Marseille, France on August 7, 1945. The original destination of the boatload of signal corps men was the South Pacific. They were on their way to prepare for the invasion of Japan.

"The *U. S. S. Harry Taylor,* loaded with GIs returning from the war, was the first ship sailing into New York Harbor after the Japanese surrendered," Robert related. "We had 5,000 men onboard a ship that was designed to hold 2,000. But after the announcement concerning the ship turning around was made by the captain, we didn't care how crowded we were. The atmosphere onboard was electric. Guys were hugging one another, and everyone had a big smile on their face – we were going home."

When the *Harry Taylor* docked in New York, it did so at Pier 88.

"I'll never forget that day," Robert said. "Someone retrieved a bed sheet from the nurses' station on the ship before we docked, and painted the name of our battalion on it. The sheet was then hung off the side of the ship."

It was a grand time, although life in the military wasn't always that good for the young man from East Gary (now called Lake Station), Indiana. But the homecoming provided a nice finish to the time he spent in Europe fighting the Nazis.

Born in Rennselaer, Indiana, Robert graduated from Edison High School on May 28, 1943. He had received a 90-day deferment from the draft on March 5 while still in high school – good until June 5 – but by June 2, he was in the U.S. Army.

"I actually only weighed 119 pounds when I took the physical examination. The minimum requirement for induction into the service was 120 pounds. I was asked if I wanted to be a 4F and not go into the service or if I wanted to go in to the military. When I told them that I wanted to enter the service, I was told to step on the scale again and lean back on my heels. When I did, my weight showed 120 pounds and it was enough that they took me."

Two busloads of young men soon left Gary, Indiana, on their way to Fort Benjamin Harrison, within the Hoosier State, and eventual induction into the service of their country.

After his induction, Robert was sent to Camp Crowder, Missouri, the home of the second largest signal corps encampment in the United States. The largest was the 1st Signal Corps at Fort Mommoth, New Jersey.

"We left Indiana by train around midnight on our way to Missouri. When we arrived at Camp Crowder, I was assigned to the 17th Signal Operation Battalion. The battalion had been activated in April 1943. The cadre teaching the new recruits was all from the south. I stayed there and trained in the Missouri heat and rock until mid-August."

Anyone who has spent any time in Missouri in the summer can appreciate what the new recruits had to endure while taking their 13-weeks of Basic Training. To say it is hot in Missouri in the summer, is equivalent to saying it is cold at the North Pole in the winter. It was hot!

"While taking Basic Training, we were given the opportunity to learn other military skills in the evening," Robert remembered. "So, while I was learning all about small arms fire during the daytime, that included training on rifles, pistols, and other ordnance, in the evenings I received training in cooking and baking. I decided to learn as much as the Army was willing to teach me."

Leaving the heat and grueling ordeal of Basic Training, he was sent to the 4th Army on the West Coast.

"I would eventually end up at Fort Ord, but first there was a stop in Sunny Vale, California, where we stayed in a walnut orchard in a valley that was fenced in."

The military area was nestled in a valley between sand dunes. The smoke from the camp hung over the tents in the valley like smoke from a steel mill, and resulted in the area being called "Little Pittsburgh."

While living in the area that resembled a steel-making town, the men were afforded the opportunity to work off-base.

"We didn't have any orders to report anyplace else, so we were kind of stranded there while the Army made up its mind as to where to send us. I worked at the Libby-McNeil Cannery while I was in California," Robert said. "Other guys worked at places like Sears. Some even used their military training to work as switchboard operators. We worked at those civilian jobs while wearing Army fatigues."

"We then went on maneuvers in February with the 69th and 89th Infantry Divisions. The place that we practiced war games at was 90 miles south of Fort Ord on the Hearst ranch property. It was beautiful. We could actually see the Hearst ranch itself, but weren't allowed near it. We stayed there for approximately three months. Our outfit was classified as "Special Troops" and we did everything from carry food to the men on maneuvers to operate the highly-expensive communications equipment we had at the time, such as the 399 radios."

"When we came back from maneuvers, we were stationed at Fort Ord in the big barracks until approximately June 21, 1944. From there, we left for Camp Shelby, Mississippi."

"While I was at Camp Shelby, I attended a box and crating school to learn how to box up equipment for the trip overseas. We had to make all of the boxes waterproof, figure out how to place the equipment inside so it would survive the trip across the ocean, make the tops for the boxes, and then label them so the equipment inside was identifiable."

It was during this time in Mississippi that Robert also worked in the supply room.

"Part of my duties in the supply room was to make out a laundry list to send all of the dirty laundry out to be cleaned. The commanding officer had to sign the list before we could send out the laundry. One day the C.O. didn't sign the list. He told me to give all of the dirty laundry back to the men. That wasn't a good sign. The next day, all of our equipment was loaded onboard a train and sent to Camp Kilmer, New Jersey. We knew what that meant."

It was September 10, 1944, and a trip across the Atlantic was imminent.

"As the men arrived in New Jersey, some who lived in that area were given overnight passes so they could go home and say goodbye." A lot of the guys in our outfit were from East Coast States such as New York, New Jersey or Delaware."

The next day, the men boarded a British ship called the *Scythia*.

"We called the ship a pocket ship because it was no bigger than a pocket," Robert recalled fondly. "The ship was being used to bring German Prisoners-of-War back to the states, then on the return trip across the Atlantic Ocean; its cargo was fresh American soldiers heading for the war in Europe."

The *Scythia* set sail out of New York Harbor on September 11, bound for Cherbourg, France.

"I worried about the possibility of German U-Boats the entire time I was onboard that ship," Robert said.

The ship landed in Normandy, France, on September 23, 1944, without any incidents at sea.

"We stayed in an apple orchard when we first arrived in France. It was the rainy season, and the entire area was a sea of mud. But, the time I spent there was probably the most enjoyable part of my time in the service. I was being carried on the books as an *Artificer,* which the dictionary defines as a person who possesses special skills. The Army said it was a person who was a jack-of-all-trades. Anything that needed to be done, they called on R.O. I was their designated Artificer."

"We stayed in that muddy area through October and into November." Then I was assigned to Rouen, France, as a depot switchboard operator. I worked at the depot where the ships came in at. I stayed there approximately three weeks, during which time I also drove a military truck and did a little cooking for the Army."

After a three-week stay in Rouen, it was off to a town in Belgium called Dinant.

"While I was in Dinant, I helped set up communications for the Army headquarters in town that was in an old Belgium schoolhouse. I stayed there until midnight on December 24, 1944."

By Christmas Eve, the Battle of the Bulge was in its eighth day, and the Germans were making advances toward Dinant.

Using a WWII era map made out of silk that was carried by paratroops during the war, Robert pointed out his location on December 24, and the route the men had to take to avoid the German advancement. The paratroopers carried silk maps because they didn't make any noise when they were opened, used, and re-folded. The map, showing the countries of Holland, Belgium, France and Germany, is now encased in Plexiglas and a marker has been used to show the "bulge" in the American lines.

"At the time we left Dinant," Robert said pointing to the location on the sixty-year old map, "the Germans were approximately four miles away. We could hear the sounds of combat as artillery shells screamed and exploded in the distance. There was a possibility that headquarters might be overran by enemy forces, so we had to cut all of the communications lines that we had there. We didn't want the Germans to have access to our communication system."

Once their tasks were completed, the men jumped in trucks and had to make a big loop away from their location to arrive safely in Suippes, France.

"As we were high-tailing it away from Dinant, we saw five-gallon cans of gasoline that our men had left alongside of the roads for our trucks to use. Someone had the idea to pour the contents from cans into our vehicles then afterwards fill them up mostly with water, with a little gasoline near the top. We then put the cans back alongside the road. We heard later that German tanks, as they advanced past Dinant in need of gasoline to continue their march toward Antwerp, used those cans of water/gasoline in their vehicles, thinking they were filled with gas. Shortly thereafter, the tanks ran out of fuel."

While he was stationed in Dinant, Robert was fortunate enough to live in a home that the Army rented from a Belgium family who owned it. The family had four daughters, and he became friends with the entire family. On a trip back to the area in 1979, R.O. and his wife looked up the family he remembered from Belgium, and spent some time with them.

Reflecting on the battalion's time in Europe, Robert said that out of the 700 men in the battalion, the only two casualties were as a result of accidents: one man drowned, another died when the Jeep he was riding in overturned.

After his discharge from Camp Atterbury, he returned home to East Gary, and went back to work at U. S. Steel Corporation, which had steel-making operations along the southern shoreline of Lake Michigan.

"I had actually worked at U. S. Steel while I was still in high school, Robert remembered. "I began by working there in the summer months. After school began in the fall, I worked weekends, and sometimes the 3-11 shift, three days a week while I was still in school."

Married in 1947, Robert was able to use the G.I. Bill to further his education in apprentice training, and further his career at the steel mill as an electrical armature winder, a re-winder of motors. He worked there for more than 42 years before retiring.

Pulling out a book from the 1940s, the Hoosier veteran pointed to the back section which listed the names and addresses of all of the men of the 303rd. One day in 1992, after looking at the book and wondering what might have happened to his buddies from his WWII outfit, Robert began making telephone calls.

"I made so many calls trying to locate friends from the 303rd, that I received a call from the telephone company when they saw my bill that month. They thought maybe there was a mistake."

As a result of the many telephone calls to friends throughout the country, the men decided to hold a reunion of the 303rd. The first reunion occurred in 1993 in Cambridge, Ohio, a central location for the aged veterans, and has taken place every September since.

"Many of the men at the reunion have joined the Veterans of the Battle of the Bulge," Robert pointed out. "Our largest reunion turnout was in 1994. We had approximately 75 veterans show up in Lexington, Kentucky, and we were shown on a segment of the *Good Morning America* program on national TV."

The mementoes saved from the war years fill a room as events are described and retold to a visitor. R.O. has kept much from that time, and looking at old photographs and mementoes brings back a flood of nostalgia.

Each picture has a story; each yellowed piece of paper a memory. The events remembered are a half-century or more in the past, but they are such a significant part of the man's life that they stay in the forefront of his memory bank, eager to be retold again.

These veterans of World War II, such as Robert Johnson, were warriors once, and the world was proud of their accomplishments. Because of that, I believe, the memories from the time they spent in Europe refuse to fade completely from their remembrance. Now, finally, they can be shared with more than just family and friends. On Memorial Day 2004, the veterans of WWII will be honored in Washington D.C. by the presentation of a monument built and dedicated to their amazing service to their country.

TROOP CARRIER SQUADRONS

75th Troop Carrier Squadron, 435th Troop Carrier Group

MICHAEL WALT – C-47 CREW CHIEF
75th Troop Carrier Squadron
Hometown: Westville, Indiana

Mike arrived at our prearranged meeting on a day reminiscent of those cold days in January 1945 when he was fighting, not only the weather, but the brutality of war as well. He came to talk about his exploits in the service of his country carrying a model aircraft—a replica of a C-47, the type of cargo plane on which he served as a crew chief during the war.

On this January day, unlike the ones in the 1940s when the actual plane was an integral part of his life and the war effort, the replica of the C-47 he carried with him would only be a prop for the many stories Mike has about his time overseas during World War II. He displayed and pointed to the plastic model often, showing where various items were located and explaining to a novice the vulnerability of its underside to enemy fire. He remembered the inner workings of the cargo plane as if he'd flown in it the day before, but it's been 59 years since Mike stepped foot inside the aircraft that he nicknamed, "The Big Dirty."

"As a kid, I made model airplanes all the time," he remembered. "I couldn't have had a better job in the military then the one I was fortunate enough to be given. Imagine, being able to fly in a plane everyday."

As he began to share details of those days flying in an airplane, the tales of the time he spent fighting the Nazis in Europe sounded like he only had fun. But as Mike related the numerous stories about being shot at while the C-47 he was riding in carried payloads that included full cans of gasoline, it became obvious that his time flying combat missions over Europe was more work than enjoyment, and his survival more luck than skill.

Mike's time in the employment of Uncle Sam began in September 1942, when he received his draft notice.

"I actually attempted to enlist in the Air Corps previously, but couldn't pass the eye test because of trouble with color blindness," he remembered. "So I waited for the draft notice that I was sure would come, and reported to Fort Benjamin Harrison in Indianapolis, Indiana, when I received it."

"I was only in Indy for a few days, long enough to find out what K.P. was, and then I was sent to St. Petersburg, Florida, for Basic Training. My total time in Florida was 10 days, as we received orders the first day we were there to report to Gulf Port, Mississippi. That's where I attended my first airplane mechanic school."

"We basically worked on all kinds of Air Corps planes while I was in Mississippi, but the primary airplane we repaired and learned the mechanics of was the P-39. We heard later that the Air Corps gave 15,000 of the P-39 airplanes to Russia to use against the Germans. They were too slow for our pilots, but because the plane had a cannon in the nose that could be used for tank-busting, the Russians loved them."

"I was actually offered the job of instructor while I was at Gulf Port, but I wasn't interested in instructing other mechanics. I wanted to fly."

Fly, he would. But Mike's next assignment took him to Chanute Air Force in Champaign, Illinois, where he attended and graduated from Prop Specialist School, and then he joined the 75th Troop Carrier Squadron in Sedalia, Missouri as a Prop Specialist.

"Not only were the enlisted men still learning their jobs while we were in Missouri, but so were the pilots who would be flying the cargo planes in combat one day," Mike recalled. "It was a little scary for awhile. We'd get in the planes with the pilots, and wonder if they were going to be able to land them or not. They eventually learned their jobs, though, just like we did. And by the time we shipped out for overseas, we were all pretty competent about what we were supposed to do in combat."

While stationed in Missouri, the men discovered there was a WAC (Women's Army Corps) base in Des Moines, Iowa.

"We'd buzz the WAC barracks in Des Moines with our planes, and by the time we landed at the airport and got to town, all the girls were there." Those crazy fly boys!

"There was a Prop Specialist in each squadron of airplanes," Mike said. "I had very few problems with the Hamilton Standard propellers so I was assigned as an Assistant Crew Chief on an airplane. Each time our planes flew, either a Crew Chief or an Assistant Crew Chief went along. I was able to get in my flying time that way."

After spending approximately three months in Missouri, the Squadron was assigned to Pope Field in Fort Benning, Georgia. While in Georgia, the pilots and crew members underwent training on flying in formations; learned how to tow gliders, and were taught the method used to ferry paratroopers to a drop zone.

When it was time to embark for overseas assignment, the flight crews flew the planes along the southern route to Europe, while the rest of the Squadron was sent to England by boat.

"It took us 11 days to cross the ocean on a British ship. We traveled in a convoy, and the weather was decent, the seas calm," Mike said.

"The troop-carrying ships landed in Liverpool, England, and from there we were transported to Nottingham. We were fairly close to London, and were able to go into the big city on weekend passes."

While in England, Mike became a crew chief on a C-47. There were 28 airplanes to a squadron, and that meant there were 14 crew chiefs and 14 assistants for each squadron. Actually, most of the Squadrons had 27 planes assigned to them, but Mike's Squadron was a Group, (there were four Squadrons to a Group) and therefore they had a plane for the Group Commander.

"I was eventually promoted to the position of Crew Chief," Mike said.

By then, he was a Tech Sergeant and with his bonus flight pay, was making about $250 per month.

On D-Day, June 6, 1944, Mike's squadron took part in missions over Normandy – the area in France where thousands of Allied soldiers came ashore.

"At the briefing, before we took off on our mission over Normandy, we were told to expect 80 percent casualties. That meant there would be a lot of planes and crews not coming home."

"Our mission for the June 6 invasion was to drop paratroopers over enemy-held territory that first night. When you're dropping paratroopers out of a plane you have to first go in low, and secondly, reduce airspeed to about 85 miles per hour. That makes you a sitting duck for ground fire, as we were flying so low that even bullets from small arms fire could reach the planes. As we were going in to the drop zone that night, there were low clouds over the drop area, and that meant the planes were scattered all over the place. Consequently, the paratroopers, once they jumped, were scattered all over the place as well. We lost one plane to enemy fire going in. I had a friend on that plane who was a radio operator. I saw the plane take a hit in the belly, veer out of the formation and then blow up."

The great moment for the Allied airborne forces came with Operation Overlord in June 1944. Their contribution to that effort alone more than justified the considerable resources that both the British and U.S. armies had poured into development of airborne tactics and training.

The drops (on D-Day) more than accomplished their mission and – to use that dreadful military euphemism – at "an acceptable cost."

The American paratroopers were less lucky (than their British counterparts) in that, due to weather, bad navigation and German anti-aircraft fire, the troop carrier pilots dropped them all over Normandy. While that may have had a direct impact on their cohesion as fighting forces, the small groups of paratroopers spread havoc and confusion throughout the Norman countryside. In particular, their actions distracted the attention of German commanders away from the landings, including that on Omaha Beach.[41]

Mike took exception to the term "bad navigation" that the author used in the quoted article above, saying that the fog that night was so bad that the planes had to disperse to inordinate lengths so they didn't fly into one another. It wasn't so much bad navigation that caused the problems as much as it was a necessity so that the planes kept their distance from one another.

"A C-47 was nothing more than a civilian plane painted brown," Mike said. "In the belly of the aircraft were four 200 gallon fuel tanks, with no armor around it to protect it from ground fire. It's amazing we didn't lose more planes than what we did."

The day before D-Day, the C-47s, as well as other American aircraft, would have three white stripes painted around the rear of the fuselage to identify them as Allied planes. Prior to the paint jobs, Allied planes flying over U.S. naval ships sometimes came under fire from the Navy because they weren't recognizable as being friendly aircraft.

"The Navy didn't like airplanes flying directly over their ships, even if they were "friendly" airplanes, but at least the white stripes identified the planes as belonging to the Allies."

After flying a second mission on D-Day, the men of the 75th Troop Carrier Squadron sat around waiting for missions for the next 2-3 weeks.

"We had to wait for the Infantry to take an area, and then wait for the Engineers to build us a runway where we could land and take off. As the Army moved farther inland from the coast of Normandy, landing strips were built, allowing us to fly supplies into the troops in those locations."

The next significant mission that Mike was part of was called Operation "Market-Garden" and it took place in Holland.

"I remember that it was a beautiful day. We flew over the North Sea on our way to the drop zone, towing gliders filled with GIs behind us. The formation of airplanes consisted of four planes, each towing a glider. The gliders being towed were the fragile, canvas-covered steel Waco CG-4A. The sun was shining brightly as we flew over Holland, and we were flying so low that we could see clothes hanging on bushes and fences that the Dutch women had hung out to dry. The next thing we knew, bullets were flying up at us and we were in the thick of the war again."

Operation Market-Garden, the failed attempt to liberate much of the Netherlands and seize a direct route into northern Germany, was the greatest airborne operation in history. But it was an ill-fated undertaking from the onset.

Despite all the command failures and mishaps, the performance of the airborne troops was magnificent.[42]

"We flew missions towing gliders behind us," Mike remembered. "During the invasion of southern France, we flew out of Italian air fields to our targets."

The air drops that re-supplied the surrounded men at Bastogne are missions that Mike will never forget.

On December 23, the damp and foggy weather suddenly broke; the day dawned bright, clear and very cold. If the 10 degree temperature turned sodden boots to icy slabs and made flesh cling painfully to gun metal, it also provided fine flying weather for the first time in days, and the men of Bastogne received word that an airdrop was in the works. As the morning wore on, all eyes searched the blue skies for dark specks. At 9 o'clock, a pathfinder team parachuted in to set up its colored panels and radar to guide the incoming planes. A few minutes before noon, the first of 241 C-47 cargo carriers droned over the drop zone. Red, blue and yellow parachutes billowed like fantastic Christmas ornaments, floating downward with priceless gifts of ammunition, medical supplies and food. Not all of the planes made it; some, hit by flack as they flew over the German lines, wobbled along, trailing smoke as their pilots tried desperately to deliver their loads before their craft broke into flames and fell.[43]

"Our planes that we flew over Bastogne had special racks attached to the bottoms of them," Mike remembered. "They were hangers, used for dropping bombs, only our payload was supplies. The pilot pulled the trigger from inside the plane, releasing the supplies in the racks, just like a bombardier would release his payload. Only our supplies had parachutes on them. There were six racks on the bottom of each plane, filled with ammunition, food, and medical supplies. It was the only time we ever used those racks on our planes."

"Inside the airplanes were other supplies such as gasoline cans. We had three cans of gas tied together, and they were dropped using one parachute. We had to push those out the door by hand – not exactly a fun thing to do when there are guys below shooting at you."

"We flew missions over Bastogne on December 22, 23, 24 and 26. Christmas Day was fogged in so badly that our planes never made it off the ground. By the fourth mission on the 26, however, the Germans knew the flight path we would take after dropping supplies over the town, and they were waiting for us. Fortunately, our officers knew that the Germans had made adjustments, and we took a different route away from Bastogne after completing our missions. Years later, I heard one of the guys who was at Bastogne say that the first day we dropped supplies to them, all he had left was seven rounds of ammunition for his anti-aircraft gun."

Before the war ended in 1945, Mike and the men of the 75th Troop Carrier Squadron hauled gasoline to General Patton's soldiers who were advancing almost faster than their supplies could keep up with them, and then their planes would carry wounded soldiers to England for treatment for their injuries.

"Our planes could each hold 24 stretchers, and we took planeload after planeload of wounded men away from the front lines to hospitals in England where they could be treated for their injuries. We saw so many guys with frozen or frostbitten feet. I felt so sorry for them."

Even after the war ended, the missions for the troop carriers continued.

"After the hostilities concluded, we flew Displaced Persons and released Prisoners of War back to their own countries. We would fly from Germany to England, drop off our human cargo, fly to Antwerp, pick up French men, and then fly them to Paris. We did that for days. There was a long line of people everyday waiting for us to ferry them someplace. There were three steps to get into our C-47s, and we had to help a lot of those freed prisoners up the steps and into the planes because of their weak physical condition. It seemed to me that the American POWs were in a worse condition than any others."

"While I was in combat, the crew chiefs stayed in their own tent, and every night after completing our flights, we would all sit around in the tent and talk about the crazy things that we had seen or had happened to us that day. That helped keep us sane," Mike said. "There is so much craziness that occurs during a war that you have to look for an outlet to keep your wits about you. Every time we took off in a plane while in combat, we didn't know if we would make it back or not."

After the war ended in Europe, the Squadron flew back to the United States. Even though he had accumulated more than enough points to be discharged, Mike wasn't. While at home on leave, Mike learned that he would be heading for Japan, where C-54s would be used to haul wounded soldiers to the rear lines. A C-54 was very similar to a C-47 except that they had four engines instead of two.

"I was home on a 30-day leave in Avilla, Indiana, when Harry (President Truman) dropped the bomb on Japan," Mike said. "That saved my butt from anymore combat missions. I was in the Army for three years and seven days and had flown 29 missions – that was long enough."

Mike would return home to LaPorte, Indiana, after his discharge, where he had moved to in 1940, and went back to work for the Coca-Cola Company in the service and production departments. He worked there for 44 years before retiring. Even after retirement though, he has kept busy, and to this day, runs a hardware store three days a week near his home in Westville, Indiana.

TAPS

Has there ever been a more sorrowful tune? Every veteran knows the mournful sounds of the 24 notes that make up the bugle call of *Taps*. Once called Extinguish Lights, or Lights Out, the call was originally used to signify the end of the military day. In the United States Military, however, it is also used at funerals, wreath-laying and memorial services.

Most veterans, when hearing the playing of the mournful notes, retreat deep inside themselves and reflect on an occurrence in their past that usually resides in some dark corner of their mind, a place that only comes to the forefront during memorial services and funerals.

When *Taps* was played at the Dedication Ceremony at Calumet Park Cemetery in Merrillville, Indiana, on May 17, 2003, more than one hundred veterans stood silently immersed in their own thoughts—the call surely bringing back memories of time spent in the service of their country; perhaps it even brought to mind the death of a friend killed in the line of duty, or of one who has died since.

It is never an easy bugle call to hear, even if one hasn't suffered the loss of a friend, because of the images it invokes and the frequent emotion that results from hearing it. And while it doesn't need any language to convey its message, and there are no *official* words to the music, there are seldom heard words that accompany the music, one version which was written in July of 1862. They are:

> *Day is gone, gone the sun*
> *From the hills, from the lake,*
> *From the sky.*
> *All is well, safely rest,*
> *God is nigh.*
>
> *Go to sleep, peaceful sleep,*
> *May the soldier or sailor,*

God keep.
On the land or the deep,
Safe in sleep.

Love, good night, Must thou go,
When the day, And the night
Need thee so?
All is well. Speedth all
To their rest.

Fades the light; And afar
Goeth day, And the stars
Shineth bright,
Fare thee well; Day has gone,
Night is on.

Thanks and praise, For our days,
'Neath the sun, Neath the stars,
'Neath the sky,
As we go, This we know,
God is nigh.

The men listed below served their country well during a time when America needed them most. They answered the call to arms and put themselves in harms way for the good of the country that they loved the most and for the sake of their fellow countrymen who they were trying to protect. They survived the perils of war and returned home to the families waiting for them and began their lives all over again, thankful for their safe return. And now they have been reunited with the buddies they left behind on foreign soil. God Bless them all.

Paul Huff
Robert Quinn
Edwin Gorzyca
Frank Cichocki
Ken Keen
William Eyer

Paul Sherbak
Joseph Gabonay
Walter Budzielek
Robert Craigin
Robert Pauley
Delmar Mounts
Thor Nygren
Morris LaFollete
Teo Esposito
George Pfeiffer
Edward Wistosky
Ernest Huffman
John Delmerico
Irvin Switzler
Devon Lewis
Leo Zdanis
Ed Engle
Eugene Johnson
Darrell Stoltenberg
Herbert Sontag
James McGhee

MONUMENT TO THE VETERANS OF THE BATTLE OF THE BULGE

On Saturday, May 17, 2003, hundreds of veterans, along with their families and friends, gathered at Calumet Park Cemetery in Merrillville, Indiana, to dedicate a monument to the memory of those brave men who fought in the Battle of the Bulge.

The inscription on the monument reads: *DEDICATED BY THE NORTHERN INDIANA CHAPTER XXX VETERANS OF THE BATTLE OF THE BULGE TO THOSE VETERANS WHO FOUGHT IN THAT TERRIBLE 41-DAY BATTLE, THE BIGGEST BATTLE EVER FOUGHT BY THE UNITED STATES ARMY DECEMBER 16, 1944 TO JANUARY 25, 1945 IN THE ARDENNES FOREST OF BELGIUM. 81,000 AMERICAN SOLDIERS WERE KILLED, WOUNDED OR CAPTURED, AN AVERAGE OF 1,976 EVERYDAY FOR 41 DAYS.*

The effort to build and dedicate the monument in Merrillville, Indiana, was spearheaded by past chapter president, Bill Tuley. Bill served in the 87th Infantry Division during the Battle of the Bulge.

EPILOGUE

Since I began work on the story of the men of Northern Indiana Chapter XXX Veterans of the Battle of the Bulge, in 2001, my world has changed dramatically.

My mother died in 2003 and will never see the result of my endeavor to tell the story of how the Battle of the Bulge impacted my father and his fellow northern Indiana soldiers.

My daughter, Laura Brown, gave birth to my first grandchild in 2004, and Avery Brown, growing up in the 21st century, will know little of the war that took place in Europe in the 1940s except what she will read in this compilation of individual stories, as there is not much to be found in school text books about the battle these brave men fought.

Eight of the men in our chapter have passed away since that day in 2001 when I decided to take on the challenge of writing about their experiences. The individual accounts of their time fighting during WWII may be lost forever.

My mentor, Bill Tuley, is 88 years old and worries that he won't ever see *My Heroes* published.

The past three years of my life, as I interviewed the men whose stories are found between the covers of this book, and met and talked with their spouses, has been rewarding beyond what words can express. I thought I knew what transpired during the Battle of the Bulge from hearing the men talk about their experiences before I began work on this project. I didn't. They have hidden their trauma well these past sixty years.

I tried not to open too many any old wounds during my interviews with the aged veterans; instead, I allowed them to dictate to me what they wanted to discuss. Some, like Roger Holloway, will tell you they still have nightmares about things they saw and did.

Others, like Bill Tuley, say that they still see the faces of the men they killed in combat.

"I wonder what they would have done with their lives had they lived," Bill has mused on more than one occasion.

One thing is certain. There is no glory in war. There is only heartache, misery, and lasting, haunting memories. The interviewees told me that they are proud they served their country in the military during WWII, but they wouldn't ever again want to go through what they had to endure in the cold, snowy reaches of war-torn Europe in the 1940s.

(ENDNOTES)

[1] 28th Infantry Division Association, the battle of Huertgen Forest: World War II, page 1

[2] Ibid.

[3] TheBattleoftheBulge@members.aol.com., page 1

[4] Outline of History of the 229th F.A. BN

[5] Combat Chronicle, 28th Infantry Division, page 1

[6] An Historical and Pictorial Record of the 87th Infantry Division in World War II, page 22

[7] Golden Acorn Memories, James R. McGhee, page 19

[8] 87th Infantry Division in World War II, page 24

[9] Ibid. page 25

[10] The 75th Infantry Division in Combat, page 24

[11] Photographic Cavalcade, Pictorial History of the 75th Infantry Division 1944-1945, page 302

[12] Ibid. page 414

[13] The 75th Infantry Division in Combat, page 3

[14] Ibid. page 4

[15] Company Commander, Army Reserve Col. Charles B. MacDonald

[16] On-line article found at http://www.grunts.net/army/106thid.html

[17] Battle of the Bulge 1944, Napier Crookenden, page 11

[18] On-line article found at http://www.grunts.net/army/106thid.html

[19] The World Book Encyclopedia, No. 14, page 455

[20] On-line article found at http://www.courttv.com/archive/casefiles/nuremberg/defendants.html

[21] Tough Ombres! The Story of the 90th Infantry Division. This is one of a series of G.I. Stories of the Ground, Air and Service Forces in the European Theater of Operations, to be issued by the *Stars & Stripes*, a publication of the Information Services, ETOUSA.

[22] On-line article *94th Infantry Division* found at **www.army.mil/cmhpg/lineage/cc/094id.htm**

[23] Ibid.

[24] Ibid.

[25] 28th Infantry Division Association, The Battle of the Huertgen Forest: World War II, page 11

[26] Battle of the Bulge, on-line article found at **www.com/user/jpk/battle.htm**, page 1

[27] The Battle of the Bulge, on-line article found at **www.tokens.myranch.com/bulge.html**, page 1

[28] The Battle of the Bulge, on-line article found at www.helios.acomp.usf.edu/~dsargent/bestbulge2.html, page 3

[29] The Battle of the Bulge, John Toland, pages 109-111

[30] The Men of Bastogne, Fred MacKenzie, David McKay Company, Inc.

[31] The Battle of the Bulge, William K. Goolrick and Ogden Tanner, Time-Life Books, page 158

[32] Ibid. page 155

[33] Inside the Vicious Heart, Robert H. Abzug, pages 26, 27

[34] Ibid. page 46

[35] Battle of the Bulge, Danny S. Parker, page 175

[36] The Battle of the Bulge, John Toland, pages 166-169

[37] History of Baker Battery From Mobilization to V-E Day, page 21

[38] Ibid. page 23

[39] Ibid. page 24

[40] Ibid. page 26

[41] Airborne Comes of Age, Williamson Murray, World War II Magazine, March 2004, pages 38, 40

[42] Ibid. page 40

[43] The Battle of the Bulge, William K. Goolrick, page 158